Red Aura

Kathryn Dorbeck

ISBN: 978-1-4834-4532-8 (sc)
ISBN: 978-1-4834-4534-2 (hc)
ISBN: 978-1-4834-4533-5 (e)

Library of Congress Control Number: 2016901106

Because of the dynamic nature of the Internet, any web addresses or links contained in this book may have changed since publication and may no longer be valid. The views expressed in this work are solely those of the author and do not necessarily reflect the views of the publisher, and the publisher hereby disclaims any responsibility for them.

Any people depicted in stock imagery provided by Thinkstock are models, and such images are being used for illustrative purposes only.
Certain stock imagery © Thinkstock.

Lulu Publishing Services rev. date: 03/07/2016

Thank you to my sister Carolyn for her enthusiasm, confidence, and countless hours of help to make this come together

Thank you to my husband Rich for all of the extra time and energy needed to see this project through to completion

Thank you to my parents for their encouragement and support in this new endeavor

I couldn't have done it without all of your love and support!

Contents

Chapter 1

I looked down at my fingernails as I continued to scrub them in the sink before heading into the operating room. Even though I had done this same thing hundreds of times, I took longer than usual today. I was thinking about Thomas Snyder and the surgery I was about to perform. I had seen Thomas last week at the grocery store, and now his life was in my hands. I was somewhat distracted, thinking about him and his wife, MaryAnne, and their two children at home. While complacency was never something I struggled with, I took extra care today. The Snyders had lived down the street from me for years, and they were good people. We were not close, but I did see them out and would chat with them periodically. I didn't know how I would be able to face them if something went wrong. I tried not to think about it. His current situation wasn't exactly something I had control over. The freezing rain had made the roads slick and the other driver had tried to stop, but skidded on the ice, coming to a stop against the driver's side door of his car. The car door had been totally smashed in and Thomas had been speared in the side, cracking three ribs and causing internal bleeding. I was called in to repair whatever damage we found inside and to stop the internal bleeding. As I finished my mental preparation for the procedure, one of the OR techs popped into the scrub room.

"Doctor, we're ready for you," she called and I nodded.

"Yeah Lauren, I'll be right there." I said a quick prayer and headed into the OR. All of the techs were in place doing their final pre-surgical checks. "Hi Thomas. Are you ready to get started?" I asked with a chipper tone to my voice.

"I'm a little nervous, but alright … all things considered," he said shakily, visibly scared about undergoing surgery.

"You'll be fine," I said, smiling behind my surgical mask. I was sure he couldn't see my mouth smile, but I was hoping my eyes would show it and my tone would help put his mind at ease. "Just relax and the next time I see you, we'll be in the recovery room."

The anesthesiologist put the mask over Thomas's face and began monitoring his patient. After a few deep breaths, his eyes started to flutter and he drifted off. "Looks like you've got an audience today," the anesthesiologist said, motioning with his chin toward the windows on the far wall of the surgical suite. I looked over to see three people filing into the small observation room: the Chief of Surgery at the hospital, the hospital's Risk Manager, and the Head of Nursing. I had gotten to know all of them in some fashion over the past five years that I had worked here and I had become accustomed to being observed during procedures. Still, I stiffened and took a deep breath as I thought about being watched during the surgery. I wasn't nervous about being observed, but it sometimes made me second-guess some of my decisions. *No, not today,* I chanted in my head. I wasn't going to let myself be distracted. I took a deep breath and began my procedure.

"Ready to close," I said as we finished up the repair work and began suturing. It had been ninety minutes of painstakingly detailed work and I was glad to be able to let my mind, and my hands, rest. "Good job everyone," I said to my team. With that, I stepped back and sighed, throwing a quick glance over to the observation room. A small smile passed over their lips and the Chief nodded approvingly at my work today. Howard was a surprisingly unassuming man in his late forties. From his lighthearted and outgoing demeanor you would expect that he was a local mailman or something equally quaint, rather than the Chief of Surgery at a major metropolitan hospital. He had a full head of light brown hair, warm brown eyes, and a tan tone to his face. The tan may or may not have been his natural skin tone. Since he and his family always went on warm-weather vacations in the winter and spent most of their summers outdoors, it was hard to tell. His almost boxy face was framed with a strong jaw line that made him photograph very well for all of the hospital promos and the publications he was cited in. He had a strong but warm handshake and a laugh that made everyone feel like they had known him for years.

Howard had been one of my mentors when I first came to Belvidere Hospital and I had worked under him for years, eventually getting to know him and his family on a personal level. I valued his friendship, and I also respected his opinion. Even though it was intimidating to have someone watching over my shoulder, I appreciated his honest and helpful feedback. He always seemed more focused on helping me better myself as a physician, rather than quickly pointing out if I had done something wrong or not as well as I could have.

The other two observers generally kept their feedback to themselves. Nurse Chapel, no one called her by her first name for fear she would be offended by such a familiar and casual tone, was the head of the nursing staff and a cold, bitter woman in her late fifties. She always wore her hair pulled back tightly in a bun with her lips pursed and her jaw set, like she was ready to hiss at you on a moment's notice. She had a nice figure and a face that would suggest that she was quite attractive in her twenties and thirties, but it looked like the years had been long and her job had taken its toll on her. I didn't know her well, but I had heard the nurses talk about her and she ran a very tight ship. In her role, it was a necessary personality trait to have, but it seemed like her people skills could have used a little bit of work.

The Risk Manager, Greg, was a typical business man. He appeared rather generic with blond hair cut high and tight. He always seemed nice enough but wasn't much of a conversationalist. He took his job seriously and treated all of us at the hospital, doctors included, like we were pawns he was maneuvering in some grand business game.

The Head of Nursing and the Risk Manager were typically there to evaluate the other people in the operating room as well as processes and workflows, and they only occasionally had feedback specifically for me. The Risk Manager in particular would more often take notes on things that had happened that could be a concern, then watch for those patterns again and bring them up at department meetings. He did bring valuable insight to our procedures and protocols, as well as helping physicians who had issues come up, but up to this point I had not had a reason to interact much with him. By the time I had turned around, they were already walking out of the observation room. I relaxed a little bit as I walked out of the OR suite and into the scrub room. I stripped off my dirty surgical scrubs and headed to the family waiting room.

I saw MaryAnne pacing nervously in front of the vending machine in the surgical waiting room. Her long, red hair was pulled into a messy ponytail and she was clearly exhausted.

"Hi MaryAnne," I said warmly as I approached her with a smile. "Let's go to the consult room." I gestured to a small private room a few yards away. She instantly got a nervous look on her face as she looked around at the other dozen or so people who were waiting to hear about their loved ones. I quickly jumped in before even getting to the room. "We just like to talk to you separately from all of the other families who are waiting. Thomas's case isn't any of their business." I gestured for her to sit down at the small conference table and I sat down opposite her.

"Everything went fine during the surgery. He has three broken ribs on his left side from the accident. The piece of metal that pierced his side had punctured his spleen. I tried to repair the damage, but there had already been enough blood loss that it had to be removed. It was ischemic, which means the blood supply was cut off for too long, so the tissue had died. You can live without your spleen, so there's no need to worry about that. Overall everything went fine and you'll be able to see him shortly."

She nodded her understanding and gave me a quick, forced smile.

"Thank you Doctor."

"You're welcome. I'll be up this afternoon to check on him in recovery and see how everything is going. And if you have any other questions for me after you've had some time to gather your thoughts, you can ask me then."

We finished up with our pleasantries and I stood up, escorting her out of the consult room over to the desk where the guide could help MaryAnne find her husband's recovery room. I made my way to the locker room to grab my coat and have a quick break outside before I started doing my rounds.

I had quit smoking about six months ago. It had taken quite a while and an exorbitant amount of willpower but I had finally kicked the habit. Even though a lot of people say that you need to break some of your routines that you associate with smoking, this was one routine I couldn't break. Truthfully, I needed these quick moments to regroup during the day.

I stood outside in the courtyard, leaning against a lamppost in the bitter cold. I loved living in Chicago, but it was days like this that I seriously entertained the idea of moving back to Texas.

I certainly wouldn't need eight layers on to walk outside in Austin in January. The cold was starting to numb my fingers, but I took in the numbing feeling and thought about the sensation from a medical perspective. I thought about each individual prick of cold in my fingertips and the sluggish and tight feeling in my fingers. I was fascinated how the human body reacted to the elements. I exhaled and watched as the steam from my breath billowed up in a big cloud and then dissipated into the light breeze.

Right now I was the only one outside and I appreciated the silence. It gave me time to let my thoughts flow freely and not be forced to make small talk with other people. I looked back at the snow covered trees and the picturesque scene in front of me, appreciating the continual rebirth of the city, something that warmer climates would never have. Even through the bitter cold and watching all of the flowers dying off, there was a beauty to it. And the certainty that "this too shall pass." These types of thoughts always made my mind begin to think about the bigger picture and deeper meanings in life, particularly right after I had a tough surgical case. How easily it could have gone the other way … A bird landed on a branch in front of me and chirped a few times, breaking my train of thought. He dipped his head, then fluttered away. I took another deep breath followed by a long exhale before continuing my routine. After clearing my head, I would mentally go back over my case before heading back inside.

It was nice to have some alone time to think about my work from earlier in the day, replaying all of my decisions and seeing if I would have done anything different. There were some minor complications, but I thought I had done a good job of reacting quickly to them, and everything had worked out fine for Thomas. Plus, complications didn't mean that I had done anything wrong. They were just a fact of life. After my mental review, a smile of satisfaction passed over my lips as I thought about how well the procedure had gone. I was sure Howard would tell me what he thought later too.

Even though it was freezing cold outside, it was nice to have had that short five minutes to myself. My fingers had gotten sufficiently stiff and slow moving in the cold, so I pushed away from the lamppost and headed back inside the warm hospital hallways. Back in my smoking days, I always opted to take the stairs on my way back up from a break. It was three flights, but I hated being in the elevator after a smoke break. I had always felt like the patients were staring at me in disapproval, like I had let them down or something. I had found it ironic that there I was saving lives every day, while slowing chipping away at my own. Some days, I would take the elevator and just smile to myself thinking that I had been free for a whole six months now. On other days, depending on my energy level, I would still take the stairs just for the extra boost of energy.

Today I took the stairs quickly, invigorated by the icy January breeze. I headed back to the locker room and quickly got ready to do my rounds. I checked in on two of my other patients before heading down to get some lunch in the cafeteria. I wanted to give Thomas some extra time for the anesthesia to wear off so that I could actually talk to him and see how he was doing. I had found that too soon after surgery the patients were not coherent enough to be able to comprehend what I was saying, let alone answer even basic questions.

After finishing lunch, I headed to Thomas's room to check on him. MaryAnne sat in the chair next to him and greeted me as I came over to the side of his bed. He was still groggy as he came out from under the anesthesia, but he seemed lucid enough to at least answer some of my follow-up questions. I began my physical evaluation as I started to talk to him.

"Hi Thomas, how're you feeling?" I asked with a calm, soothing tone. Overall, he seemed to be doing pretty well. He didn't answer right away, but instead nodded a slow, sleepy nod. "The surgery went really well and we were able to repair all of the damage from the accident. We had to take your spleen out since it was damaged, but you'll be fine. We're going to keep you here for a few days and watch how the recovery is going, but I wouldn't anticipate any problems," I said, waiting for him to speak and show some signs of having understood.

"Thanks doc ... I really appreciate everything you did for me." Thomas didn't show much sign of pain, but then again he had enough morphine going through him that he shouldn't been feeling much of anything right now. He paused, looking like he was about to say something else, but wasn't sure if he should. After a few more seconds, he continued. "It must've been quite an interesting case today."

"Oh? How so?" I asked, my eyebrows instinctively coming together as I tried to figure out what he was getting at.

"Well, I just mean having an audience."

"Oh, right, the observation team. They come in from time to time to observe the doctors and nursing staff during surgery. Nothing to be concerned with," I said very nonchalantly, not telling him that they sometimes made me nervous too.

"They just seemed ... I don't know ... almost menacing or something ... Especially that dark haired guy on the end." He had an almost anxious look on his face as he remembered the observation team, but right away he seemed embarrassed to have said anything at all. He looked off in the other direction, probably hoping I would let it go.

I continued my physical exam as I thought about what he said. I was remembering back to the observers and how they might appear to a patient who hadn't been introduced to them. I could definitely see how someone could find them intimidating, or menacing as Thomas had thought, especially Nurse Chapel. I knew Howard so well that I couldn't imagine him to be intimidating, but Thomas must have meant him. His strong jawline and boxy face could come across as threatening. The Risk Manager just looked too generic to be intimidating.

I shook it off and continued my exam, not wanting to make Thomas feel awkward about his admission. He didn't bring it up again, so I changed subjects to get his mind off of this topic that seemed to bother him. I asked him how the girls were doing, which made him smile a lazy, groggy smile. He began telling me, in fairly slow speech, about how their Christmas had gone.

"Well, Taylor is eight and she's been really into Disney princesses this past year, so we got her new sheets and decorations for in her room," he said with a smile. His smile almost instantly turned to a grimace and I could see the tears well up in his eyes. "And then the accident happened, and I thought to myself "This can't be happening. I haven't even had a chance to get her room ready for her."" He sucked in a sharp breath and I saw one lone tear slide down his cheek. I glanced over at MaryAnne who reached for his hand and gave it a squeeze.

"You will, very soon. What about Alex, what did she get for Christmas?" I asked as I continued to look over his chart. He coughed and regained his composure.

"She is really getting into volleyball at school, so we got her all outfitted so that she can practice and try out for the team next year," he answered with a small smile.

"That's great! How old is she now, ten?"

"She turned twelve in November. Can you believe it?" We both laughed and I noted the clear cognitive status in his chart. I knew his daughters ages, but wanted to make sure that he could recall those details clearly as well. By the time I was finished with my evaluation, he had relaxed again.

"Everything looks good for now. Let us know if you need anything else for the pain, otherwise I'll be back to check on you again tomorrow," I said with a warm smile.

"Thanks doc. I really appreciate it," he answered as his eyes started to get heavy again. Within a few moments his eyes had completely shut and his arms went limp by his side as he drifted off again.

I squirted sanitizer onto my palm and was rubbing my hands together as I headed back to the nurse's station. The station was pretty chaotic for a Tuesday afternoon with a half dozen nurses and a handful of doctors packed tightly in and around the small space. There were four workstations for the shift nurses, and a bank of shelves with forms and charts and reference manuals on one wall. It always seemed to me like the lighting in here was a little too bright; too institutional. If I had to actually work in that station, I'd probably end up with a headache in less than an hour. Each of the four workstations had a phone, computer and printer, and all seemed to have an overabundance of papers, files, and binders. I had to chuckle to myself at how cluttered with paper this 'paperless' hospital seemed to be.

As I walked up to the counter, I caught Janice's glance and motioned to her that I wanted to talk to her. She was the shift nurse who was going to be taking care of Thomas tonight. I gave her my final orders for the day on Thomas and all of my other patients and headed briskly to the elevators. I was just hoping to not get drawn into any long conversations on my way out.

Luckily, when I made my way to the physicians lounge, I found it to be relatively empty. There were a couple of doctors sitting at a small table by the window reading newspapers, and a third doctor sitting on the couch drinking her cup of coffee and watching the news on the flat screen television. I walked over to the water cooler and got a quick glass of water. As I stood there with my cup, a bright orange flyer on the announcement board caught my eye. The spring fundraiser was coming up in a couple of months. It was a black tie event at the Planetarium, which sounded promising. I definitely preferred this to the fall golf tournament. They always asked me to play because I was one of the few female physicians who could actually keep up on a golf course. Unfortunately, most of the men didn't quite know how to react to that. I felt like they would either overcompensate by complimenting me on every shot, even the lousy ones, or they hardly spoke directly to me, afraid they might say the wrong thing. Occasionally, they would put me in a women's foursome, in which case they would always put us last so that we wouldn't 'hold anyone up.' That was equally as frustrating because we would be the last ones done and wouldn't have much time to clean up before the dinner portion of the evening.

I much preferred the black tie events. Any excuse to go shopping and have a day of pampering. Plus, Chicago was a great location to have black tie events. There were so many classy venues, and I adored getting dressed up and dancing. My sister, Cassie, had been very involved with a local charity and we would go to their fundraiser every year. A few years ago, their event had been at an art museum, and I still had the hand painted stars the children had made as auction items. I continued reading about Belvidere's gala and was sure my boyfriend Steven would be excited to go to it with me. Last year, it was at the Field Museum and we had a great time, so I was sure he would want to go again. I grabbed a flyer and took it with me so that I could talk to him about it tonight.

I finished up my water before making my way to the far right corner of the lounge and into the ladies locker room. I took off my lab coat and gave it a quick once over to see if it needed to go in the wash. This was a fresh coat this morning and still looked clean, so I hung it back up in my locker and grabbed my toiletries bag. I went to the panels of mirrors and brushed through my long, auburn hair. The static in this building was miserable. I ran my brush under the faucet and rebrushed my hair, which at least helped a little bit. I pulled my makeup bag out, touching up quickly around my eyes before spritzing with my Tearose perfume. *There*, I thought to myself as I looked in the mirror. *Not too shabby for the end of the day.*

Back at my locker I put my toiletries away and grabbed my long, grey ruffled trench style sweater. I tried to look nice at work without overdoing it. I had to laugh at one of the other female doctors who seemed to always have on fitted skirts, silk blouses, and stiletto heels that couldn't have been comfortable. Granted she was a gynecologist and only wore that on her non-surgical days, but I always wondered what her patients thought. Did they think she was getting ready to go out on a date after their appointment? Today I had gone with a pair of black pants, a pink scoop neck knit top, and low black heels. Just the right combination of feminine, professional and practical.

After layering on my hat, scarf, and overcoat, I grabbed my gloves and headed for the door. The cold air outside the hospital sent a quick shiver down my spine. Luckily it was only a block and a half to the subway station. It was already dark out when I left, and I walked quickly to the underground station, wanting to make it home by seven. Steven had promised to make dinner tonight and I hated when I was late. It was 6:20, but the actual train ride itself was only fifteen minutes, so I relaxed knowing that I would be home on time. I made my way down the steps and onto my platform just as the train pulled up. I quickly found a seat and settled in for my ride.

I would have stared out the window, except that we were in the tunnels so there was nothing to look at. Instead, I reflected over my day and smiled to myself. I loved being a doctor. Ever since I was little, I had wanted to be a doctor. I don't really remember what had initially piqued my interest in medicine, but I adored playing doctor with my parents and sister. I had the little plastic stethoscope and would always find some awful disease that would require a concoction of M&Ms and orange Tic Tacs to cure. As I got older and took biology classes in school, my interest grew even deeper and I couldn't wait to get to college to start diving into all of my pre-med classes. The part I liked the most was the mystery to be solved. You were given all of the clues, but there was no final chapter you could flip to and see if you were right. You had to come up with the answer on your own and there were no shortcuts to be had either.

Med school was everything I thought it would be, but my residency program could not come fast enough. I loved the hands on time with patients and getting to see how I was able to help real people. I felt like I had actually found my place in the world. Sure, they worked us ragged during those years, but looking back on it now, it all seemed worth it. I really got a chance to bond with my fellow residents during those years and build some lifelong friendships. For new doctors, it's pretty difficult to find time to make new friends outside of work. That was actually one of the reasons I had chosen Chicago. Some of my friends from college and med school also ended up in the city and I figured that would make it a bit easier to adjust to a new place.

As flashbacks of my first few years in Chicago danced through my mind, I listened to the rhythmic sound of the el and glanced out the window now that we had come above ground again. The el pulled up to the next stop and the woman announced the station name – the station before mine. As we pulled away, I looked down at my watch and put my gloves on, getting ready for my stop that was coming up next. The streetlights flew by and I stood up to walk toward the door while the train began to slow down once more. I stiffened and got ready for the burst of cold air that would hit me as soon as the doors opened. I walked across the platform, maneuvering through the crowds that were huddled waiting for the brown line train, and listening to the deep, hollow sounds of my footsteps on the wooden planks. The el station was old, but it had character. I had been on the transit systems in some other cities, like DC, and while they were nice and state-of-the-art looking, they lacked the character that the Chicago transit system had. The rickety old train cars that would screech around the corners in the loop added something to the commute.

The old el station fit perfectly into my neighborhood. The houses lining the street were mainly brownstones. All of them were unique with ornate stonework facades and regal stairways leading up to the porches. During the warmer months, most of the homes had beautiful little gardens and well-kept lawns. Albeit, it was pretty easy to keep the lawn well-groomed when there was literally less than two hundred square feet of grass to mow. Despite the small size of yards, it never ceased to amaze me how some of the residents had gardeners to take care of their yards and gardens. I thought it was actually kind of fun to take care of ours. It was small enough that just a couple hours was plenty of time to make it look beautiful, and adequate time to make you feel productive for the afternoon. I even went out and bought a little push mower, like the old style ones you see from years ago. I certainly didn't want a gas mower because then I would have to drive to the gas station that was not particularly close and pay twice what the normal gas prices were in the city versus the suburbs. Gas prices were a huge drawback of living in the city, so that was part of the reason I took public transportation so often, even though I had a car and the hospital had parking for physicians.

The two blocks from the station to my house seemed to be a long two blocks with the bitter wind blowing in my face. I passed the time looking at each house to see who still had their Christmas decorations up. For years, I had loved to keep the decorations up until late January, but Steven preferred to take them down right after the holidays. As a compromise, I left the wreath and red bows up, but the rest of it was already packed away until next year. Most of the houses in our neighborhood still had lights up, but the trees were out of the front windows, especially the real trees. Those had already drooped, forcing their owners to drag them to the curb a few days ago for trash day.

I walked up to the ornate iron gate and it creaked loudly as I opened it. I grabbed the mail from the mailbox and closed the gate behind me. About ten paces from the gate was the base of the stone steps. The house was actually much more grandiose than the homes our friends lived in. My grandparents had bought this brownstone in the 1940's when they first moved to Chicago and my grandmother lived in the house until about 10 years ago when my parents had moved her to a nursing home. My grandmother insisted that I take the house when she found out I was moving to Chicago. She said nothing would make her happier than to see family making memories in the house she loved so much.

From the stairs, I could see the lights on inside, and as I stepped up to the porch I could see Steven cooking in the kitchen. Roxie, my dog, was watching intently, hoping he may accidentally drop the entire pan of pasta on the floor. I walked through the front door and could smell the sweet smell of fresh bread, and the vodka cream sauce. He already had the table set beautifully, complete with fresh flowers in a crystal vase and candles lit. *Impressive,* I thought to myself.

"Hi guys! Smells fantastic!" I exclaimed as I walked through the door, setting the mail on the round mahogany table in the foyer. Roxie jumped off her bed and ran over to me, jumping and panting as I bent down to scratch her behind the ears. She was always so excited to see me. I hung up my coat and hat on our antique hall tree next to the door and looked at my hair in the adjacent mirror. The static from taking my hat off made it stick out in every direction, so I tried to smooth my hair before leaning over to pick Roxie up and wandered into the kitchen. Roxie was a mutt, but I loved her. The shelter had told me exactly what her breed was, something like a schnoodle, or a yorkiepoo, or something like that. I didn't really care, so I hadn't paid much attention. All I was looking at was that precious little face of hers and that had me sold. She was small enough for me to carry her around and was mellow, which was a must given my crazy work schedule. She nuzzled her little brown nose into my arm as I continued to scratch her head.

"Welcome home honey," Steven cooed as he leaned in to kiss me. "Would you like your wine?" he asked as he held up a glass of cabernet.

"Why thank you sir," I said, sipping my wine and evaluating the damage he had done in the kitchen. Actually, for him this wasn't too bad. I think he might have left a couple of clean dishes this time.

Within about fifteen minutes he had finished preparing dinner and we were sitting down eating. Both of us recapped our days to each other, showing the normal amount of enthusiasm that couples show after two years of dating. I told him about the surgery today with Thomas and how I felt bad that Howard had spooked him. Steven had met him before, so he knew how laid back Howard really was. Then Steven filled me in on the deals he was finalizing today and what the rest of his week looked like. He was in banking and was very good at it. His calm and collected personality had saved him during a number of tense business deals. No doubt this, and his tenacity, contributed to his success.

I had met him when I first moved to Chicago and even though he continued to pursue me, we didn't start dating for a couple of years. I really wanted to focus on my job to make sure people didn't pigeonhole me as someone who only wanted to do the bare minimum, or someone who was cocky enough to think they didn't have to put in their time and pay their dues. After two years of being friends, and dozens of rejected proposals for a date, I finally gave in and let him take me out to dinner and I hadn't looked back since. I smiled to myself, and just then he caught me in thought. He reached across the table to gently trace along my cheek with his index and middle finger as he got up from the table to grab the bottle of wine and top off both of our glasses.

We continued the chit chat for most of dinner, and then I remembered about the black tie event. He listened with interest as I filled him in on all of the details. He enjoyed going to black tie events with me, which was a good thing considering that we went to these types of events multiple times per year. He sat back in his chair with his left arm crossed over his chest, holding his wine glass in his right hand. In the candlelight his cool gray eyes sparkled and his warm smile gave me butterflies in my stomach. I smiled as my eyes wandered across his wiry frame and up to his cleanly shaven face. He had a sexy smile playing across his face and it made my breath catch. It seemed silly that he could still give me butterflies after two years, but I loved it. He leaned across the table and stroked my hand gently. "Of course I'll go with you sweetheart," flashing that irresistible smile. "And the Planetarium will be an awesome setting with the view and the patio. And romantic too" he threw in with a quick wink, tipping his glass to clink with mine.

After the main course was finished, we settled into the living room on the warm, sepia colored couch in front of the fireplace. Like most other brownstones in the neighborhood, we had twelve foot ceilings, meaning that most winter nights were on the cool side. On the especially cold nights, like tonight, Steven would build a fire to help warm up the house. Tonight, it made for an especially nice effect. I could hear him rattling around in the kitchen, and then he appeared holding a plate with tiramisu and two forks. He paused behind me and kissed the back of my neck before walking around the end of the couch and putting the dessert down on the dark cherry coffee table.

The tiramisu was delicious, and the wine went perfectly with it. I cuddled up next to him with my glass of wine and pulled a blanket over the top of us. I always felt so safe and warm in his arms. He stroked my hair as we continued to talk and look out the window at the snow that had started to fall late in the evening. After about an hour, he took my wine glass from me and grabbed my hand, pulling me towards the bedroom. "It's getting late. Time for bed," he whispered in my ear as he pulled me up from the couch.

* * *

It was a warm, sunny day in Austin and I was running around in my backyard with my sister. She was two years younger than me, but we got along really well, especially considering I was ten and she was eight. Most of my other friends couldn't stand their siblings at this point, but I thought Cassie was pretty cool to play with. We had been playing on the slip'n'slide all afternoon, but we were starting to get bored with it. The grass was too mashed down now and waterlogged to be soft anymore, so we turned off the hose and were onto the next thing to keep us entertained.

Ours was one of the few houses in the neighborhood, at that time anyway, that had an in-ground pool, and we definitely got good use out of it. We would swim almost every day during the summer, and would practice our diving and synchronized swimming. When I wasn't dreaming about being a doctor, I would pretend I was a synchronized swimmer. That afternoon Cassie and I had been playing in the pool, diving for rings, and having contests to see how long we could hold our breath under water.

As the afternoon wore on, my mom would come out and check on us and bring us snacks. She would always have some little comment to us, like 'you better be careful or you'll shrivel up so small you won't stretch out again,' but she would always leave us to play. We had been around the pool long enough that she trusted us to be careful. And she was always in the kitchen baking or cooking, so she could look out the window and see us at the pool. As it started getting later in the day, we heard her voice call to us from the kitchen window that it was time to get out of the pool and come inside since it looked like rain was coming. Knowing we would get to play in the pool again tomorrow, we didn't protest. Cassie started picking up our toys from around the yard and I jumped back in the pool to get our diving rings out. I had five of them on my arm and swam over to the sixth ring that was under the ladder on the side of the pool. I grabbed it and started to head back to the surface when I felt something pulling from around my waist. I opened my eyes, looking down at my waist and saw the edge of the ruffle on my swimsuit, caught on the edge of the ladder. I tried to pull harder, and the fabric ripped a little, but the seam was strong and it was wedged between the side bar of the ladder and the rung. I started to panic. My arms started flailing, flipping the rings off and sending them sinking back to the bottom of the pool. I gasped, taking in a mouthful of chlorinated water, then quickly gritted my teeth and snapped my mouth shut again. I knew I wasn't close enough to the surface to get my head above water. I had to get loose. I tried to turn around to get a better angle on the edge of my suit, but the snag kept me from being able to turn around all the way. I was finally able to

19

make my legs stop kicking me towards the surface long enough to fall closer to the ladder. With all my strength, I pull on the edge of my suit as hard as I could and I heard a rip, then a thud and everything went black.

I had the sensation of slowly falling backwards, and I opened my eyes. I could see the shimmering water up above me and I could hear a silky voice telling me to start swimming. I felt so confused and weak right now. Then all of the sudden, I felt my body lurch upwards, almost like a reflex and the voice shouted at me to swim. My mind told my arms and legs to kick, but it was like my body was not listening to my mind anymore. The voice started to shout at me and now I could see the outline of a man's face. He had dark hair, but the chlorine was stinging my eyes and I pulled them closed tightly against the burn. My mind kept ordering my body to move, but it still didn't seem to be listening. I opened them in time to see an arm plunge into the water and grab my wrist.

Chapter 2

"A hhh!!!" I shot straight up in bed, gasping for air and clutching my chest. I was so disoriented, so I just sat upright in bed for a minute, trying to catch my breath.

"Honey, what's wrong?" Steven asked, still half asleep, only partially mentally engaged in his question, and still hugging his pillow. "Bad dream?"

"Yeah, I guess so. I was dreaming about that time in the pool with Cassie. I'm fine," I said with a sense of exhaustion in my voice. I got up to get a drink and splash some cool water on my face. I had had this dream before, but I had been having it more often these past six months than I had in the past. The first few times I'd had the dream when Steven was over, he had snapped up on full alert, expecting that someone was breaking in, or some other emergency that required him to spring into action. Now he waited until I would shake him in the middle of the night before he would fully wake up. I threw on my robe and slid my feet into my slippers. It was entirely too cold to go to the kitchen barefoot and in just my nighty.

The floorboard by the door to our bedroom creaked as I walked by, and I could hear Roxie's collar jingle as she shook her head and got out of her bed to see if she could be of any comfort. I picked her up and walked into the kitchen to grab a glass out of the cupboard. The filtered water from the front of the stainless steel fridge was cold and helped to soothe my jitters from the sudden jolt of waking up screaming. Thank goodness I didn't have any surgeries this morning, otherwise I'd be needing a brisk run and a couple of cups of coffee in order to stay alert in the morning.

I sat at the table and tried to clear my head before going back to bed. I didn't want to toss and turn for hours and keep Steven up. I looked up at the top of the windows in the dining room at the ornate glasswork. All of the tall windows in the dining room and the living room had beautiful stained glass window panes along the top edge. The sunlight cast a gorgeous pattern on the hardwood floor when the sun would hit it just right, but the dim light from the streetlamp didn't do it justice.

I finished my glass of water and Roxie looked up at me, cocking her head to the side. She gently licked the edge of my wrist and rested her head on my forearm. I filled up her water dish again and we both headed back to the bedroom. This time, I made a deliberate effort to step over the threshold so that it wouldn't creak and wake Steven up again. I took off my robe and threw it over the arm of my chair, and stepped out of the plush purple slippers. Usually Roxie slept on the floor, but tonight I slid under the covers, and put her on top of the blanket right next to me.

My eyelids were getting heavy, but I continued to pet her until I started to nod off. This time, I hoped, I wouldn't dream of swimming pools.

As I drove down my street the next morning on my way into work, I glanced over at the Snyder's house and I could see an older woman playing with Alex and Taylor in the living room. I'm sure MaryAnne had spent the night at the hospital with Thomas. I would be checking in on them first thing when I got to the hospital. During my drive, I reflected back on my evaluation with him yesterday after the surgery. He seemed like he was okay, but I couldn't shake the look on his face when he mentioned that Howard was "menacing." At first I had thought it was sort of funny that someone would view him that way, but something in the way Thomas looked at me when he said that, it felt very … ominous? No, that didn't seem like the right way to describe it, but I couldn't place the words.

As I continued to mull it over and think about each of the people in the operating room and in the observation room, it suddenly struck me. The team doesn't come into the observation room until the patient is anesthetized for exactly that reason. They wouldn't want the patient to feel anxious or worried that they were being watched. I would have to ask him about this again when I checked on him this morning.

I made it to the hospital a little before eight. I usually liked to be in earlier, but given how poorly I had slept the night before, I was pretty impressed that I was in before nine! As soon as I walked into the physician lounge I could smell the sweet smell of fresh muffins and pastries. Some drug rep must be in today pitching a new line. At this point I'd gladly take the free muffins since I hadn't had a chance to stop for breakfast on the way in. I quickly settled in and then headed out to check on Thomas. I would grab breakfast after my visit with him.

"Good morning," I announced as I came into Thomas's room. MaryAnne was already awake and reading a magazine, but stood when I walked in. I began going through my regular follow up questions and evaluation, trying to think of how I was going to bring up his comments from yesterday "casually" in the conversation.

"The accident was just so crazy," he was saying, "almost like everything was happening in slow motion. Like I could see it all happening but couldn't do anything about it. And everything after that seemed like such a quick blur. Riding in the ambulance, coming here, and getting prepped for surgery. But then things slowed down again and I remember talking to you before we started," he said with a comforted smile.

"Thomas," I asked in a very laid-back tone, "you mentioned you saw the observation team in the operating room. I'm curious, what else do you remember from the surgery?"

"Well, I remember hearing muffled voices, mainly yours and another lady. It sounded like the one who was here when I first woke up. I couldn't hear exactly what you were saying, but I could hear your voices. And I had an overall numb and limp type of feeling, like a sort of darkness or cloud or something was passing over me. And then I remember looking over at those guys watching us. I mainly just remember the guy on the end, with his dark eyes, watching over the scene." He paused for a second, trying to read my expression. That was one thing we got really good at during our residency: keeping a straight face. When I didn't respond right away, he followed it up with "Why, is something wrong?"

"Oh no, it's just that usually the patients don't remember much from during their surgery. Usually the last thing they remember is me telling them I'll see them in the recovery room." I looked up from the tablet with a pleasant, but detached smile.

"Well, does that mean that there's something wrong with me that I do remember more?" He gave me a little half smile, his face registering a hint of worry. He looked anxiously over at MaryAnne who was watching me carefully.

"No, I'm sure it just took the anesthesia a little longer to set in with you." I said, not entirely sure whether that was the truth or not. I finished up my exam and told him that one of my colleagues would be back again the next day to check in with him, since it would be Saturday. If all went well over the weekend, he would probably get to go home early next week. Both he and his wife smiled at the thought and thanked me again.

I walked back to the lounge and continued to mull over what Thomas had said. I walked through the door and immediately saw Howard leaning up against the counter talking to another doctor that I didn't know very well. His eyes caught mine and he nodded, letting me know he wanted to talk to me after I got settled.

After I grabbed a muffin and some coffee, I took a seat at the table by the window. Howard politely excused himself from his conversation, topped off his coffee and joined me.

"So what'd you think of the surgery yesterday?" I asked, not particularly anxious, but just curious as to his observations. He grinned widely, showing a long line of perfect, sparkling white teeth.

"How do *you* think it went?" This was his typical approach he had used when mentoring me. He didn't like to show his cards first, so he would hold his comments until after I told him what I thought. He was always examining my deeper thought process versus just evaluating my results, since results can be misleading. You can do everything right and a patient may still die, or you can make a big mistake and the patient can still pull through. As Chief of Surgery, he was making sure we were thinking about things correctly not just looking at final outcomes.

I started with my overall assessment of the case and its outcome, then went back to go through the narrative of Thomas's case step by step and the decisions I had made. There were some minor complications that were quickly addressed but we still dissected the events leading up to that point, my possible courses of action, and the reason I chose the path I did. After I had finished, Howard went through his perceptions of the case in the same detailed manner as I had. We didn't go through all of my cases in this much detail, but since he had observed, I figured it was a good idea to get his feedback. As we started to wrap up our review of the case, I decided to ask him about Thomas's comment.

"Howard, one last question for you. Did you notice anything weird with the timing of the anesthesia?" He paused for a moment, his eyebrows coming together.

"No, not that I can remember. Why do you ask?"

"Well, it's just that the patient said he remembered looking over at the observation room and saying that "the guy on the end looked menacing." Typically, he should have already been under by the time you came in." Howard started thinking about it, but before he could get too far in thought he started chuckling.

"What? What're you laughing at?" I asked, with a smile on my face now too.

"It's just that I've never been described as 'menacing' before. I didn't realize I had that effect on people!"

"Yeah, I guess he would have been talking about you. Greg wouldn't exactly be considered menacing. But you didn't notice anything with the anesthesiologist?"

"No, but maybe it was actually just a very vivid dream he had while he was under, and since the setting was the same he assumed he had really seen it."

"Yeah, that's true. Well thanks Howard for your feedback. I really do appreciate it," I said with a warm smile.

"Oh, one more thing," he added as I started to get up from the table, "we have a new batch of residents coming through in about six weeks or so. Could you take one for a 90 day rotation?" he asked.

"Yeah, sure. Just let me know as we get closer." He smiled broadly as I agreed. "And thanks for the feedback on yesterday's case," I said as we both walked away from the table.

"Anytime Suzanne. Alright, I'm off to do rounds so I'll see you around" and with that I was off to start checking on my patients too.

I was getting excited thinking about our date tonight, which helped the day to pass more quickly than most days. It was a Friday and Steven was taking me out to dinner tonight. He had chosen a chic little sushi place along Michigan Avenue that we had heard great things about, but never had a chance to try.

As soon as I got home, I quickly showered and started deciding on what to wear for the night. I settled on a knee length blue satin dress, with a halter top neckline and ruching along the left side. Whoever came up with the concept of ruching should be given a medal! Between the slimming effect and concealing any little bulges, it was perfect for a dinner date, or any occasion really. Given the temperature outside, I opted for a dressy black cardigan so that I wouldn't be shivering in the restaurant, as I so often did.

I could hear the grandfather clock in the foyer chime seven, so I quickly finished up to meet Steven in the kitchen. Rounding the corner I could smell his intoxicating cologne and a smile automatically crept over my lips.

"Well don't you look beautiful," he whispered as his arm dropped to my waist, pulling me towards him for a kiss.

"Not too bad yourself," I cooed, passionately kissing him back. "Are you ready to go?" I smiled as I readjusted my skirt.

"Yep, and I even called for a cab so we wouldn't have to walk to the corner in the snow to hail one," he smiled, proud of himself that he had thought ahead, and smiling as he looked down at my tall heels that I had picked. Definitely a good choice to have the cab pick us up here. He ushered me towards the door and helped me with my coat before grabbing for his own.

We chatted aimlessly in the back of the cab as it made its way through the city to our restaurant. He filled me in on his day, informing me of a last minute business trip on Monday and Tuesday to Indianapolis to close a deal they had been working on for the past few months. Hopefully once this was done he wouldn't have to travel as much. Not that he was gone on long trips, but Indianapolis and St. Louis were far enough away that it usually wasn't feasible to be there on time for an early morning meeting, so his trips often were overnight trips.

The cab stopped in front of a small restaurant, crammed in between a bar and what looked like some sort of office space. From the outside, I would guess you could have about forty people max in there, but maybe that was a good thing. Walking in, we could hear music in the background that seemed just a little too loud for a restaurant, but too quiet for a bar. The music was upbeat, techno style music with no lyrics. It did seem to fit the ambience of modern/chic in Chicago. The interior of the restaurant was surprisingly sparse, or I suppose 'minimalistic' from a décor standpoint. Most of the tables were small, dark wooden tables intended for just two people. The floors and walls were all smoothed concrete, with one having a rocky texture to it and water cascading down the length of the wall. The sushi chefs were behind a long, stainless steel counter with spotlights accenting this feature of the restaurant. Other than the chefs and the waterfalls, I noticed no other artwork or attractions in the small space.

We were quickly escorted to our table near the waterfall and at the end of a line of two person tables. Given the volume of the music, I decided I should move my chair to the side of the table so that Steven and I wouldn't have to be shouting over the music all night.

After savoring our delicious meal, the waitress cleared our plates, asking if we wanted to see a dessert menu. Despite how full

I was, it was a crime to not at least look at the dessert menu. Steven nodded and she disappeared with the dirty plates. A few moments later she quietly dropped off a small menu on the edge of our table.

"You really do look breathtaking tonight," he whispered in my ear, kissing my neck before pulling back to get a good look at my face. His gray eyes sparkled in the candlelight from the small globe on our table.

"Aww, you're just buttering me up, aren't you?"

"And if I were?" He smiled a cheeky little smile and gently kissed me on the lips, his right hand on the back of my neck underneath my hair. "So, what are you thinking about for dessert?" He said, keeping his hand behind my head, and grabbing the menu with his free hand. "Anything catching your eye?"

He typically let me choose whatever I wanted for dessert, and then would nibble off of mine. "Oh, you mean besides you?" I asked in a playfully seductive tone, to which he chuckled.

"That'll have to wait til later," he said, in an equally seductive tone, with a quick raising of his eyebrows for emphasis.

"Um … I'm thinking maybe green tea ice cream."

"In the middle of the winter?" he chuckled, and the waitress returned to our table. "One order of green tea and one order of red bean ice cream," he said, barely taking his eyes off of me.

"Sure thing" and she disappeared again.

We finished our dessert with the same low, seductive tone before braving the cold outside. Luckily, Michigan Avenue had cabs available about every fifteen seconds, so we weren't in the cold for very long. That was certainly something I appreciated about Chicago. If you lived in the city, it was so easy to make your way around without a car. Between the el and cabs, you could get just about anywhere really quickly and fairly cheaply. The late night cab smelled a little musty, but I didn't mind. I was too busy cuddling up next to Steven and taking in his scent to notice much else around me.

When the cab finally came to a stop outside of our house, Steven graciously helped me out and led me up the stone pathway to our front door, kissing me gently at the top of the stairs before unlocking the door. He pulled me inside and continued to press his warm lips against mine, kissing me tenderly as he unbuttoned my coat and hung it on the hall tree.

He smiled at me, captivating me with just one, smoldering look. I followed him to the bedroom without a second thought.

* * *

Monday was like any other day at the hospital. I had some pre-surgical consults to do with patients who would be coming in later in the week for procedures, as well as a few patients who were considering surgery and wanted to discuss all of the pros and cons, as well as alternative treatments. After my regular office appointments, I wandered back over to do a final check on Thomas. He had been progressing nicely and if everything checked out, he was going this afternoon.

"Hi Thomas," I smiled, "How're you feeling today?" He looked very alert, with good coloring. I pulled his chart up on the computer in his room and reviewed the nurse's updates on his conditions over the past two days.

"Oh, I'm feeling pretty good. It still hurts a little if I twist to the side, but I can get up and walk around by myself now."

"That's great Thomas. I'm glad to hear you're up and moving now," I said as I walked towards him to do a physical examination of his condition and ask him some additional questions about how things went over the weekend. I was finishing up when I noticed him shift and look down at his hands.

"Hey doc? Um … About the other day … I was kind of jab-bering on, wasn't I? I hope you don't think I'm crazy or anything like that." He looked down at his hands, embarrassed that he even had to bring this up.

"Don't worry about it," I said with a sincere smile on my lips, "Dr. Howard Barrett, the Chief of Surgery, was watching during the procedure, so you probably saw him. From a distance he can look intimidating, but he really is a nice guy."

"Dr. Barrett? I do remember seeing him there. He also checked on me over the weekend. He wasn't the guy I saw. It was a differ-ent dark haired guy. That other guy just looked … out of place or something." Thomas paused for a long moment, remembering back to his visions during the surgery. He began shaking his head, "No, it definitely wasn't Barrett … Listen to me!" he said with a tone of 1950's housewife in his voice, "going on and on about ghosts … You're gonna have me committed!' He said, waiting for me to deny his fears.

"Nah, I'm not gonna have you committed. Too much paper-work!" I teased, remembering back to what Howard had said. "It was probably just a very vivid dream that you were having. A lot of people get that when they're under anesthesia."

"But, Dr. Jacobsen, I know I wasn't dreaming. I've have very lucid dreams before and this was definitely not that. I know there was a guy watching me and you, and all of us in the room." He looked away from me with a torn look on his face, a look of newly found determination, but also fear of continuing to talk about this. "Oh well …" he sighed.

"Well Thomas," I declared emphatically, interrupting the si-lence, "everything checks out with you physically, so you're free to go home this afternoon. If I don't see MaryAnne again before you leave, tell her to call me with any questions. I'm just a few houses down."

I didn't want to push anymore on this watcher, or ghost, or whatever it was. I hadn't seen anyone and no one else from the OR commented on seeing someone out of place, so there was not really anything I could say to Thomas about this. I did believe, however, that he saw something. Whether what he saw was real or only in his head was a different story.

I stopped by the brightly lit nurse's station on my way off the floor to give them final orders and sign off on Thomas's discharge. As I was standing at the counter finishing up with Thomas's chart, I heard the overhead speaker chime and then a very monotone voice drone "Paging Dr. Forrester and Dr. Jacobsen."

I leaned over the counter at the nurse station and motioned for the nurse to hand me the phone and dial the operator. "This is Dr. Jacobsen" I said when the voice on the other end of the line picked up.

"Doctor, you're needed in surgical suite three immediately for an emergency procedure."

"What's the case?" I asked as I quickly finished with Thomas's file.

"A seven year old boy just presented to the ER. He fell from his roof and was impaled on some sort of bush or small tree. There's massive internal bleeding that needs to be stopped and his condition assessed. Dr. Forrester will meet you there."

"Thanks. I'll be right up," and with that I hung up and started walking towards the elevator.

I made my way to suite three and suited up for surgery. I walked over to the sink to begin my scrubbing ritual when Dr. Colin Forrester slipped into the scrub room and came to the sink right next to me.

"Doctor," he said in a low, jokingly serious voice. I looked over at him, just as his eyebrows were coming down from their playful expression. He had a lopsided smile on his face, with a playful gleam in his eye, but he didn't take his focus off of his scrubbing. He was a good eight inches taller than I was, so it was pretty easy for him to glance over in my direction without taking his eyes off his work for more than half a second.

"Doctor," I chimed back with a nod of my head and smirk running across my lips. Colin and I had been friends for the past four years, and this kind of joking around was a common type of interaction for us. In our early years, we had danced around the idea of possibly dating, but ultimately decided that dating someone who worked in the same hospital was probably a bad idea. Neither of us wanted to leave Belvidere, so we settled on just being close friends instead.

He had gone down the path of trauma surgery, so I knew this must be a pretty bad case if they had called both of us in. We were coming to the end of our scrubbing ritual, so it was time for both of us to be serious about our work ahead. He must have read the change in my posture, because he spoke first.

"So, did they brief you on this case yet?" His tone suggested he hadn't been told any details except to get into surgery.

"Just a quick overview. They said a seven year old boy fell off his roof and into some bushes, or shrubs, or something like that. Apparently he's been impaled, presumably through the upper thorax if you're here, and has some internal damage and bleeding in his lower abdomen, which is apparently why I'm here." We both finished up as the nurse came to help put our gloves on.

"Man, I hate it when it's kids. And what the hell was a seven year old doing on a roof anyway? Aren't his parents watching him at all?"

Colin was right. Pediatric cases were always tough from an emotional perspective, but also because all of the structures were so much smaller. We both took a deep breath and walked into the operating room. The boy was already prepped up and fully under at this point. I could only guess from the large opening in the blue paper that there was a tremendous amount of damage to his torso. I walked over to his midsection and Colin walked around to his far side, up at shoulder level.

"Oh Christ …" Colin whispered as he assessed the injuries. I could tell he was grimacing, even though his mouth was covered by his mask. His eyes and furrowed brows spoke volumes. This wasn't going to be an easy case. I looked down at the injuries in front of me with an equally pessimistic response. Coming straight up out of his right side was a branch about three quarters of an inch thick. The area around the puncture looked tattered, no doubt due to the boy flailing after he landed. I shuddered to think what we would see when we actually cut into him. I looked over at my tech, Lauren, who was going to be assisting me on my portion of this case.

"Alright, let's get to work. Scalpel," and I held out my hand for the familiar pat of the instrument. After I had a chance to take a look at the extent of the damage, I stepped back from the table for a moment to get my plan together.

"How do things look down there?" Colin asked without looking up from his work.

"There's some damage to the large intestine, right kidney and his appendix will need to come out for sure. I can't tell how much other tissue damage is here. How about you?" I asked as I stepped back up to the table, ready to get started on the large intestine.

"I don't know …" He trailed off, with a pessimistic sound to his voice. "The main part of the branch went straight through his lung. He must have started thrashing around because some of the surrounding valves and tissue are severely damaged, including possibly the left ventricle … I can't even see the extent of the vessel damage yet either. He's been slowly bleeding out for at least twenty to twenty five minutes."

There was a pregnant pause, and his tone said it all. It may be too late for this boy. "The best I can do is to try to stop the bleeding first, and then work on repairs."

"Let me know" I murmured as I got underway.

Almost forty minutes had passed and I was finishing up on the tricky parts of my surgery. The last thing left was to remove the appendix and I would be done. Based on the sighs coming from the other end of the table, I was not optimistic about how things were going with Colin's piece. Appendectomies were pretty straight forwards, so I relaxed a little as Lauren and I worked swiftly and almost silently. I straightened up as we finished ligating the vessels and prepared to make the final cuts to remove the appendix.

"Scalpel," I said quietly as I looked up and held my palm out. I felt the metal strike my hand, and started to close my fingers around it when something caught my eye. I jerked my head quickly to the right, and my eyes locked gaze with a man standing in the OR. My fingers released.

"Shit!" I gasped as I felt a searing pain shoot up my arm from my hand. Lauren grabbed the scalpel that now lay, flat side down luckily, on top of the drape over the boy's belly. "Damn it!" I said, looking down at the incision to the inside of the first knuckle on my left hand.

"What's going on down there?" Colin asked, with a hint of panic in his voice. "Are you alright?"

"Yeah, I'm fine. The scalpel slipped and I cut myself," I replied, with notable embarrassment, and irritation in my voice.

"Do we need to call in a back-up for you?" He asked, still keeping his eyes focused on his work ahead of him.

"No, I'll be back in ninety seconds. Nurse," I motioned to one of the techs to come with me back to the scrub sink. The cut seeped slowly as I took the surgical gloves off. *Damn!* I thought to myself. I was always so careful during surgery. I hardly ever had any accidents. I ran the water over my hands and started cleaning out the cut. I gasped through gritted teeth as the water stung the open cut and sent ripples of pain up through my arm. I would have to take a closer look at this once we were done here. I may need stitches, but I was close to finishing up with this case and wanted to get my part done to see if I could help Colin on his work. I held my hands out, careful not to touch anything as the nurse bandaged up my cut and put on fresh gloves.

"Alright Lauren, lets finish up with this appendix," I said calmly as I walked back into the operating room. She had a very sheepish look on her face and kept her head down, making sure not to make eye contact with me.

"I'm sorry, Doctor," she said in voice low enough that it was practically a whisper.

"Don't worry about it" I said gently. "It wasn't your fault at all. I got … distracted."

"What happened Jacobsen?" Colin asked from the other end of the table. He usually referred to me by last name during surgeries. Somehow 'Dr. Jacobsen' seemed too formal or distant, and first names seemed too common. Even though we were friends, we had a job to do.

"I … I thought I saw something."

Chapter 3

*T*he boy's surgery had taken us long enough into the afternoon that the next shift of physicians had already arrived by the time the surgery was done. For all of his efforts, Colin hadn't been able to save the little boy. The damage had been too extensive and he had been bleeding for too long before he arrived at the hospital.

This wasn't the first time that we had been in surgery together where the patient didn't make it through, but it never got easier. While I could recognize that it wasn't Colin's fault, it would take him much longer to come to that point himself, if he ever did. The worst part about it was having to go back out to the waiting room and tell the family that the patient hadn't made it, especially when the patient was just a child. One of the hardest parts about it was not even being able to say you're sorry. Those two little words, I'm sorry, always seemed to be the appropriate sentiment for people who had just lost a loved one, and it was almost impossible to try to empathize with the family when you couldn't even say that.

A law had been passed in Illinois a few years back that said doctors could apologize right after the incident, and that it wouldn't be held against them later as admitting they had screwed up. Now that law had been thrown out so you had to be very careful in how you spoke to families. Typical lawyers. Maybe if they were the ones delivering this news they would feel differently. I had offered to Colin to go talk to the family, given how upset he was. Granted, I too felt like I was going to throw up right now, but he had even more of a guilty feeling on his shoulders, whether it was valid or not, since it was eventually the boy's heart that gave out.

"No," he let out a long, defeated sigh. "Thanks for the offer Suz, but this one's on me," he said, shuffling solemnly out towards the waiting room. I knew he'd be gone for at least fifteen minutes, maybe more, so I used this as a chance to go outside for my quick 'not having a cigarette' break. The numbing cold would be soothing about now.

Back in the physician lounge, I headed to the locker room to change into my street clothes. With the new shift coming on, we were able to go and clear our heads. I caught up with Colin and we opted to go out for a cup of coffee to talk, rather than talking in the lounge. While most of the doctors were sympathetic when another physician lost a patient, you couldn't help but think that some of the more egotistical ones were thinking to themselves that they would have done better and that the patient would have pulled through.

We left the hospital in silence, heading down a block and a half to local coffee shop. This one was always less crowded than the Starbucks across the street from the hospital, so we would be able to talk a little bit more openly without being worried that someone would overhear us.

I went up to the counter to order our drinks and he settled down in a round little booth at the back, facing the windows so we would be able to see if anyone walked in that would require us to change topics. A few minutes later, I joined him with our hot cups of coffee. Putting my hands around my cup gave me a weird stinging sensation against my numb fingertips.

I glanced up at Colin, trying to read his sad blue eyes. His lips curled down as his fingers traced around the handle on the mug. I wasn't going to ask him what he was thinking about right now, or what he was feeling. I knew that feeling all too well. I waited for him to speak first.

"So what happened in there today?" he asked, looking up at me, his eyes locking in on my gaze. I looked down awkwardly, knowing full well how silly it would sound when I explained it to him. I took a long sip of my coffee and got my thoughts together as to how I was going to explain it to him without sounding totally insane. I figured I may as well start at the beginning.

"Remember that car accident case I had last week?" Colin nodded in agreement. "Well, when I was talking to him post-op, he said that he saw a dark haired man watching us. I thought he had meant Howard, since the team was observing that day, but when I visited him again today he said that Barrett had been in to see him and that wasn't the guy he saw in the OR. I've known Thomas a long time, and he's not an irrational or superstitious guy, and he's not easily ruffled, but he seemed really scared by what he saw. And he is dead-set that it wasn't a dream or a hallucination or anything like that." I paused to see if Colin was giving me a look like I was completely crazy yet. Surprisingly, he actually seemed to be listening intently. Maybe he was just looking for something to take his mind off his other feelings right now.

"So were you just thinking about that this afternoon?" His voice seemed to have a hint of disappointment in it. Daydreaming during surgery was unacceptable, and usually a sign that you were losing your edge.

"No, not exactly," I said, letting out a long sigh. "Everything was going just fine. I had finished ligating the appendix and was ready to cut it out. I had relaxed a little bit since the hardest part was over, and I had my hand out for the scalpel. I had looked up as Lauren was putting the scalpel in my hand, and I swear I saw someone in the OR. He was about five feet away from me on the other side of the operating table." I stopped and shuddered at the memory of it.

"So I take it that's when you sliced yourself?" he said, with an understanding look on his face.

"I didn't actually slice myself, I just lost my hold on the scalpel and it fell on my other hand and cut it open." I looked down sheepishly at my hand as I recounted my accident to him.

"Here, let me see it." He reached for my hand and lifted back the bandage to take a look. I hadn't actually gone back to re-examine it after surgery, so it was probably a good idea to see how deep it was. Colin had a warmth and gentleness to his touch that I wasn't quite expecting. He lifted my hand up closer to his face so he could get a good look at it. As he gently placed his fingers on either side of the cut, I winced a little, instinctively twitching my hand. "Sorry Suz."

"That's alright. I'm just being a baby."

"Well, that's kind of an awkward spot. You may want to get a couple of stitches, just to make sure it heals quickly," he said gently as he lowered my hand back towards the table, his thumb rubbing the back of my hand quickly before he released it.

"So who was this guy you saw?" He picked up his coffee cup with one hand, leaning forwards over his other arm. His eager face had a mocking grin on it, like he was gossiping with girls about a cute boy across the room.

"No, you're just going to laugh at me. I know how dumb it sounds," and his expression turned to genuine interest.

"Try me," he said, raising his eyebrows and shooting me a smile.

"Well, he looked like he was maybe in his late twenties, with short, dark brown hair. He had a boxy jawline, and dark eyes."

I paused to take a drink of my coffee. I had only seen him for a moment, but that image had been burned into my mind.

"Now, when you say dark eyes, do you mean like a creepy 'devoid of life' black or just dark brown?"

"Dark brown."

"And what was he wearing?"

"You mean like all black?" I asked with a ridiculously dramatic tone and to that he smiled, the light dancing in his eyes. I smirked.

"Seriously, was he?" he teased.

"Oh ha ha, very funny. No, and he wasn't holding a big sickle either."

"Hey, I didn't say that! I didn't even suggest it. You came up with that one all on your own." He may not have said it, but he was certainly getting a kick out of this. Maybe it was a bad idea to share this with him. I squirmed in my seat before continuing.

"No, actually if I had passed him on the street he wouldn't have stood out at all. I mean, in the OR he stuck out like a sore thumb, but that's just because he wasn't gowned. He was just wearing jeans and a white button down shirt with the sleeves rolled up. When I looked up and caught his gaze, a weird expression flashed across his face, like he was surprised that I had seen him or something. Then I cut myself and looked down at my hand, and by the time I looked back up he was gone."

"That does sound crazy. No wonder you didn't want to tell me. I should have you committed," he teased, but it did make me somewhat uncomfortable. I fidgeted again in my seat and took another drink of my coffee. He could tell I was agitated.

"Sorry, I'm just playing. I don't think you're crazy. If you said you saw something, I believe you." His honesty made me smile slightly. And I did believe he was being honest with me, rather than telling me what I wanted to hear. Colin was one of the few doctors I knew that seemed to be open minded to things that were not yet fully explained by science and medicine.

"Thanks Colin. I'm still sorry I screwed up in the middle of surgery. I can't believe I did that!"

"Don't worry about it. It happens to the best of us," he said with genuine sincerity.

"Yeah, but I still feel like a newbie letting something like that happen." I wasn't sure if I should continue or not, so I chose my words carefully. "I hope that my having to leave in the middle didn't throw you off."

"Oh Suz, don't you dare think that. I mean, yeah, I was concerned about you when I looked over and saw you bleeding, but that didn't ... That didn't have anything to do with me losing that kid. I just ... I don't know what happened." He stiffed in his seat and stared down blankly at his coffee.

"Hey, it wasn't your fault," I began. "You know if I thought you had done something wrong I'd tell you, right?" He nodded thoughtfully. "You said so yourself when we first assessed his condition that it didn't look good. Not everyone can be saved," I said quietly. I reached over and took his hand him mine and squeezed it gently, rubbing my thumb along the side of his hand.

"I know me telling you this doesn't really make it better, but I think you did a really good job with him." He gave me a dutiful little smile and pulled his hand away, reaching up to run his fingers through his wavy, dark blond hair. As much as I hated to see him in pain, I caught myself noticing how especially handsome he looked right now. I don't know if it was the vulnerable side that I was seeing, or maybe the fact that he had feelings that ran so deep. His sharp cheekbones gave his face a tough look, but his soft lips accented his face and gave it an unexpected contrast.

"I don't know. I suppose so, but it doesn't make it any easier. I mean the kid was just seven years old." I thought I could see the signs of his eyes watering up. He rubbed his hands down along the side of his face, bringing his hands together in front of his chest and stretching them out in front of him.

"Okay, new topic," he declared with a smile. "So how're things going with you and Steven?" He had met Steven a number of times at parties and work events, and I think Colin genuinely liked him. They always seemed to get along really well, even beyond the required politeness for the situation.

"Pretty well actually. We were planning on going to the black tie thing in March, so that'll be fun. Are you gonna go?" Colin wasn't much of a schmoozer, but he knew how important these types of events were to the hospital, so he would usually go for a least part of the evening.

"Hmmm, well I haven't really thought about it yet. I'll have to see how things go over the next month or so."

"Are you dodging this because you don't have a date?" I prodded with enthusiasm on this question. I was an easier way for me to ask him about his love life. "You know, I do have friends who are *dying* to go out with you, so I'd be more than happy to hook you up."

"Thanks for the support mom, but I don't want to ask someone two months in advance of a date. I'll get back to you a couple weeks before hand if I'm going to need another date from you." In the past I had set him up a few times with my friends. It seemed so hard to casually meet people considering how many hours we always worked.

We stayed at the coffee house for another hour or so, catching up on our personal lives, and occasionally back over to work. By the end of the conversation, he was smiling again and seemed to have shaken the melancholy he had when we first walked in. I smiled to myself, thinking that at least I had done some good today. We finished up and headed towards the subway together.

He took a different train that was also going north, so we picked it up at the same stop.

"So what're you up to tonight?" I asked him casually.

"Oh, some buddies and I are going to Murphy's for a few drinks. One of our friends from college is in on a business trip. How about you? Any big plans?"

"Nope, Steven's actually out of town on a business trip, so I'm going to have a relaxing night in. You know, watch a chick flick, do my nails, that type of stuff." He knew me well enough to know that I was completely serious, otherwise he would have offered an invitation to join him and his friends. I had met some of them before, and had always thought they were a nice group. I considered whether I would be interested in a night out without Steven, but opted for girly night instead. By the time I had finished my contemplating, we were already at the subway station and heading down the stairs to the platforms.

"Sounds like a blast," he chortled. "You have fun with that," he said as he gave me a big hug at the foot of the stairs. "And thanks again for this afternoon. You always make me feel better," he said candidly.

"You're welcome Colin," I said as I squeezed him back. As he pulled away from me, I could see a slow smile start to form. "See you later," I said softly, with a slight sigh, taking in this very sincere moment with him. I headed to my platform and waited for my train. I got my cell phone out, ready to call Cassie as soon as I got on the train.

As soon as her husband Bob answered the phone, I could hear Cassie in the background playing with the kids and laughing loudly over the squeals coming from the little ones. She had three kids, all under the age of six, so she was usually running around after one of them. They were all well behaved, most of the time anyway.

"Just a second, Suzy. Cassie, it's your sister!" He called out to her, loud enough to be heard over the playing in the other room. I could hear her jog to the phone, and the dog's nails grappling on the floor as he tried to chase her.

"Hey big sis," she panted into the phone, obviously out of breath from the romping around, "what's new with you?"

"Oh, you mean besides my waking up screaming in the middle of the night?" I said sarcastically, with a forced laugh. I had told Cassie last week about the swimming pool dreams coming more often now. She hadn't known what to make of it, but always listened as I recounted the dreams. She had been there that day too, but obviously it didn't leave the same scar on her as it had on me. She just remembered being scared and running inside to get our mom and dad.

We talked on the phone about once a week, so she was usually pretty up to date on what was going on with me, but I hadn't told her about Thomas's vision yet. I filled her in on how it may or may not be related to my accident today in the OR. I went through all of the events of both in excruciating detail. Even though she was constantly busy with the kids, it always seemed like she had as much time as I needed. The time we had on the phone made the long distance between us seem a little bit easier to take.

Three years ago she and her husband had moved out to Nebraska for his job. The move had been really hard on both of us, but it also made me realize that I needed to make more female friends here in the city. I had a couple of guy friends, like Colin, but Cassie leaving created a huge void of other women to talk to.

She intently listened to everything I said, chiming in with the expected *yeah* and *uh-hums* throughout the story.

"So Cass, do you think I'm crazy?" Even to myself I sounded desperate.

"Well, if you are, you've always been that way then," she laughed quickly as she drew her thoughts together on what advice she should give me on the subject. My mind raced as I tried to figure out where she was going with this.

"What do you mean by that?"

"Well, even when we were younger you seemed to have an overactive imagination," she said in a very motherly tone. Her tone started to irritate me.

"So you think I'm making this up, like a monster under my bed or something?" I was clearly a little agitated and she immediately realized that we were not on the same page and not remembering the same events from our childhood.

"No, no Suzy. Not monster stories, or the tooth fairy or stuff like that. Don't you remember, after dad pulled you out of the pool, you swore you saw someone in there with you ..." She paused, waiting to see how I would take that piece of information. I honestly didn't know what to do with it. I hadn't really put the two together, despite how much time I had spent mulling things over and analyzing the events of the past week.

"A guy?" was all I could manage to say. She had a photographic memory of events, which was helpful, but also meant that it was sometimes hard for her to let things go. My memory of events tended to be a bit spottier than hers, usually just remembering the pieces I wanted to and the way certain events made me feel, rather than the details of it. Cassie could probably tell me exactly which swim suit I was wearing that day if I asked her.

"Yeah, the dark hair guy with dark brown eyes and that nice, sweet voice? You said you saw his face and that he was telling you to swim. How do you not remember that? You had dreams about him for the next month." I sighed, as a flood of memories came back to me. Again, they tended to be light on the details, but I remember how sad I was when I would wake up and realize that he wasn't real. I couldn't remember his face very clearly, only that he had been there with me in my dream.

"Do you remember what color towel dad wrapped around me too?" I said in a sarcastic tone that came across a lot snippier than I had intended.

"Yes I do. It was red with Strawberry Shortcake on it," she responded emphatically and we both laughed.

"Yeah, I guess I do remember that. I honestly hadn't even given that a second thought that they might be related. But if they are … Oh great, so I'm a thirty five year old woman with an imaginary friend. That's really awesome." Now I definitely felt stupid. Thank goodness my conversation with Colin hadn't taken this detour.

I exited the train and made my way back home while I continued to talk to Cassie about this. Luckily we managed to change topics away from my grade school problems of an imaginary friend by the time I got to my front door.

"So what's new with Steven?" She asked eagerly. I knew she was really happy in her marriage and with her family, but sometimes I think she liked to live vicariously through me.

"Oh, he's just out of town tonight on a business trip, so I'm having a girly night. But overall things are going really well! He seems super excited about the black tie event in March, so I was happy about that. He also liked the idea of having it at the Planetarium. He said it was very romantic," I said in a mock hoity-toity voice.

"Really?" she asked eagerly. "He liked the idea of a *romantic setting*?" Her voice went up a pitch as she asked this, clearly getting excited about something, although I wasn't exactly sure what.

"Yeah …" I said cautiously, with a hint of curiosity.

"Do you think he's going to propose?!" she squealed, but in a hushed voice.

"Frankly, I hadn't even thought that." Which was true. "Do you really think so?"

"Well, you've been dating for two years, and living together for almost eight months! Haven't you guys talked about it yet?"

"Well, not anything specific." I tried to remember back to some of the conversations, my heart quickening as I thought about the possibility that I might be getting engaged in a couple of months. Oh my gosh! There was so much to think about with – *wait!* I stopped myself mid-thought. I wasn't going to let myself get this excited about something that may not even be happening. "No Cassie, I'm not going to let myself go down this road just yet. If he does do it, I want to be surprised."

"Okay, okay. I just got a little carried away," she said. I could tell, even over the phone, that she was absolutely grinning ear to ear right now. Cassie loved weddings, especially if she got to help plan one. Given that I worked non-stop, I knew she was excited at the prospects of helping me plan mine.

"Look, I'll absolutely let you know as soon as anything happens, but I don't want to jinx it."

"Right, right, right!" She said excitedly. "Mum's the word!" And with that we said our goodbyes as I reached down to pick up Roxie.

I loved talking to my sister, but sometimes she would fill my head with crazy ideas. As much as I tried to forget that little seed that she had planted in my head, I couldn't help but let my mind wander to the fundraiser and Steven finding some clever and romantic way to propose, to our wedding, and the honeymoon in Tahiti …

I picked up Roxie, put her leash on her and took her outside in our little yard. It was still bitter cold outside, but the thought of Tahiti kept me nice and warm. We came back inside and I put on the kettle for a cup of cocoa as I went and got changed into flannel pants and a sweatshirt. I didn't feel like going to the effort of starting a fire tonight, but I threw on a chick flick, made my cocoa and wrapped up in a blanket. I loved the way the girly movies always gave you the butterflies in your stomach and that warm, fuzzy feeling all over. I suppose that was the hopeless romantic in me.

My movie was over by eight. For me, this would be an early night. Dealing with the little boy's death earlier today had taken so much out of me that I really felt exhausted, even at such an early hour. I did one last walk through of the house, taking in the soft sound of my bare feet plodding across the old hardwood floor. I got ready for bed, smiling at the thought that Cassie had planted in my mind about a possible upcoming proposal, and snuggled in under the sheets. I had given some thought to my future wedding, naturally, but I wasn't one of those girls who had the whole thing planned out by the time she was twenty. I tried to push the thoughts out of my mind though. When the time was right, it would happen. I was certainly glad though that Steven was not here tonight. I was sure he would have been able to tell that something was preoccupying my thoughts. Instead, on a night like tonight, I once again let Roxie sleep on the bed next to me. Within minutes, my eyelids were getting heavy and I was off to sleep.

It was about three in the morning when I heard my phone ring. It took me a minute to even realize that my phone was ringing in real life, and not just in my dream. With a groggy hand, I reached over to the night stand to answer it. Who could be calling me at this ungodly hour? As I reached for my phone, the caller ID lit up and I could see it was the hospital. Great, just what I needed right now, another emergency case to take.

I dutifully picked up my phone and answered "Jacobsen" in the most alert voice I could muster at this point.

"Suzanne, I'm sorry to wake you, but there's been an accident. Could you come down here right away?" Without even mentioning it, I could recognize that the voice was Howard's voice. He usually didn't wake people up in the middle of the night unless it was really important.

"Howard, what's going on? What type of accident do you mean?" I asked, still not completely awake yet.

"It's Steven. He's in the emergency room."

Chapter 4

I was half in a panic, half in a stupor as I got changed. Instinctively, I let Roxie out as I finished getting dressed to go down to the hospital. Usually I would call a cab, or take the train if I wasn't fully alert, but I definitely did not want to go walking to the train in the middle of the night by myself. And at this hour, the trains were not running very regularly anyway. I would have to call a cab and then wait, which I didn't want to do either. That left driving in as my best option. Since I was not going into the hospital to work, I didn't worry about primping like I normally would before work. I grabbed a pair of jeans and a soft brown sweater and dark brown leather boots. I ran a brush through my hair and I quickly washed my face in cold water to help wake me up before heading to the kitchen for a can of soda for in the car. I gathered up my purse and keys, let Roxie back in, and made my way to the garage and into the car. I normally didn't like driving in the middle of the night after having just been woken up, but I figured I wouldn't run into much traffic. The panic over what was happening with Steven mixed with the jolt of cold air and how cold the inside of the car was, kept me alert enough to make it quickly and safely to the hospital. Even though the Volvo SUV had heated seats, I didn't use them tonight. I figured it would just make me sleepy.

One perk to being a doctor was that I didn't have to drive around looking for a spot. Even though I was here for personal reasons, I parked in the physician's parking deck and rushed over to the main hospital entrance. I wasn't as familiar with the ER, but got there quickly enough, asking for Howard as soon as I found the nurse on duty. She showed me back with a look of irritation. She must not have realized that I was a doctor on staff here and assumed I was just name dropping to get 'better service' in the ER.

"Dr. Barrett," the nurse politely asserted as we came around the edge of the nurse's station. He was leaning over another patient as we walked up. His face immediately brightened when he saw me and motioned for a nurse to take over whatever he was doing with his current patient.

"Hi Suzanne. I'm sorry to have called in the middle of the night, but Steven was brought in to the ER in an ambulance less than an hour ago." Howard had met Steven before at hospital functions and Howard had a skill for remembering names and faces. This was something I'm sure he learned as part of his schmoozing for his job. Howard and Steven had been cordial to each other, but it always seemed like there was a tension between them, some sort of forced civility. "He has a head injury and was unconscious on arrival. Other than the head trauma, there didn't appear to be any other noticeable injuries. I just thought you would want to be here when he woke up."

"Thanks Howard. Which room is he in?"

"He's in twelve. Feel free to stay as long as you want. Hernandez is taking care of him, so she'll be back shortly to talk to you."

I thanked him and walked over to room number twelve and let myself in. Steven was hooked up to all of the regular heart monitors, and had an IV in his arm. He had a white bandage wrapped at an angle around his head and his face was mildly bruised up. It looked like he had gotten into a bar fight with someone and lost. I was giving him a once over when the sound of the curtain stopped me. I turned to see Dr. Antonia Hernandez standing by the curtain. She was a pretty woman in her late forties who had been here for at least ten years. She was great at her job and I trusted her opinion.

"Hi Suzanne," she said with a cheery tone for the middle of the night. I was flattered that she remembered my name. I had only met her a few times, and I was awful with names. I wondered idly whether she remembered it on her own, or if Howard had prompted her. I always like to know when my patients, or the family or spouse of my patient was a doctor. Not that you do much differently, I would just use a different tone in talking to them and provide more clinical details than when I would talk to non-physicians. She filled me in on the clinical details that she knew from her examination of him. He was sound asleep from the pain meds, and probably also since it was the middle of the night. After she finished filling me in, I was still left with some questions.

"I was wondering, do you know where the ambulance picked him up?" I asked with curiosity. The longer I was here, the more I worried as to why Steven was here. He was supposed to be on a business trip tonight, so unless there was a last minute cancellation or car troubles … I didn't even want to think about any other reasons as to why he might be in here.

"Yeah, the EMTs picked him up somewhere in Bucktown. I'm not exactly sure where, but they're bound to be back tonight with another load, so you could probably ask them."

I asked her a few more questions, then thanked her for everything she had done. I stepped into the hallway and caught one of the nurses on duty. I told him I wanted to be informed as soon as the EMTs arrived for the next drop off. I pulled up a chair next to Steven and settled in for a long night at the hospital.

About an hour and a half later, I awoke to the sound of him sighing and coughing as we woke up. He looked like hell and seemed totally unaware of his surroundings. As soon as his eyes locked on mine, his cheeks filled with blood and he looked away, pretending to be looking over himself for other wounds. Within seconds he looked back over at me and smiled his warm, loving smile.

"Suzy," he cooed, "what're you doing here? What's going on? I can't even remember how I got here or what happened." He had a genuinely confused tone about him, but something seemed wrong. His eyes seemed too calm, and his smile just a little too forced.

"I'm not sure what happened. The EMT's picked you up in Bucktown, and once you were admitted here, they recognized you and called me." I didn't know how much to push right now given his condition, but it wasn't life threatening, so frankly I didn't feel like babying him. "So what happened to your business trip?"

I had barely gotten the question out when the nurse popped his head in from around the curtain. "Excuse me, Doctor. You had asked to be notified as soon as the EMTs arrived, and they've just dropped off another patient. They're waiting for you by the nurse's station."

"Thank you, I'll be right there," I said politely. I hated to break this conversation with Steven, but I knew the EMTs had to get back out and I didn't want to keep them waiting. As I stood, I shot a suspicious look at Steven. For all of the wonderful thoughts I had earlier this evening after talking to Cassie, I didn't have the strength to muster those to the forefront of my mind right now.

It was easy enough to locate one of the EMTs by the nurse's station. I walked up and introduce myself to him as a doctor, deciding not to mention that I was Steven's girlfriend. I didn't want to give him any excuse to withhold information. He said that dispatch had sent them to a home around Damen and Armitage after a report of a domestic disturbance. Neighbors claimed that the couple was arguing loudly and that the argument had made its way to the front porch. One woman had seen a woman throw a vase at the man's head, knocking the man backwards, and down the half dozen steps to the front path leading to the curb. When the EMTs arrived on the scene, the woman was crouched on the ground with her arms around her legs, rocking back and forth and the man was unconscious.

"Was a police report issued?"

"I'm not sure," the EMT responded. "They were taking the woman's statement when we left with him. They'll probably be over later to see if he's going to press charges."

I thanked him for the information and walked back into room number twelve. Steven was sitting upright, with a calm, but not particularly happy look about him.

"So, are you going to tell me what happened?" I asked in a very direct manner. He looked at me, curiously, for a moment before speaking.

"Well, I was all packed up for the trip and one of the other closers from the office was going to ride with me, but she needed to grab a few more things from home, so we stopped by her place on the way out of town."

"Uh-huh," I said, dripping with disdain, "just a couple hour stop by her place?" I looked at him with piercing eyes, making him squirm in his bed.

"No, no, it wasn't like that! Her boyfriend came over and all hell broke loose. I must have been caught in the crossfire." He actually looked somewhat sincere, but I caught myself before I let that thought totally sink in. *What a line!* I screamed in my head.

"Sure Steven … I know I always wait til 2:30 in the morning to leave for *Indianapolis* for an early morning meeting," I said with a controlled, calm tone that I was actually quite proud of, given the circumstances. Not to mention, the EMT said nothing about another person being there.

"No, Suzy, you've got the wrong idea!" He was quickly trying to steer me in a different direction, but he seemed to be struggling as to how to do that.

"Oh really? Then what idea should I have about this?" I stared straight at him, my eyes boring into his.

"Honestly honey, it's just a misunderstanding!"

"Well, you can tell that to the cops when they show up to take your statement and see if you wanna press charges after your domestic disturbance. After all, the neighbors called the cops when the two of you took your fight outside and she threw a vase at your head." He opened his mouth like he was going to speak, but the pause was too long. He was searching. He snapped his mouth closed and looked down sheepishly.

"You're a lying sack of shit, Steven, and I want you out by the end of the day." I may have been fuming inside, but I delivered the line so coolly through gritted teeth that I barely even flinched. "All of your crap will be in the foyer. I want you gone by the time I get home from work tonight," I hissed at him through my still clenched jaw. "I have a late shift tonight, so I'll be back at around midnight. You better not be there when I get home. Just lock up and put your keys through the slot," I gave him one final scowl and turned on my heel, not giving him a chance to protest.

I walked out of the room in a trance like state, hardly even comprehending what I had just said to him. All I knew was that I wasn't going to make a scene, especially not here. The last thing I needed was the physician lounge buzzing about some dramatic break up scene in the middle of the night in the ER. Even if Antonia had enough courtesy not to mention it, the nurses would surely gossip about a reality TV moment at work, and the entire physician staff would end up hearing about it soon enough. Steven had too much pride to mention it to the doctors or nurses, so I would be able to deal with this in my own way.

My hands were shaking and I felt nauseated as I walked through the sliding glass doors at the hospital. I felt like screaming and crying at the same time, but didn't really want to do either of them at this precise moment. I looked over towards the parking garage and at least had enough common sense to realize that now was not a good time for me to be driving. I knew that as soon as I was alone and out of sight of other people, I was going to totally lose it. Instead, I walked the half block to the corner and hailed a cab.

No sooner had I set foot in the house, I collapsed onto the floor in tears. At this point, I didn't have any strength for anger, just an overwhelming sense of pain and betrayal. Just hours ago I was talking to my sister about the possibility that Steven and I would be spending the rest of our lives together, and he was out screwing some other woman … A wave of anger flashed over me and I picked myself up off the floor and headed to the bedroom.

At least most of the furniture in our house was either already here when I moved in, or pieces that I had bought before Steven moved in. The majority of his possessions here were clothes, movies, books, and other small things. That should make it easy to pile it all up in the foyer. I stormed into the closet, having to use every ounce of self-control not to put my fist through the wall. I threw open the closet doors and began throwing things over my head and behind me onto the floor by the bed. Roxie whined and hid behind the edge of the bed, not wanting to get in the middle of my rampage.

As I was tossing things onto the floor, I thought back over the past few days and everything that he had said to me … That was such a nice surprise that he had volunteered to make dinner, especially after having been on … a … business trip!

"Ahhh!! You bastard!!" I screamed as I started chucking things over my head with new enthusiasm. Now I didn't even know what to believe. Had every business trip been a lie? Was I really that naïve? I moved on to the drawers in the bedroom, pulling them so hard that the drawers themselves practically fell out onto the floor. I yanked entire handfuls of clothes out of the drawers and threw them onto the pile I had made on the floor outside of the closet. The drawers were quickly emptied and I slowly walked over to the heap of clothes, examining the pile suspiciously, like I expected some bright red lipstick stain to jump out at me.

Defeated, I bent over to grab an armful of clothes and start kicking some of the others towards to front door. Roxie still stayed well out of the way, cocking her head to the side, trying to figure out what I was doing. I looked down at the rug on the middle of the floor and dropped my armful of his crap onto the pile I had kicked over. I smiled with a small sense of satisfaction, seeing all of his nice suits balled up in a heap on the floor. He could pay for the damn dry cleaning himself. I was half turned around when I heard a faint thud on the hardwood that caught my attention. I turned back to my pile and eyed a small red box, lying on its side on the bare floor. My hands trembled and my head spun as I looked at this little box. I wearily took two steps over and crouched down in front of it for a few moments. I cautiously extended my hand towards it, like it was a scared animal that was going to bite me.

I took a deep breath, not wanting to open it, but knowing that I had to. I closed my eyes, and opened the box, hearing the hinge squeak quietly. I took one last deep breath before opening my eyes.

Just as I suspected. From inside that harmless little, red lacquered box was a band, holding a large princess cut diamond, with two smaller baguettes on either side. My hands trembled as I crouched there. A thousand questions had been flying through my mind all night, but now there was just one. Was this ring even intended for me?

Furious that I even had to ask myself the question, I let out a shriek and threw the little lacquered box as hard as I could at the wall. A shattering sound interrupted my scream, followed by the sound of glass raining down on the floor. Great, just my luck that I happened to hit the one mirror in the foyer ...

My anger gave way to anguish as I made my way over to the shattered mirror. I stooped down to the floor, looking at the mess I had just made. I reached back and grabbed one of Steve's shirts and started to rake up the pieces, ignoring the couple of pain pricks in my hands where the glass was poking through the thin shirt. My emotions were flying back and forth so quickly between hurt and anger that I wasn't even sure myself what I was actually feeling. In an instant, I looked down at the broken pieces of mirror in the crumpled up shirt, catching a glimpse of my distorted face and a wave of depression and anger ran over me at the same time. Without even directing them to, my hands started to clench around the broken pieces and move instinctively towards my chest, as if to grab the pieces of my broken heart that were falling down around me.

My loud sobbing had given way to quieter gasps as I fell to the floor. *Let them go ...* I heard a voice say.

"What?! Who's there?" I shot upright, still sitting on the floor with my fists clenched around the glass, but now I was at full alert. Hearing those magic words of 'who's there,' Roxie came running out of the bedroom barking. I turned my head from side to side, looking to see who had spoken, but I couldn't see anyone. I opened one of my hands, letting the broken pieces of the mirror fall to floor. I could see a few small cuts and chastised myself for having grabbed those pieces without thinking. I honestly hadn't meant to do that but at this point I was too tired to care. Exasperation set in and I folded over on the floor, one hand covering my head and the other one clenched around the glass as I lied there on the floor sobbing.

Just let the glass go Suzanne ... He's not worth it, the voice said, and I passed out on the floor from sheer exhaustion.

I awoke to the familiar but distant sound of my alarm clock going off in the bedroom. I didn't realize until I got to the clock that my alarm had been going off for twenty minutes, I just hadn't heard it from the other room. Unfortunately, I had only gotten two hours of sleep on the floor of the foyer. If only I could call in sick today ...

I didn't have to be into work until lunch time since I had a late shift tonight, so I climbed into bed. I laid there, staring up at the ceiling for a solid hour, completely awake and alert. I looked down at my hands that had been aching and saw a smattering of little cuts in my palms. None of them looked particularly deep. The overall effect was a dull, throbbing feeling coming from my hands. With my mind already at work, I figured I would have no luck in falling back asleep.

I got up and out of bed, feeling completely defeated. *But,* I said to myself, *as long as I was going to be awake, I may as well make myself useful for the next couple of hours.* I really didn't want Steven to come in to a shattered mirror on the floor, so I tended to that mess first. It wasn't that I wanted to make the house look nice for him, but I did not want him to think that he had broken me. I wanted him to see that I was stronger than he would give me credit for and that I did not need to put up with this. I deserved better. I spent the next hour going through his things, much more calmly than the night before and putting, instead of throwing, them in a pile on the floor. He can figure out for himself how he was going to get all of this to wherever he was going to be staying. I knew he had some friends in the city, but I really didn't know where he would go, nor did I really care at this point. For all I knew, he was going back to Bucktown to make amends with her.

As I went through all of his belongings and tossed them onto the pile, waves of memories flowed over me. Every pair of clothes reminded me of a special dinner or event; every movie of his was one that we had snuggled up on the couch to watch; every picture frame was one that I had to pause at to consider whether to keep it, give it to him, or let it go the way of the mirror in the foyer.

At some point halfway through the purging, I came across a small framed picture from our second anniversary. I ran my finger across the two smiling faces in the photograph. Looking at it now, they both seemed so fake and so distant to me. For a minute, I allowed myself to consider whether or not I was doing the right thing to boot him out like this. After about fifteen minutes of going back and forth on it, I came to the realization that if he behaved like this at such an early stage of our relationship, how would he behave ten years from now, or twenty? I now questioned every business trip he said he had taken. If he really was going over to her place each time, that meant this had been going on for well over a year. It was odd, but I started to wonder if he was even any good at his job. He was talking about these big deals that he was working on, but was it all just a front to get a night out of the house? Maybe his confidence was actually coming from successfully pulling one over on two women at the same time. Maybe that air of confidence wasn't related at all to his job like I had thought. That realization made me wonder what else I thought I knew about him that really was not true.

After a couple hours of thoroughly removing all of Steven's presence from my house, I walked into the bathroom to take a hot shower and to make myself not look like hell warmed over.

I tried to stay focused as I showered and got ready for work, but there were too many little things that I had missed during my cleaning. I knew it would take weeks to get the last few pieces of evidence cleaned up. Even in the shower, Steven's bottle of body wash made me break down into tears. I tried to zone out while I finished getting ready, but was only mildly successful in my attempts.

I paid little attention to the clothes I picked to wear today, except to make sure they actually matched. Today would be a day for a bun. I wasn't in the mood, and I didn't have the time, to style my hair this morning. I took one final look at myself in the bathroom mirror, thanks to my destroying of the mirror in the foyer. I would hardly say that I looked good today. The dark circles and the bloodshot look in my eyes gave me away. Too bad I had broken the mirror in the foyer. That light out there always made me look a little bit better than the lights in the bathroom.

Oh well, I thought to myself, *I guess today will have a lot of coffee in it.*

Almost as soon as I got to work, I ran into Howard. This had been the moment that I was dreading since I left the hospital last night. I knew he would ask about Steven, so I had been practicing my straight face on the el the whole way into work.

"Hi Suzanne," he said in a very normal, low key tone. "How's Steven feeling? That was quite a blow to the head."

"Oh, he's doing fine. Just a little bit of a headache," I giggled nervously as I answered. He looked over my face slowly, and then nodded. He must have realized there was something more to the story that I didn't want to share, so he let it go. Instead he just nodded with his lips pursed into a frown.

"Well, that's good to hear," he paused, looking down at his tablet. "I'm observing a new surgeon today. He's coming in for a procedure in a couple of hours. Care to join me? He specializes in liver transplants, and comes very highly recommended."

"Sure! That sounds like fun. What time should I meet you?" My afternoon was mainly flagged for administrative work, so I had room in my schedule for this. I would just have to catch up on paperwork later.

"Come by suite five at 2:30."

"Alright, thanks Howard. See you then."

It was somewhat of a rare occasion that I got to observe potential new surgeons at the hospital. The fact that Howard was interested in my opinion of this doctor was an honor, and a compliment to my skills. I anxiously finished my work that afternoon with an eye on the clock for my 2:30 observation.

I met Howard outside the surgical suite at 2:25 and we chatted for a few minutes about things to look out for during the surgery. As soon as the patient was under, we walked into the observation room and got settled in for the procedure. I was continually amazed every time I would watch other surgeons at work. I would study their every movement, trying to play through the same scenario in my head and ask myself if that was the same thing I would do. Watching the quick and steady hands of a surgeon was, for me, like watching something of a cross between a magician and a concert pianist. The grace and precision of their movements would captivate me and I felt like I could watch them for hours. As I watched him, I made a few mental notes of techniques I would like to try and maybe incorporate into my repertoire. Being in this room and in my element was really a nice distraction to both my mental and physical exhaustion.

About ten minutes later, I heard the door open and looked back to see the Risk Manager join us in the observation room. We all exchanged pleasantries and filled him in on what he had missed. As he joined us, I felt a strange sensation wash over me. Just a week ago when I was out in the OR and Howard and the Risk Manager were in here, I had felt intimidated. Now the situations were reversed, and I smiled to myself wondering whether the doctor out there was feeling as intimidated as I sometimes did when I was observed.

As I turned back to watch the end of the procedure, my eyes caught on a shadow in the edge of the observation room. By the time my head and eyes had reached forwards, I could see the reflection more clearly. It stood there, motionless, in the glass between us and the operating room. As I focused my gaze on the reflection, I saw that it was the same face as the man I had seen the day I dropped my scalpel. My heart quickened and I snapped my head around to stare at the spot in the room where the man should be standing.

By the time I turned to that spot, there was no one there. I shook my head and looked straight forwards again. *I must be imagining things*, I thought to myself. Apparently the lack of sleep was catching up to me after all. I refocused my attention back on the surgery. I didn't want to miss anything, and I didn't want to appear to be daydreaming. I considered it praise from Howard that he invited me to observe, and I didn't want to give him the impression that I was taking this opportunity for granted.

A few minutes later, I saw the same reflection. I whipped my head around sharply, but when I looked at the spot that should be the shadow's source, there was no one there.

"Dr. Jacobsen, are you okay?" the Risk Manager asked me.

"Yes, thank you. I'm fine, just felt a bit of breeze on my neck." Both he and Howard looked at me. The Risk Manager kept a straight face, presumably thinking nothing of it. Dr. Barrett noticed my distraction, but he only commented that I looked tired. I examined his face, to see whether he appeared irritated. I would understand if he perceived this as me not paying attention, but there was no evidence of any unhappiness. He simply had a mildly concerned look on his face. I agreed that I was a bit tired from my long night and then returned my focus to the OR in time to see the surgeon closing. I walked out of the observation room and back to the physician lounge. I would need more coffee to stay alert for the rest of the day.

After what seemed like one the longest days in years, I put on my warm, gray cashmere hat and scarf and headed to the train station to catch my train home. At almost 11:30pm, the bitter cold seemed worse than usual for winter in Chicago. I walked quickly, partially from the cold, and partially because I didn't want to dawdle given how late it was. I never was particularly scared to walk around the city by myself, but for whatever reason, I felt a little anxious tonight. Probably because of how tired I was right now, and having mixed feelings about getting home. Even though I told Steven not to be there when I got back, I was a little nervous to find out whether he had listened to me or not.

At the bottom of the stairs, I could hear the southbound train approaching, so I knew mine would be a couple of minutes still. I checked my watch and sighed impatiently as I waited for my train. The train arrived a few minutes later and I wearily climbed on board and took the first available seat. If it wasn't so late, I probably would have called Cassie to fill her in on everything that had happened in the last twenty four hours, but at this late of hour and with such young kids at home, I decided against it. Instead, I just stared blankly out the window for my fifteen minute ride home. I stood up at the stop before mine and started to make my way to the door. I could feel the train slowing and I got ready to exit as I noticed a man standing in the doorway next to me. The doors opened and the man looked over at me and smiled politely as I stepped off the train.

Two steps later I realized that I recognized that man.

"Hey! Hey wait!" I shouted to him, probably too loud given that it was almost midnight and he was only ten feet in front of me. Instinctively, the man turned around to look at me, but quickly turned back and kept walking.

"Hey wait! I want to talk to you!" I said, running to catch up with him. I reached out and grabbed his arm, and he whipped around to face me. He had a probing look in his eyes, but I could also see a hint of fear on his face. He let his arms hang straight down beside him, but I could see his hands tighten into fists beside him.

"Yes? Can I help you with something?" he asked, in a very polite manner. I stammered, suddenly feeling very small and not quite sure what I should do next. Why the hell was I confronting a stranger at midnight on an empty el platform? Not my smartest choice.

"Who are you?" was the best I could muster. I shook my head, feeling silly for having asked such a basic question, but looking up at his face, I realized it may have been a better question than I had anticipated. His eyebrows came together slightly, almost to imply that he was searching for that answer himself. My impatience got the best of me and I continued without giving him the chance to answer.

"I recognize you from the OR. What were you doing there?" my tone now turning more accusatory than curious. He recoiled at this last statement. I studied his face in more detail as he appeared to search for an answer. I could see his jaw clench and his eyes darted down and away as he searched for an answer. I had not had much of a chance to really take him in during the split second I saw him in the OR. Maybe it was just my imagination playing tricks on me, but in this light he looked absolutely flawless. I couldn't remember a face that looked so smooth and perfect up close. The tan hue to his skin gave it a healthy and fresh glow on this cold, dark night. His dark, warm eyes seemed to flicker in the light coming from the lamps on the platform. They had an almost pleading and yearning quality to them. I had to look away to keep myself from staring rudely at him.

"I don't know what you're talking about," he said with a very forced look of confusion.

"Yes, you do. You were in the operating room yesterday. That little kid had fallen off of his roof. I was removing his appendix and I looked up and you were there! I'm sure it was you," I said, surprising even myself at the conviction of my words. He looked down and shifted his weight back and forth between his feet. As he looked back up, he opened his mouth thoughtfully, and then closed it again, obviously having decided against saying what he was originally thinking. I watched this movement of his mouth and how perfectly his dark pink lips moved as he stammered.

"That little boy died on the table. You have to have remembered that ..." I trailed off, in an almost imploring tone.

"I know." His tone was compassionate, but there was something else that I could not quite pinpoint in his tone. It was a hint of cockiness or something along those lines. He had stopped fidgeting, at least for the moment, and instead he stood up straight and returned my gaze. When he stood like this, his shoulders looked very strong and commanding. They were wide enough to impress, but not so wide as to draw unwanted stares.

"What ... what do you mean 'you know'?" His face flushed and he stammered briefly, then started to turn around to leave. Without even thinking, I grabbed his arm again, feeling his bicep tighten under my grip.

"Wait, what do you mean? Did you have something to do with him dying?"

"Not exactly," he said softly, turning his head back towards me to look straight into my eyes as he said those two little words. His voice had a deep, rich tone to it, almost soothing despite the topic of conversation.

"But sort of?"

Silence.

"Well, did you drug him? Or poison him? Or something like that?" He flinched and shook his head slightly, his warm eyes flashing a look of disgust at the idea that I thought he had poisoned a child. Of course, thinking about it like that did sound particularly crass.

"No, of course not!" he said as he took a noticeable step backwards, pulling his arm out of my grasp.

"Well, explain yourself. How is it that you were in the OR, unscrubbed and ungowned."

"I'm sorry, I can't …" he said as he started to back away again.

"Okay wait. For starters, what's your name? I can't keep calling you "you.""

"It's Ben."

"Okay, Ben, then if you didn't poison him, were you the one who pushed him off the roof?" I prodded, with just a little tact as my first assumption.

"Yes, I push little kids off of roofs," he said sarcastically, shooting me a look like he deserved more credit that than. Of course I could not really give him much credit at all since I knew nothing of this man except his first name. He probably also thought that I was a little on the crazy side right now, and clearly not fit to practice medicine. I was starting to wonder that myself.

"Well, then what? Why were you there?" He paused for a moment as he decided what to say. I could see his chiseled jawline tighten as he looked up and over my shoulder.

"Let it go Suzanne," he said in a surprisingly soothing voice, but I shudder at the simple phrase. I was caught completely off guard by his newly found calming tone. I was looking off, taking in this new sentiment before I realized that he had started backing away slowly and was almost to the top of the stairs.

"But ..." I said, reaching my hand up to my face, and feeling very confused by this whole interaction. Maybe I was just tired and hallucinating. This time I didn't yell after him or chase him. I just stood there letting the numbing coldness overtake my body, while I thought back over the brief conversation. I shivered, then straightened up and headed towards the stairs down.

By the time I got home it was almost twelve thirty, and even the pot and a half of coffee I had this afternoon couldn't help keep me awake right now. I trudged up the stairs and wearily fished through my purse to find my keys. I could see a few lights on in the house and I was just praying that Steven wasn't there. I didn't have the energy to talk to him right now.

As I opened the door, I could see Roxie running across the tidy hardwood floor to greet me. Much to my surprise, and satisfaction, the house was empty and the massive heap was gone from the middle of the foyer. As I opened the door further, I could hear the tinkling of Steven's keys drag across the floor. At least he knew how to follow instructions. As I surveyed the room, I saw an envelope in the middle of the floor with my name on the outside. I walked right over the note and to the bedroom. It was a long day, and all I could think about was going to bed.

Chapter 5

I awoke the next morning in a cold sweat. I had been dreaming about my interaction with Ben. My mind was racing, replaying those few short minutes over and over again. As I got ready for work, I was so preoccupied thinking about that conversation that I didn't even notice the small pieces of Steven that had made me break down the day before. I made a mental note as I was walking to the train station today that I would have to remember to drive home. In my stupor the day before, I hadn't even remembered that my car was still in the garage from the night I went to see Steven.

* * *

The rest of the week flew by in a blur. Things at work were slow, which I was incredibly grateful for, and I successfully dodged Steven's phone calls for three days. Each time he called, he left a message apologizing and asking me to call him. As the week wore on, the requests to call began to turn into pleas. I knew I would eventually talk this through with him face to face, but I was determined to have that conversation on my timetable, not his. After all, he was the one who wronged me, so he could sweat it out a little bit longer.

But mainly the problem was that I didn't really know what I was going to say. I had dated a few different guys in school and during the early part of my residency, but only one had been a really serious boyfriend. When Joshua got offered a job in New York, it was the chance of a lifetime and he couldn't refuse. I was still in med school in Chicago, so I was not willing to follow him just then, but we tried to make it work. The plan was to do the long distance thing until I graduated and then I would apply for a residency position in New York as well. We were very optimistic in the beginning, despite the distance and the expense of flying back and forth to see each other. The first few months went really well with two or three in person visits and countless hours on the phone. But as his business trips became more frequent and I began getting into finals, the in person visits got fewer and further between. The phone calls slowly got shorter and sometimes turned into just texting conversations. It wasn't either one of our faults, and neither one of us blamed the other. Eventually, we had our final in person meeting when he had a trip to Chicago. We both knew it was over, even though we both still cared for each other. My mind drifted back to that conversation and that relationship as I thought about how to deal with Steven. I was hopeful that I could find something from that situation to use here.

But this was different. We had not both decided that this wasn't going to work. My whole heart was still in it when his heart, or other parts of him I suppose, was no longer in our relationship. I know people say you can get past infidelity, but I never really thought you could. Especially considering we weren't even engaged. It just felt to me like if he was bored and distracted already, that certainly wouldn't get better over time. If anything, it would get worse. My heart had changed after finding out about him, and I couldn't, and more importantly, didn't want to go back. Of that I was certain.

* * *

I finally broke down and talked to Steven on Saturday morning. I kept it brief and opted to set up a time to meet him for a cup of coffee later in the day. I really didn't want to be completely alone with him, and a public setting should also keep things from getting ugly. I got ready and put more thought into my choice of clothes for the day than I should have. A part of me considered it a challenge to find the most unflattering, lumpy sweater in my closet, while the other part was intentionally looking for something to make him reconsider why he would ever think about another woman. The better part of me settled on something in between, but still warm. The last thing I needed was to be cold and have him make some gentlemanly gesture like giving me his coat.

My sudden disdain for him caught me off guard. I realized that I really had not spent much time thinking about him over the past week. Part of me wondered whether it was because I knew this was for the better and that he was not the right man for me. Even still, change, especially sudden change, can hurt so I tried to let myself go numb. If I could do that for a week or so, then when I allowed the emotions to flow again they would not be so overpowering. When I wasn't numb, my thoughts kept drifting back to Ben, and trying to make sense of who he was and why he was in the OR. I still was not completely certain whether I had really seen him or if I had just imagined him. Having a mystery to solve was a nice distraction from the Steven drama, so I gladly let my mind wander.

Considering it was late January, it was surprisingly warm outside. I decided to take advantage of the weather and go to the park before my appointment with Steven. Appointment seemed too formal of an expression for our meeting, but date was certainly not the appropriate term. I needed to clear my head. I wasn't this nervous before my final encounter with Joshua, but then again we knew each other so well, and we both knew what was going to be happening and accepted it. Given the umpteen voicemails from Steven over the past week, I knew he was going to try to change my mind. Or make up some stupid excuse or lie or justification for why he did what he did. I usually was not the one to have these hard, serious conversations. I felt like I was too accommodating to fare very well, but right now I had to stand my ground.

I kept giving myself little mental pep talks and trying to anticipate things he might say. Those tangents made my mind race, and I began reading too much into my every thought. I sighed and shook my head in frustration. I wanted to have my thoughts in order a little bit better before this conversation, but this churning was not helping. I opted to head out in hopes of keeping my mind from getting overwhelmed. While a walk in the park on an April afternoon would have been a bit more enjoyable, the cold air would help me think clearly too. I got myself bundled up and headed out for the park.

I truly enjoyed days like today. As I exited the el station and made my way to Millennium Park, I looked up and took in the beauty of the city. For some people, a big city like Chicago would be overwhelming. Too busy and too chaotic for some people's taste. On a day like today, it was easy to see why Chicagoans fell in love with it. The streets between the el station and the park were lined with little shops and restaurants, including my favorite purse store in the city! Even though the gala was some time off and I hadn't picked out a dress yet, it was never too early to start looking for accessories. Or at least that's what I told myself. I didn't end up buying anything, but it was a nice distraction to think about something fun coming up on the calendar. I thanked the clerk as I walked back out into the cold and continued on my way to the park.

As I crossed the street and started to enter the park, I could hear the people laughing from the ice rink that was a fixture here in the winter. I took a seat on one of the nearby benches and began watching the skaters. I loved to people watch, especially the families. It reminded me of the times I had come here with Cassie and the kids. The fun memories made me smile and helped calm my rising nerves.

I glanced around and my eyes fixed on a young girl who appeared to be an aspiring figure skater. She was gracefully weaving in and out of the other skaters and towards the center of the ice. As she came in, she prepared for some elaborate trick. She started well enough from what I could tell, but then must have lost her footing and went tumbling to the ice, knocking into another couple. It may be a mean thing to do, but I couldn't help but chuckle a little. This hardly seemed like the appropriate place to practice your routine when there were so many other people on the ice.

I watched a few of the couples skating and tried to guess how long they had been together. It was usually pretty telling when one of them would fall and then you would get to see either an overly attentive partner help the other one, or an argument would break out, with each not quite sure how loud to be. Then there were the gooey-in-love couples that that Steven and I used to be.

It didn't take long for my mind to fill with memories of me and Steven, but I quickly stamped them down. I knew the conversation coming up later today would be tough, but I had to convince myself to be strong. I let myself drift off into thought for a long while before returning my gaze to the ice and the people watching for a few more minutes.

With that, I stood up to stretch my legs and continue to make my way through the park. Not far off I saw The Bean and headed in that direction. The Bean, as the statue or the artwork was referred to, was not far off from the skating rink. I didn't actually know the official name for it, but the silver, reflective sculpture looked like a giant jellybean. It was positioned parallel to Michigan Avenue, and when you stood in front of it you could see the city sky line and, on a nice day, the clouds overhead. Because all of the surfaces were reflective, you could make your way around, and underneath, The Bean and see yourself from different angles, like in the carnival mirrors. It may be a touristy thing to do, but I didn't care.

There weren't many tourists out today, so it was pretty easy to navigate around the Bean. I walked towards it, looking up at the skyline in the reflection and I smiled. This was such a picturesque view! I could stand here for hours, just taking it in. I started to make my way underneath the structure, watching carefully as my reflection shrank and grew in the shiny surface. As I was coming around the other side, still looking up at my reflection, I noticed another person in the reflection next to me. I whirled around to see if I was right.

"Ben? Is that you?" I asked in a very chipper tone. He turned to look at me as I said his name. This must be quite a change from my accusatory and rude tone earlier this week. The truth was, I really was glad to see him. I had been playing back over our partial conversation and was curious to ask him more.

"Suzanne," he replied politely. He was standing with his hands clasped behind his back, a look that seemed too formal given his casual attire. His posture seemed more fitting for a funeral director right now.

"What are you doing here?" I continued, without giving him a chance to reply. "It can't be a coincidence that I keep seeing you. This is a pretty big town after all."

He nodded, and a trite smile came across his lips.

"Are you following me?" I asked in playful, and almost flirty tone. Was I really flirting with someone I didn't even know? It must have been my nervousness about my upcoming meeting with Steven. My heart beat faster as I pondered what that would mean if he *was* following me. Would I be worried, or would I be flattered by a handsome, dark haired man following me around? If he had any ill intentions, surely he would have acted on them already. Being on a secluded el platform at midnight was about as wide open an opportunity as he would get.

"No, I'm not following you," he answered, with a genuine, but almost regretful look. Almost as if he wanted to follow me. How ridiculous! This man surely had better things to do with his time.

"So if you're not stalking me," I nodded my head teasingly, "then what brings you to the park today?" He shot a glance over to the ice skating rink and then back at me.

"Just out and about." He sounded so serious, but I wasn't convinced. "I actually should be going," he said as he smiled politely and nodded his head.

"No wait, please." There wasn't the demanding tone in my voice like I had that night on the platform. "Will you go for a walk with me?" I asked as I looked up at him with hopeful eyes and smiled. Okay, so maybe I was flirting with a complete stranger. But I felt like I knew him somehow, so maybe I shouldn't consider him a *complete* stranger. Something seemed very familiar about him but I couldn't quite place it.

"I really do have some things to tend to today," he apologized. As I listened to his very formal and reserved tone, I tried to decide whether I thought it was charming or whether something seemed off about his manner. When he smiled at me, though, I got a warm fluttery feeling in my belly, so I decided his mannerisms were charming.

"Please? Just for a little bit?" I was sure he could hear the sincerity and the pleading in my voice. To my delight, he seemed to weaken. I took that as my chance and started to walk past him to where some of the paths through the park started. "Come on," I encouraged. A very satisfied smile crept across my face as I approached him and dragged my hand across the back of his arm, in a motion like I may pull him along with me.

"You can't just keep showing up around me and then avoid all conversations, now can you?" I said playfully. He reluctantly gave in and joined me as we made our way down one of the paths. I had so many questions running through my mind. I wanted to know why he had been at the hospital, and what he had seen, but I didn't want to scare him off either. He had hurried off the last time I tried to ask so many questions, so I decided to keep this interaction a bit more lighthearted. Would I get to see him again if he didn't think I was hounding him with questions every time I saw him?

As we started down the first path, I decided to go with the usual introductory conversations.

"So Ben, I take it you live in the city?"

"Yes, as do you I assume," he mirrored my tone and depth of conversation with a smile on his face. I think he knew that there were much bigger questions on my mind, but got a kick out of this type of conversation.

"And what is it that you do here in Chicago," I asked with a faux serious tone, mirroring that of a talk show host interview. I was hoping this would reveal some sort of detail that could help give some more meat to our conversation. He stiffened as we walked, and paused for a quick moment before responding.

"Oh, I stalk pretty girls," he said with a laugh, looking back over to me for my reaction. My heart skipped a beat, in a good way.

"So you're saying you think I'm pretty," I replied lightheartedly, with a smile creeping across my face.

"Of course I do." A wistful smile passed over his lips, but he quickly started talking again to conceal it. He was walking close enough for us to have an intimate conversation, but far enough that he wouldn't accidentally brush against me.

"So you're a doctor," he said, abruptly changing the topic of conversation.

"Yep."

"What made you go into medicine?" He must have figured that would make me start talking and take the focus off of him. I wanted to be polite and answer his question, but I didn't want to spend all of our time talking about me. I would rather listen to him talking. He had such a beautiful, rich voice. I could listen to it for hours.

"Ever since I was little I wanted to be a doctor. I loved the idea of solving the mystery and making people better. My small contribution to society I guess."

"I would hardly call your contribution small. You save people every day. It must be very rewarding," he said, exhaling deeply and swinging his arms forward, clasping his hands together.

"Well, I don't save them all …"I trailed off, thinking about that little boy Colin and I lost.

"Sometimes, people's numbers are just up. It isn't your fault," he said in a very reassuring tone.

"It would be nice to know when that was the case, then we wouldn't feel so bad about it I suppose." We walked for a few moments in silence, just looking at the flower beds that were so beautiful in the spring time. Now they were all covered in snow, with just the twigs pointing out of them. At the next intersection of paths, there was a vendor cart selling drinks, so I used this as a chance to break the silence.

"Hot cider please," I ordered and fished out my wallet.

"And for you sir?" the vendor asked, looking at Ben.

"Nothing, thank you," he answered with a polite smile. We continued walking as I took a sip of the steaming drink.

"You're thinking about that little boy, aren't you?" I was silent and just nodded. A melancholy look had come across my face and I looked over at Ben. His deep eyes seemed to be speaking to me, and I smiled at the gentleness in his face.

"It was just his time Suzanne. There was nothing you could have done."

"It just doesn't seem right. He was so young. How could it have been his time already? And what parent is that oblivious anyway?" A hint of anger had come into my voice now. I really did blame the dumb parent who would let their kid be so reckless.

"You know, just because they're young, doesn't make them little angels." He paused for a moment, but decided it was best to keep me talking, rather than give me a long enough break to ask questions.

"So have you always lived in Chicago," he asked, taking the conversation back to a lighter note.

"No, I actually grew up in Austin. I had a grandmother here who left me the house I'm in now."

"Were you close to your grandmother?"

"Well, as close as you can be living so far away. We didn't see her too often growing up, but we always had a good time coming to visit her. She would take us to the parks, or museums, or something fun like that."

"Were you planning to move to Chicago? Is that why she had left you the house?"

"Definitely not. At the time, I thought I'd live in Texas all my life. I was actually really shocked when I found out she wanted me to have her house. I guess because my sister had already settled down with her husband."

"So you moved up here when you got the house?"

"Well, I came up to take care of everything with the house. I was up here for a couple of weeks and just fell in love with the city, so I decided to go to med school here."

"Do you ever miss Austin?"

"Yeah, sometimes. These winters are something to get used to, but overall I like Chicago. There's so much to do here, and it's a big enough city you can get yourself lost all day," I smiled, thinking how much I would love to get lost all day with him. But enough about me, I wanted to get him talking again. "How about you? Are you originally from Chicago?"

"I lived in Kansas City for a number of years, and then came here about two years ago."

"Really?! I was born there, but my family moved when I was just a few months old. I've never been back there since we moved to Austin. What's it like?"

"Didn't your parents ever show you pictures or anything like that?"

"Nope," I responded wistfully. "They never really talk about it."

"Well, it's quite beautiful. The plaza is gorgeous in the summer. You can walk along by the fountains and just take it all in. The city is big enough that you have everything you could need, but not as overwhelming as a city like Chicago."

"You sound like you really loved it there."

"I did. I'd love to move back there someday," he said as he looked off into the distance. No doubt he was off in thought, thinking of how his life may be able to get him back there. I took another drink of my cider and then looked back over at him.

"Then if you loved it so much, what brought you here?"

"Work," he answered in a polite but short tone.

"Oh, you mean your stalking profession?" to which we both laughed. "You never did really tell me what you do." We walked on in silence for a short time.

"I'm an observer," he said in a forced, nonchalant way. He intentionally didn't say anything else, and I was going back and forth in my head as to whether I should ask him more about this or leave it be. What the hell, be bold!

"Like observing people during surgery in the OR," I said, in more of a statement than a question.

"Yes, something like that." He seemed to stiffen again and look uncomfortable with our conversation. As we rounded the next curve, I could see the skating rink again and hear the sounds of kids laughing as they went whirling by.

"I don't mean to be evasive, Suzanne, but I'm not supposed to talk about my work."

"No that's fine. If I were sneaking into an OR, unscrubbed, I would want to keep that under wraps too," I said, with more bitterness than I had intended. I looked down as we continued to walk, and began to fidget with the edge of my cup. He slowed to a halt and turned to face me. My heart raced, wondering whether he was going to be upset with me for being rude, or if he was going to cave and explain his cryptic behavior.

"Well, I really do need to get back to work, but I'm glad I ran into you Suzanne."

"Oh, you have to go already?" I said as my heart sank a little. I would have loved to have had more time to talk to him, but I could tell he was not going to be the type of guy who would let me in that quickly. Something inside of me was telling me that he was different than any of the other men I had met, so it was best not to push my luck.

"Yes, unfortunately. I was supposed to be working when I first ran into you, so I don't want to be slacking off on the job," he replied sincerely, with a wide smile passing over his lips. His deep brown eyes seemed to dance as he looked at me, like they were trying to tell me something.

"Okay, well, will I see you again?" I said with the hopefulness of a teenager talking to her crush. I could feel myself blush as I looked down, embarrassed that I was actually thinking that.

"I'm sure we'll run into each other again," he said with a nod, and an almost mischievous smile that lit up his eyes. I looked back up and smiled back at him.

"Take care, Suzanne," he said, with a quick stroke of my arm as he started to turn and walk back towards the skating rink.

"You too Ben," I said in a soft voice and a very pleased smile. And with that, he hurried off. I stood there for a moment, taking in our whole conversation; each word; each expression. I'm sure I would analyze every detail of it later tonight, but for now I just stood there, content with the feeling I had right now. In the distance I could hear a bell tower ring. *Darn it,* I thought to myself.

I hurried off to go meet Steven.

Chapter 6

*A*s I got ready for work the next day, I thought back to my two conversations from the day before. My meeting with Steven was as I had expected it to be. He apologized profusely, asking what he could do to make it up to me. For the most part, I let him say his peace, with only a few interruptions. I'm not sure whether it was my curiosity about Ben that was distracting me, or whether it was the realization that I didn't want Steven anymore, but when I looked at him, I no longer had any sense of personal attachment to him. I looked desperately into his eyes to find that shred of him that sent my heart racing, but all I could see now was the shell of a man I used to love. My reflections on all of the times he would 'go on a business trip' and then come home in a better mood made me question the entire basis of our relationship. And it made me nauseous. The fact that most of me didn't even want to believe him or give him a chance to explain was answer enough for me. He swore that he still loved me, but I couldn't honestly tell him the same. I wasn't angry or bitter, but my desire to make that relationship work had faded.

But that was yesterday. Since that meeting, I had been thinking back through our conversation, wondering whether I had made the right decision. I hoped to God that I didn't make the decision based on my newfound interest in Ben. I hoped that he wasn't the reason that I did not want to give Steven a chance. I hadn't been able to get Ben out of my mind for the last week, but how well did I know him? It was extremely rash to blow off a legitimate relationship for a 'what if' with someone who was pretty much a stranger to me. Given how calm I felt about the fizzling relationship with Steven, I decided that it must be what I really wanted, deep in my heart. It just seemed like my head was telling me that I was being a little rash. I shook my head as I continued to get ready for work.

The nice thing about working on Sundays was that it mainly consisted of checking in on patients and catching up on paperwork. Occasionally, we were called into surgery from the ER, but luckily that didn't happen too often. Since Sunday's were usually not as long and stressful, I decided to drive to work. I simply wasn't in the mood to brave mass transit today. Another plus was that I could turn my music up and, hopefully, get lost in the lyrics until I got to work. I was tired of spending so much of my time playing out scenarios in my head, so I opted for something upbeat and fairly mindless. I definitely didn't want something sappy that would get me teary-eyed before heading into work.

I was still happily singing along to the music when I pulled into the parking garage at the hospital. The physician's floor was packed full of shiny, expensive sedans and SUVs. As I made my way down the row, I was happy to see Colin's car here. I could use someone else to bounce at least my Steven scenario off of.

As luck would have it, I passed Colin in the hall on the way to the physicians lounge.

"Got any lunch plans for today?" I asked in a casual manner as I walked towards him.

"Apparently I do with you. What time?" he asked as he kept walking, but at a slightly slower pace.

"12:30. Meet you in the lounge?" I turned towards him but kept walking in the other direction.

"It's a date," he said with a smile as he turned and kept walking down the hall. I made my way towards the lounge and shook my head. I committed to myself that I would not think about Steven or Ben again until lunch time. And surprisingly, I was able to hold myself to that.

When I met up with Colin, we both decided that we needed to get out of the hospital for a little while during lunch, so we went across the street to a small café. As luck would have it, we missed the main lunch rush. As we got our food and made our way over to a table by the window, Colin started in on the teasing immediately.

"So, have you seen any reapers lately?" When I turned to look back at him he had a huge grin on his face and his eyes were twinkling so much that I could swear they were laughing at me too.

"Ha ha," was the best I could come up with. I wasn't sure that I wanted to start off our lunch like this, but maybe this is how it was going to have to go. We grabbed our seats and I tried to look coolly out the window as I replied.

"As a matter of fact, I did see our grim reaper again," I said, taking a sip of my drink.

"Are you shittin' me?" His eyebrows had come together and he was starting in on his sandwich.

"Yep, and just my luck it was when Howard asked me to observe that new guy."

"At least this time you didn't have a scalpel in your hand," he said as he looked up and caught my stare. He shot me a quick smile as I blushed slightly, embarrassed by my scalpel incident. "Let me see," he said as he held out his right hand and motioned for me to show him the hand I had cut open the week before. Playing the compliant patient, I placed it gingerly in his hand like a lady would present her hand for a man to kiss, rather than for a doctor to examine. He turned my hand over in his and looked it over thoroughly.

"It's healing nicely. We shouldn't have to amputate," he delivered in a very dry tone.

"Well isn't that a relief," I responded as I played along with his tone.

"That's pretty impressive that Barrett asked you to check out a new doctor. You must be turning some heads, medically speaking," he smiled as he started in on his lunch.

"Thanks for the clarification," I smiled with a sarcastic tone about me. "Yeah, I was pretty excited that he did. The guy has some good techniques that I'd like to try out. In our debrief afterwards, it sounds like Howard's gonna give him a shot at the position. I think he has another doctor to look at too, but this one is a contender."

I took a few more bites, deciding how I was going to continue with my story. I was getting it organized in my head when Colin interrupted my thought process.

"So?"

"So what?"

"So back to your ghost story."

"He's not a ghost," I said, a little defensively.

"How can you be sure? Has anyone else seen him?" If anyone else were to ask me a question like that, I think I would have been offended and taken it as an attack. I could tell from the expression on Colin's face that he genuinely wasn't questioning my sanity. He was only trying to understand what I was talking about and make me see all sides of my situation, which was exactly what I was hoping to do.

"Well, if it would have just been in the observation room, I probably would have chalked it up to just being tired from having not slept much the night before."

"Oh that's right. I heard about you and Steven," he interrupted.

"Yeah, well we'll get back to that in a minute," to which he just nodded and kept eating. "I saw him outside of the hospital too: once on the el platform by my house the night after the little kid, and then yesterday by The Bean."

"Did you talk to him?"

"Yeah, I stopped him on the platform, but didn't get much out of him besides that his name is Ben and that he *was* the one in the OR that I saw when I cut myself."

"What was he doing there?" Colin's expression had now changed to a more serious one. I hoped this wouldn't turn into a bad conversation.

"He said he was observing."

"Observing who? Us or the patient?"

"I'm not really sure. He didn't say …" I trailed off as I thought about what exactly Ben would have been observing that day.

"That's just really weird that no one else saw him there."

"You're telling me! I love feeling like I'm crazy and seeing people. But the drink vendor at Millennium Park saw him too, so then I can't be crazy, right?"

"What else did he say? Why was he observing the kid?" Given that he totally ignored my sort of question about whether I was crazy, I could tell now where his irritation was coming from. He didn't like the idea that there may have been an outside person involved in a case where we had lost a child on the table.

"That was really it from the conversation on the platform. I think it lasted a total of ninety seconds. I did bring it up again at the park. He didn't say why specifically he was there that day in the OR. He just said that it was the little boy's time and that not all little kids are angels. I don't know what exactly he meant by that." I looked down bashfully at my food.

"So his time was just up?" Colin said in an irritable tone. "Who's he to say when someone's time is up? Is he some angel or someone that hangs around hospitals waiting to take people to the pearly gates?" Colin had pushed his chair back a little and was visibly annoyed by the conversation now. I hated to see him like this. We hadn't spoken much about the boy that we lost since our initial conversation at the coffee house. I didn't want to bring up bad memories right now or to send him down that spiral again of beating himself up about that case. I tried to do what I could to calm him and to divert his frustration from me.

"Look, Colin, I don't know. All I'm telling you is what I saw and heard. I'm sorry if I upset you. I shouldn't have mentioned anything at all. It's just … You know I don't really have anyone else to talk to about stuff like this," I said in a lower voice as I leaned in towards him. While I wasn't trying to give him the puppy-dog-eyes look, I felt like I probably at least had a hint of that on my face right now. His expression seemed to soften a bit, so I continued.

"You're one of the few people I know, particularly in terms of doctors, who believes that there may be things out there that we don't fully understand. I'm not saying that this is something magical or anything like that," I paused as I reached my hands across the table, "just that I don't really understand it yet, and I'm looking for some help."

There was a long pause as we both looked at each other. Colin was visibly trying to work things out in his head and decide what to say next, and I was trying to follow along with his internal thinking. At this point I didn't feel very successful.

He finally broke the silence. "So what were you doing at the park yesterday?" and with that he continued his lunch. I guess he wasn't sure what to make of the situation with Ben, so he was changing the subject. Accordingly, I let our conversation flow in a different direction.

"I was actually trying to clear my head before my conversation with Steven."

"Ah, yes, the Steven story," he nodded, remembering from earlier on in the conversation that this was something we would get back to. I filled him in on the ER incident and Howard calling me in, as well as a few other details. I figured it wasn't necessary to tell him that I had broken our mirror and cried myself to sleep on the floor in our foyer. Correction: MY mirror and MY foyer. It was going to take a little while to get used to using the singular again. Colin listened patiently as I made my way through the story, and then I paused at the point where Steven had left a note on the floor.

"Man, what an asshole!" he said and we both started laughing. "Suz, you really do deserve much better than him. I always thought that guy was a punk."

"I thought you liked Steven? You two always seemed to get along pretty well." I was somewhat surprised by Colin's comment about Steven. I had never noticed any tension between them, and I generally considered myself pretty observant. I wondered whether he was just saying that to make me feel better.

"I must be a better actor than I thought! I was really just being nice to him for the sake of our friendship," he looked down for a moment, and I thought I could see him blush ever so slightly.

"What do you mean, for the sake of our friendship? If you don't like my boyfriend, you can tell me. I'd rather you did actually," I said in a very sincere voice. I think I even believed what I said too.

"Suzy, I did tell you once, very early on in your relationship that I got a bad vibe from him. Remember? We were at that Mexican place over the summer. Sitting outside drinking margaritas?" I slowly nodded my head and he continued. "You didn't break up with him, so I figured you had made up your mind that you wanted to see things through. If I didn't at least pretend to like him, then

I knew it would be awkward for you to feel like you had to choose between us. So I decided not to put you in that position. Our friendship means more to me than that," he said earnestly. I looked up at him, and he quickly glanced away out the window. "Plus, you'd probably have chosen him over me anyway. He was your boyfriend after all," he said as he took another bite of his sandwich.

"I'm sorry I didn't listen to you at the time. And I'm glad you acted the way you did though. You're one of my closest friends and I hate to think I could have lost you over some stupid guy."

"Thanks Suz. I guess it wasn't all selfless though. I also wanted to be around when you were single again!" he said with a school-boy gleam in his eye. He quickly grabbed for his soda as an excuse to look away.

"Colin, I'm flattered, but I really don't-"

"Whatever, I don't want you now! You're screwed in the head! You think you're seeing ghosts in the OR. I probably shouldn't even be talking to you," he teased me, laughing to let me know that he really wasn't serious about thinking I'm screwed up in the head. And he did it to change topics. I think he could sense that I wasn't ready to have a conversation like that with him, so he kept things lighthearted.

We finished the rest of our lunch on lighter topics and then bundled back up to head over to the hospital.

That night when I got home, I took Roxie for a walk and my mind went straight to Ben. For the past week I had been captivated thinking about this mystery man who somehow managed to be showing up in random places. I kept getting so lost in his dark eyes and the velvety sound of his voice that I hadn't thought much yet about why exactly he was appearing to me. I had hoped to find out some of these answers, but I never seemed to have enough time with him to get through my whole list of questions.

Since my lunch with Colin when he referred to Ben as an 'angel,' I had started to consider what that would mean. I took a long deep breath as Roxie and I made our way down the street. What if he *was* an angel? I could see that. I could see him being sent to protect and reassure people. I pondered this as we crunched through the snow that covered the sidewalk. Given how short Roxie's legs were, we walked at a pretty slow pace.

I continued to mull things over and I suddenly stopped in my tracks. What if he's not an angel? What if he's a demon or dark spirit? No! No, that couldn't be the case ... Could it? I had to line up all of the facts in my mind. I started making my mental laundry list.

First, the little kid. He was there when the little kid died, and he admitted to me that he had something to do with it. Granted I didn't know what ... Does that make him a demon? But then why did he say that the kid wasn't an angel? Does that imply that he was justified in taking the kid's life if the kid was evil in some way? I would have to make sure to ask him what exactly his involvement was with this boy.

Second, the reflection I saw when I was observing. He was there during that surgery and no one had died. That patient had pulled through just fine. So maybe he was there as a guardian? Or maybe just observing like he said? Or did he only take my patients?

Third, that night on the el platform. Well, hmm. I really had no clue as to what that meant. That wasn't at the hospital. No one died, but then again, was anyone's life actually in danger? I had no idea what to make of that. Was he following me that night? I suppose it's possible that he lived around here ... At that thought I started to look around at the houses along the street. It was pretty silly to think I would happen to see him standing in a window looking at me at precisely this moment, but I looked anyway.

The last time I saw him was yesterday at the Bean. He had said he was working that day. But doing what? Just observing the people skating in the park? There must be a connection between his observation of people in the park and in the hospital. I just had to figure out what that connection was.

And was he the one that Thomas had seen? It seemed like he might be that person based on Thomas's description and that I started seeing Ben after Thomas told me he saw him. As I thought through all of the times I had seen him, most of them appeared to be positive, or at least not menacing. He didn't really seem like a demon to me, but then again I suppose I didn't have much of a frame of reference. As I was settling on the conclusion that he was not a demon, Roxie and I had made it back to our front gate. It creaked when I pushed the gate open and we walked up the stairs to the front door. I got ready for bed and grabbed my book from the coffee table before heading to the bedroom. Ever since Steven had left, I had been letting Roxie sleep on the bed next to me. It was probably a bad habit to get into, but at this point I really didn't care.

I tried to focus on my book, but tonight I couldn't keep my mind engaged in the story. I generally preferred to read fiction, and I had found this story engaging a couple of weeks ago, but now I just couldn't stop thinking about Ben and what his presence in my life meant. I stared at the same page for fifteen minutes before I finally gave in and turned off the light to go to bed.

That night I dreamt about Ben. I was in surgery on a middle aged woman. It looked like a fairly straightforward procedure and we were about halfway through. I heard the tinny jingle of bells ringing, like the bells above the door in a convenient store. I looked up from my patient and saw a man and three younger children come in. They all appeared to be dressed in their Sunday best on a spring day. He ushered them over to the operating table, and I realized that I was alone in the OR. None of the usual staff were there to assist me in the surgery. I was on my own.

"Doctor?" the youngest child, I would guess about five years old, said to me. She was wearing a little blue dress, and her wispy blond hair was in short pig tails. "Are you going to save my mommy?"

"Of course I am sweetheart. Your mommy will be just fine," I said with a smile on my unmasked face. I looked down and continued with the surgery as the family stood there, just a few feet away from the operating table, watching my every move. I didn't feel the nervousness like I did when the observation team was there. When I looked back up at the family, I saw Ben standing just a few feet away from the father.

"That's the breaks, Suzanne," he said to me. "It's just her time."

"Wait a minute!" My heart started to race and I began to panic. I looked back down at my patient and she was already bleeding out. Seeing the panicked look on my face, the little girl started crying and buried her face in the edge of her father's suit coat.

"NO! Don't take my mommy!!" She screamed, with tears streaming down her face. I looked over at Ben and he stood there coolly.

"Sorry Suzanne," he said, without a hint of remorse, and turned and walked away.

I awoke the next morning with clenched fists and tufts of sheets in my hands. My pillow was wet and I could tell that I had been crying. I had dreams of losing patients before, but never ones like this. Never ones with Ben in them, or someone who seemed to be in control of the situation. And I had never heard that heart wrenching sound like that little girl screaming as she watched her mother die on my table.

I got out of bed, walking into the bathroom with my face in my hands. Part of me wanted to forget the dream, but another part of me wanted to go over every detail in my mind so that I could analyze every aspect of it to see if there was any deeper meaning or anything else I had missed.

"Ughhh," I moaned aloud. *Another day awaits,* I thought to myself.

Chapter 7

I got to the hospital and settled in to my routine without much trouble. I checked my schedule for the day, and my heart skipped when I looked down and saw that I had a gallbladder removal procedure this afternoon. Immediately, I wondered if I would see Ben today during surgery. But then my heart sank thinking of my horrible dream last night. Even though the last time I saw him during surgery we lost the patient, a part of me so desperately wanted to see him again. They didn't always die when he was around, so I should not assume that seeing him meant my patient was not going to make it. I reminded myself to stay focused on my other patients for the morning, and that I would have time later to work through this issue.

I headed over to the institutional looking nurses station and checked my tablet for the list of patients for the morning. A few routine consults, a couple of follow ups … It looked to be cases I could handle pretty easily before lunch time. I smiled to myself as I noted that one of the patient's last names was Benjamin. Luckily I caught myself before any of the nurses noticed that I was standing there grinning like a Cheshire cat. I looked up at the clock. Still three hours until lunch.

The rest of the morning seemed to drag on this way. I found myself checking the clock every few minutes, counting down the time until I could shut off and day dream a little bit. By the time lunch came around, I felt like I had been in the hospital for days, rather than just a few hours. I had decided to stay in the cafeteria today so that I could review my patient's chart in a bit more detail before the procedure. While I would always do final review and analysis before every case, I took an especially detailed and thorough look at this patient, probably as a way to distract myself from my other thoughts of the day. And, given my awful dream from the night before, I wanted to calm my nerves before surgery. The procedure looked straight forward enough, but something felt out of place. I looked through all of the patient's background information, not knowing exactly what I was searching for. My eyes wandered over page after page of progress notes and test results, and then I froze as I came across her personal profile. Mrs. Rosemer was married with three children.

My mind began to run away with itself, and I tried to remember back to the surgery from my dream. I focused on the part when I looked back to my patient and saw that she was bleeding out. What exactly had I been doing during the surgery? My mind strained back to see all of the details, and in hindsight, I saw that it had also been a gallbladder procedure. My heart sank and I pushed my chair back from the table, staring straight ahead, but not focusing on anything in particular.

Demoralized, I grabbed my tablet and headed back to the physician lounge to prepare for the afternoon. *It's just a coincidence,* I kept telling myself. I do dozens of gallbladder procedures every year. It's not like this is a strange procedure for me to perform. But if Ben does appear today, then what does that mean? What if he's here to take my patient? Does that make him a killer? I prayed that today's surgery wouldn't be a reenactment of my dream from last night. I don't think I could stand losing a second patient in such a short time.

I slowly closed my locker and took a deep breath, holding it in for a minute before loudly exhaling. One of the other doctors who was standing in front of her open locker shot me a concerned look. I didn't know her well, and certainly didn't feel like engaging in a conversation with her, so I smiled politely and walked out of the room. I stopped for a glass of cold water in the kitchen area on my way up to the OR. I savored every cool drop, probably as my way to procrastinate.

I spent an inordinately long time scrubbing. My mind kept racing in different directions and I had to keep mentally telling myself to refocus. *If this is a reenactment of last night's dream, then this patient is going to die and there's nothing I can do about it,* was one of my directions. A part of me was ashamed to be thinking that. As I was starting to beat myself up for it, another part of me broke in. *Snap out of it! It's just a dream and don't you dare condemn a patient you haven't even started on because of a stupid dream! You're a doctor. Now act like one.* Yes, this second voice sounded more like me. This was the one I was going to listen to and believe in. With that, I finished my scrub, gloved up, and confidently walked into the operating room.

"Doctor," Lauren said with a compassionate smile on her face as she stepped to my side beside our patient. I looked over and noticed that this was the same anesthesiologist that was on Thomas's case. I was going to pay close attention to what he did today, not that I didn't trust him, but simply for my own curiosity's sake. I wondered again if Thomas's vision was induced by the anesthesia, although I was becoming more convinced that it was Ben.

I checked in one final time with Mrs. Rosemer and then signaled to everyone that we were ready to begin. The anesthesiologist started giving instructions to the patient as he put the mask over her face. I, too, inhaled deeply and took a long look at Mrs. Rosemer's face before studying the faces of each of the other people in the operating suite. I held the cold scalpel in my hand, taking in the texture of the handle against my gloved hand. I looked up, half expecting to see her husband and three children standing across the table from me. I was relieved when I did not see those four in my OR suite, but a short twinge of sadness came over me as I found myself looking for Ben. Much to my disappointment, or maybe it was relief, he wasn't there either.

I took another deep breath and pressed the scalpel into her flesh. I felt the skin give way as the blood came pouring out over the blade of the scalpel. A quick rush came over me as I remembered back to my dream from the night before. I quickly regained my senses and continued with my task at hand.

Throughout the entire procedure, I would catch myself sneaking a quick glance up from Mrs. Rosemer to check the room for any people who should not be there. I also would look over periodically at the anesthesiologist. So far, I had not noticed anything that would seem out of the ordinary with what he was doing. I had now firmly decided that the person Thomas saw was Ben, and I doubted it had anything to do with the anesthesia.

As the time passed by with no hint of any observers, my nerves subsided. In their place was a dull, somber feeling that seeped through me. The surgery concluded without any complications. While a part of me was incredibly relieved by the fact that my dream from the previous night did not come true, a small part of me was disappointed that Ben had not been there. I thought about that as I cleaned up in the scrub room. Could I really feel sad that things had worked out the way they had? A woman's life was saved today, and I was down trodden because I hadn't seen a man that I had been fixated on for the past week. I shook my head in disappointment with myself as I finished up scrubbing. I tossed the paper towels into the trash and headed back to finish up my afternoon appointments.

It had started to snow by the time I left the hospital that night. The traffic wasn't bad, but just a little slower than usual. Roxie wasn't a huge fan of the snow, so nights like tonight were quick trips out for her. After taking her out I headed to the kitchen to fix something for dinner. Since Steven had moved out, I hadn't been as motivated to cook real meals for myself. There was something very unsatisfying about spending all of that time on just yourself. It either ended up being a tiny amount of food, which seemed like a waste, or you would end up eating the same leftovers for a week. After making a quick sandwich instead, I made a fire and opened a bottle of red wine. I loved wood-burning fireplaces, even though they were significantly more work than gas fireplaces. My solution to that was throwing a few fire starter logs in with the real wood. They would catch quickly and burn long enough to catch the other logs. Within about five minutes, the fire was blazing and filling the room with warmth and with a soft glow. The light from the fire was bright enough that I didn't need many other lights on. I walked over to the stereo and I scrolled through my music to find a playlist that suited my mood for this evening. It mainly consisted of what I would consider to be sappy, mellow music. I cuddled up on the couch with Roxie and a crocheted green and brown blanket that my grandma had made for me and stared out the window. Watching the falling snow was so peaceful and it kept my focus long enough to quiet my mind.

By the time I got to my second glass of wine, Ben was all I could think about. Every morning for the past week, he had been the first thing I thought of when I woke up, and every morning I got ready for my day with a smile on my face. I would find myself replaying our couple of conversations over and over in my head. Every glance he had given me made my heart skip, even now when I was thinking about it a week after the fact. The thought of him was constantly in my head, to a point of pure distraction.

Every time I would think about him, I would get butterflies in my stomach, and start smiling. I had had crushes on guys before, but never like this. There was something different about him, something very familiar. I felt like I had known him for years. And now, especially sitting at home in my living room, curled up next to the fire, I wanted him here with me more than ever.

Part of my heart ached that he wasn't here right now, and then a part of me was almost mad at him. Mad and disappointed that he hadn't shown up in the OR today. Not that I had wanted my dream to be reenacted, but I had desperately wanted to see him, even if just for a few moments. I closed my eyes and remembered the first time I saw him during surgery. My mind replayed every curve of his face, every sparkle in his eyes.

As I poured myself another glass of wine, I tried to line up all of my emotions into some logical order. There was the clear physical attraction I had to him. Probably the same attraction the majority of the female population would have towards him. Moving on slightly from the physical side was his voice. The few times we had spoken, his voice had been smooth and rich, like pure sweet chocolate. I smiled at the analogy given my love for chocolate. I let my mind meander down the path of remembering all of his physical traits again.

But there was the side of him, truthfully it was most of him, that I really did not know anything about. There was a little voice inside of me that told me he was complicated. That there was something unnatural about him, even though I couldn't quite pinpoint it. That on its own frustrated me to no end. It was as if there was an image that I could almost see, but it was blurry. The harder I tried to focus on the image, the blurrier it would become. Just like I was drawn into the field of medicine to solve mysteries, I was drawn to Ben to find out what was so different about him. I wasn't sure what his involvement with some of these patients had been, but my mind was okay with not knowing that at this exact moment. It gave my mind something to think about and process. And I had thought about worst case scenario. What if he really was, for all intents and purposes, killing people? I had thought over that question a hundred different times, and I kept arriving at the conclusion that if that were the case then there must be a good reason. I would need to know more before making any final decisions.

As I went through some of these different scenarios, I realized that I had been intentionally avoiding the obvious emotional question for the last week. I knew the question was looming, but I had not wanted to acknowledge it, for fearing of having to come to some sort of an answer. Instead, I kept telling myself how ridiculous it was that I even be thinking about Ben at all, let alone daydreaming about us. I had spent so many hours daydreaming about going for walks along the beach on Lake Michigan, and just spending time together. Granted I had also had much more vivid daydreams, but they seemed to be all encompassing. Although I felt like I had looked at my feelings from so many angles, I still had not dared to ask myself the one question I did not know if I wanted to hear the answer to. So, after a few more sips of wine to fuel my liquid courage, I asked myself the most basic of questions: was I starting to fall for him?

No sooner had I thought those words, the butterflies returned and my heart started to race. I smiled as I realized that the answer was yes.

Chapter 8

*T*he next day I had a new sense of peace when I woke up. For whatever reason, answering the question of how I felt about Ben had somehow given me much more clarity. While I wouldn't necessarily call it a logical or sane conclusion, I did feel at peace knowing what to make of my feelings. I was glad that I had stopped playing mind games with myself.

I got to work early and welcomed the smell of pastries when I walked into the physician lounge. Even though I wasn't in a hurry this morning, I had skipped breakfast. I had been so preoccupied this past week that I hadn't been to the grocery store, so the house was void of anything that resembled breakfast food at the moment. I was standing at the counter getting my croissant and coffee when I heard a familiar set of voices and laughter. I turned around to see Howard and Colin walking through the doors together. They got along really well, although now I wondered with Colin whether it was genuinely getting along or whether he was once again just being a good actor. Colin still had his coat and messenger bag with him and he gave me a quick nod as he headed off toward the locker room.

"Good morning Dr. Jacobsen," Howard said as he joined me at the counter. "You seem to be doing better than the last time I saw you." His tone was more of a concerned tone, not sarcastic. I smiled and turned to face him.

"Yeah, things are going much better." I had a surprisingly sincere tone, but then again after last night I could honestly say that I was doing much better. "So have you decided which surgeon to hire?"

"Yep, we're going with Carpenter. He's the one you observed with me. He's really good and anxious to start."

"That's great, I'm sure he'll make a wonderful addition."

"Yeah, I think he will. Well, I've gotta run. Catch up with you later," he said as he flashed his row of pearly white teeth at me. He turned on his heel and walked hastily out the door. As I turned to walk over to one of the little tables, Colin walked out of the men's locker room and when his eyes caught mine, they sparkled. His smile gave away his true feelings and I could tell he was definitely in a chipper mood today.

"Hey Suz, how's it going?" he asked as he picked up a muffin and grabbed a chair across from he.

"Oh, not too bad. Pretty much the same ol' same ol'."

"I hear ya. It's been a pretty uneventful week on my end too. Hey, I'm going out with a few friends tonight. Do you wanna come with us?" I could tell by his tone that it was strictly a friendly invite, but that he was anxious for me to come along anyway. I thought about it, but I wasn't sure if I felt like going out, or if I just wanted to stay home and have some quiet time. Apparently my delayed response was being taken as a rejection.

"Come on, it's a Friday night. Plus, how long has it been since you've been out? Besides going out somewhere with just Steven?" I smiled at that. It was true. I hadn't gone out much in the past six or eight months unless it was Steven and I going somewhere. It wasn't that he didn't like me going out with friends, the problem was that I didn't have many friends up here. It was hard to make new friends, particularly female ones, and it was different hanging out with guys when your boyfriend was standing right next to you. Even though Colin and I were good friends, I had always felt weird telling Steven I was going to be going out with another man, and 'no,' he wasn't particularly invited to go along.

"Well, where are you guys going? If you're going down to Rush & Division, I'll probably pass." Rush & Division was an area downtown that had a lot of dance clubs and I would guess that the average age of the people in that area on a Friday night was about twenty-two.

"Nah, nothing that hard core for tonight. We're going to Irish Eyes, probably around eight-"

"Seriously? Aren't you a little old for-"

"Hey now, we're not that old," he said with a huge smile. "But really, one of Paul's friends is playing there tonight. Apparently the regular guys for Irish Eyes cancelled so Paul's friends got the call. Come on, you can go out and party like you're in college. But legally. It should be a good time," he said with a friendly smile.

"Yeah, it sounds like it." I thought about the offer. I didn't really have anything going on tonight, except tentatively going to the grocery store. But, on the other hand, if I turned him down with no good reason, he may stop inviting me out. The truth was I really did miss having a more active social life. Sad that it would take someone this much prodding to decide to go out on a Friday night ...

"So you're in?"

"Yeah, I'll text you when I'm leaving my place to make sure you guys are there," I said with a smile. The more I thought about it, I actually was looking forward to going out tonight. Going to the grocery store on a Friday night just made me feel mildly pathetic.

"Awesome! See ya later tonight," he said with his beautiful smile as he got up from the table. "Gotta get to my rounds," he explained as he turned to head out of the lounge, tossing his napkin and muffin wrapper dramatically into the trash as he went. A hint of a smile passed across my face as I finished my breakfast and prepared myself for the day ahead.

I was on the train headed home for the day and I was actually pretty excited about going out tonight. Not that I was thinking anything crazy would happen, but I reveled in the thought that I could do whatever I wanted tonight and didn't have to worry about checking in or getting home too late. I checked my email on my phone as the train clicked along. My personal email account was full of the usual junk mail about low priced meds, discount vacations, and a whole bunch of other crap that I wasn't even going to read to find out what it was.

As I scrolled down my inbox, one particular email caught my eye. It was an email yesterday from Mandy Shaylands. I hadn't heard from her in ages! We had been roommates in med school and had been really close friends for quite a while. I felt a brief moment of guilt as I saw her name appear, thinking it had been entirely too long since I had last spoken to her.

I opened the message and read the very short email. "Moved back to Chi-town. Wanna hang out? Here's my new number." That was very much her style. Nothing too lengthy. She would rather get together in person and catch up than let email be the setting for our interactions. I added her number to my address book and then sent her a quick text message. "Irish eyes @ 9. U in? SJ" Within thirty seconds my phone beeped that I had a new text message. I swear that girl was permanently attached to her phone. "See you there!"

I got home around six and took Roxie outside while I thought ahead to my evening out. I decided I should have some sort of substantial food for dinner since I would be drinking tonight. I didn't want to get out of hand and make an ass out of myself the first time I was out on my own in the past three years.

After dinner, I headed to the closet to decide what to wear tonight. Irish Eyes was a laid back pub. Anything dressier than jeans and you would look out of place. I tried on a couple of my pairs of jeans to see which ones fit the best right now, finally settling on a pair of boot cut, dark jeans. I never got on the "skinny jean" wagon, never thinking they looked good on me, or very many other people for that matter! I probably could have gotten away with wearing a sweatshirt to Irish Eyes, but opted for something slightly more flattering. I always felt like dressing in flattering clothes in the winter was a challenge. Most of my cute tops were all short sleeved, although it was probably going to be warm in the bar, so I decided to brave it for tonight. I chose a fitted brown and blue shirt that wasn't too low cut. I didn't have much in the way of cleavage, and so I typically didn't like to draw attention to that area. But this shirt had a cute brown lightweight coat to go with it, under my heavy winter coat of course, and brown healed boots.

After I finished getting dressed, I moved into the bathroom to do my hair and retouch my make-up. About twenty minutes later, after futzing with the same few pieces of hair over and over, I was finally done. I checked myself in the mirror and I was actually pretty happy with myself. I heard my phone beep and went to the kitchen to take a look. It was Colin letting me know they were at the bar. I checked the clock and it was about ten til eight. I did one more quick trip out with Roxie, then came in to finish getting bundled up. Instinctively, I looked over to the wall to do a final check, but I still had not gotten around to replacing the mirror after my temper tantrum a couple of weeks ago. I would probably wait until spring when I could go to some flea markets or antique shows to find one with character. Given the style of my house, a plain one would just look out of place. I went to the bathroom to do one final check and then I was out the door.

It was just a quick cab ride over to Irish Eyes, and luckily I hadn't had to stand out on the corner for too long before I caught a cab. I was glad that I had worn at least somewhat practical shoes for tonight. Even though I was able to catch a cab to the bar, finding one after would be another story. I may have to walk a few blocks to the train station rather than waiting around forever in the snow to catch a taxi. Irish Eyes was on a long and fairly busy road that had bars up and down the street. Granted, these weren't the crazy dance clubs down on Rush & Division, but they were packed nonetheless on a Friday night. Even though there would be lots of cabs driving around, there were tons of people looking for cabs too.

I walked into the bar, and smiled appreciatively when they carded me going in. The bar was already fairly crowded given how small it was. I could see people getting the tiny stage in the corner ready for the band later tonight. The interior of the bar was a warm, dark wood, but the décor made it look like a drunk leprechaun had thrown up all over the place. Just about every three foot section of wall space had some sort of Irish, green, or shamrock something adorning it. The funny thing was, despite how cheesy this place looked from a distance, it really was a fun place to hang out and grab a few beers.

I looked around and was able to spot Colin standing over by a table with a group of four other guys. I recognize a couple of them from other parties or things that I had gone to with Colin. Most of his friends were really nice and pretty outgoing. They all had good jobs, and none of them were doctors. It was a nice change to be able to talk about non-medical topics. I made my way through the crowd and over to their table.

"Hey Suz, you look great" Colin said as he gave me a hug. "I'm glad you made it out tonight. Here," he said as he handed me a Guinness. "This one's on the house."

"Thanks," I said as I took my coat off and took the beer from him.

"You remember the guys, right? Joe, Marcus, Paul, and Charlie," he said, gesturing to each one as he went through their names.

"Hey guys," I said with a nod.

"And how's the good doctor been? It's been a while!" Charlie said. Of all of Colin's friends, I knew him the best. He had lived with Colin for a couple of years when I first moved to Chicago, so I had seen him a lot. He was sitting closest to me, and was grinning ear to ear with him arms wide open. I think that they already had finished at least a couple of rounds before I got here.

"Not too bad," I replied as I gave him a one armed, sideways hug. "Are you still causing trouble?"

"You know it," he said with a laugh as he picked up his pint and resumed conversation with the other guys. I turned back to Colin who was watching me and smiling.

"I hope you don't mind," I took another sip, "but I invited one of my friends from med school to meet us here. She just moved back to Chicago, so I thought it'd be nice to introduce her to some other people."

"Yeah, no problem. I'm sure the guys won't mind having another girl hang out with us." Colin and I stood around talking for the next twenty minutes as the bar gradually got louder. A little before nine my phone buzzed in my pocket and I pulled it out to check on Mandy's status. Her cab was pulling up outside, so I excused myself from Colin for a minute to go closer to the door to meet her. It took my beer and I a couple minutes to wade through the crowd, and I met her about halfway between our group and the front door. She smiled and threw her arms around my neck when she saw me.

"Suzy! How *are* you?!" she exclaimed. "You look great!"

"Damn! So do you Mandy!" I exclaimed as I looked her up and down. She always had a curvy, voluptuous look to her. I had to admit, I had been a little bit jealous of her. While a lot of girls in college were stressing out about wanting to be pencil thin, Mandy had always had a very healthy glow about her. I never considered her to be overweight, she just curved in all of the right places. Her long reddish brown hair tumbled effortlessly around her shoulders, drawing attention to the low cut shirt she had on. She had a way of dressing that accented her features, but without looking slutty like so many other girls did. I think part of it was the way she carried herself. She was confident and well spoken, so she was able to turn heads in a number of ways.

"Thanks! Gotta love all of those free samples, right?" she laughed as she gestured to her face. She was a dermatologist and they were always getting free samples from new companies.

"Must be nice! Let's go get you something to drink," I said as I grabbed her hand and made our way to the bar. As we stood there waiting in line, we began catching up.

"So, how's Steven? Things were going pretty well l when I visited last fall," she asked as we scooted up in line and she turned to face me so that we could talk.

"Actually we broke up a couple of weeks ago."

"I'm sorry to hear that. Are you okay?" she asked as she put her hand on my arm. She studied my face for a moment to see if I was really okay or if we need a quick subject change.

"Yeah, I was the one who broke it off. He wasn't the right one, so why waste time, right?" I realized that as I said this I fully believed every word of it, and it didn't even make me sad to think about Steven now. I looked back at Mandy and saw her smiling and looking over my shoulder.

"So what're you doing back in Chicago?" I asked her. Without breaking her gaze, she answered.

"I got an offer to join a great practice downtown." And with that she looked back towards me. "Three years and I'll be a partner. Good hours, and it's big enough that we don't have to cover vacations or weekends that often, so I'm pretty excited about that!" She laughed and turned back to the bar and held out a twenty.

"That's great Mandy! When do you start?"

"Next Monday. I get a week to settle in and then back to it!" She had caught the bartender's eye and was now ordering. She looked back over my shoulder as she waited for her beer.

"What're you looking at?" I asked as I turned around. "Is it someone we know?" I said still panning the crowd that would have been over my shoulder.

"I wish! No, it's just a gorgeous blond over there," as she motioned slightly with her chin. She wasn't as gaudy as to point at someone she was interested in. "And I think he's been looking over here too," she smiled, pleased that we had caught someone's attention. I turned again to look as she paid for her drink and I caught Colin's gaze. As Mandy turned back towards me to walk away from the bar, I waved at Colin and he waved back.

"Oh, you mean the guy waving at us?" I asked Mandy.

"Yeah, why's he waving? Do you know him?" She seemed optimistic that I knew him and would introduce her.

"Actually that's who we're here with tonight," I said with a smile. I liked playing matchmaker.

"Is he Steven's replacement? Not too shabby!"

"No, he's not my boyfriend. He works at the hospital with me."

"Oh, well then lucky me!" she giggled.

"Come on, I'll introduce you," I said as I grabbed her hand and pulled her towards the table.

As the night drew on, I had made my way around the table, talking to all of Colin's friends as well as catching up more with Mandy. She and Colin had seemed to hit it off and were now chatting away. Both had visible smiles on their faces and I had noted some of the 'casual touches' throughout the night. Mandy was a very direct person, and that, coupled with her looks, tended to keep men's interest for as long as she wanted to keep their interest. It was funny that she had ended up being a dermatologist, when she herself had such naturally flawless skin.

At this point the live music was in full swing. Paul's friend was occasionally called in as a backup when one of the regulars couldn't make it in. A crowd like this was very particular about the music: it had to be loud, pretty fast, and something that everyone could sing along to. Usually the main theme of all of the music was Irish drinking songs. After a few beers, I was one of the loud mouths who was singing along to some of the songs too, but I didn't mind because almost everyone else in our group was singing too. When the first set was over, they took a short break before the next set started.

I was standing next to Joe, one of Colin's friends that I hadn't met before. He seemed really nice, and we struck up a conversation. Given how loud the bar was, I didn't mind that he was doing most of the talking, otherwise my throat would probably be raw the next day from all of the yelling.

He was telling me about his job, and how he knew Colin and the rest of the guys. I looked over towards Colin as Joe was describing some of their exploits, and Colin happened to look up and over at me at the same point. He smiled when he saw that I was looking at him, and then he nodded towards Joe and grinned.

I returned the gesture. He looked back down at the table and noticed that Mandy was holding an empty glass, so he nodded to me and we both headed to the bar to get another round. I looked back and saw that Mandy had quickly started up a conversation with Charlie.

"So, has Joe talked your ear off yet?" he laughed as we got in line. Like a gentleman, he gestured for me to go ahead of him. Even though the live music had stopped, the crowd was now louder than before it had started, so I stood very close to Colin so I could hear what he was saying.

"He's very social," I said with a smile and a nod.

"Very politically correct," he said with a quick laugh.

"And how about you and Mandy? Looks like you two are hitting it off over there." I was sure Mandy would fill me in on her side of it later, but I was curious to hear his side too. I liked to see how two people saw the exact same interaction in two (sometimes) very different ways.

"Yeah, she seems nice," he answered in a lighthearted tone, but not as much fire or conviction as I would have expected. Although, it was pretty difficult to pick up tones in a loud, crowded bar.

"Nice, huh? That's a very generic comment," I said with a pause, in case he wanted to jump in with anything else. "And those are very nice shoes you have on," added with enough sarcasm that could be read over the noise.

"Thanks, I thought so too," he paused as we moved forwards in line. "No, she really seems very smart and like she'd be a lot of fun to hang out with."

"And she's hot too, so that's a plus," I chimed in with a lopsided smile.

"You think?" he asked with an expression on his face that I couldn't read. But I could definitely see a smile on his face.

"Like you didn't notice," I said teasingly.

"Should I?" he asked, as we took another step forward.

"Okay, I'll stop harassing you. For now."

"Thank you Doctor."

"You're welcome sir," I said as I took a step up to the bar. "I'll have another pint of Guinness," I said as I got my money out. Colin put his hand over mine and shouted over the noise of the bar to make it three, then put his money down on the bar.

"Thanks for the drink."

"You're welcome. Thanks for coming out with us," he said with all seriousness as we picked up our drinks and headed back to the table.

Even though the bar didn't close until two, by about midnight I was noticing myself starting to get groggy. All around, it had been a pretty long week for me, and I wasn't used to staying out this late. I made my way up to the bar to buy another round, this time with a soda for me. I got back to the table to drop off a couple of beers and to down my soda. Hopefully the caffeine would give me a little bit of a boost. I walked over to a beaming Mandy.

"So it looks like you two are hitting it off?" I said as I motioned with my chin towards Colin, who was turned away from us talking to Paul.

"Suzy, he is so hot! And he seems like he's a really nice guy, and smart and funny too." By this point I could tell she'd had a little too much to drink, but not by what she was saying. She would have said almost the exact same thing sober, less the overly enthusiastic smile.

"He's the total package Mandy," I said with the utmost sincerity. The two of them actually would make a good couple.

"Thanks sweetie! And you'll find someone too. Maybe he's right under your nose and you don't even know it!"

"Who knows, maybe he is!" I humored her given how good of a mood she was in. I had finished my Diet Coke at this point and was ready to brave the cold weather. "Hey, I think I'm gonna take off. Are you okay to get home?"

"Oh yeah, I'm fine. You be careful on your way home too, okay?"

"Will do," I said as I gave her a hug. "I'm so glad you're back in Chicago now. I need another girl to hang out with. Alright, I'm gonna say bye to Colin and I'll see you later."

I scooted past her in the bar that seemed even more crowded now. I walked up next to Colin and put my arm around his waist. He put his arm around my shoulder and leaned in to hear me over the noise.

"I think I'm gonna take off now. It's been a pretty crazy week and I'm dead on my feet." Saying it out loud made me even more tired than before.

"Are you sure?" he asked as I nodded.

"Yeah, I'm just gonna hop a train. It's only a couple of blocks away," I said, my eyes fixing in on Charlie, who was putting his coat on and saying his goodbyes too.

"Hey Charlie," Colin shouted and motioned to get his attention. He nodded and made his way over to us. "You headin out?"

"Yeah, I've gotta head into the office in the morning."

"Can you walk Suzy to the train?"

"No problem, I was heading that way too," he responded and looked over at me with a quick smile. I eyed Colin a little suspiciously, but he shook his head. At first I thought he was trying to set me up but his expression told me otherwise.

"Hey, text me when you make it home."

"Alright dad," and I leaned in and gave him a quick peck on the cheek and motioned to Charlie to head out.

As soon as we hit the brisk air outside, we both shivered. Charlie had his hands stuffed in his pockets, but he turned to me and extended his elbow in my direction. There was still some snow on the ground and all of the people out walking around had packed it down, making some spots on the sidewalk slippery. I was also freezing so I grabbed onto it and huddled in close to him as we walked to the el stop. He lived up in Wrigleyville, so he would be heading in the opposite direction, but at least it was nice to have someone to walk to the station with me. As I suspected, despite how many cabs were driving around, there weren't many that were available.

We talked the whole way to the train, partially because he was so easy to talk to, but also just to distract from the bitter cold. The wind was whipping tonight, sending shivers down my spine as we trudged through the snowy streets. Luckily, when we got to the station there was space under one of the heating lamps, so that helped keep us warm. My train arrived first, so I gave Charlie a hug and thanked him for walking with me. He said his good nights too and I hopped on board my train to call it a night.

When the doors to train opened, a rush of warm air washed over me and I was relieved to have my muscles relax slightly from being clenched the whole walk over. I looked around the train car, which was pretty empty except for a few stray passengers, and two sets of couples. I walked down the aisle towards an empty seat, and as I was passing by one of the other riders, my mouth dropped wide open.

It was Ben.

Chapter 9

"*B*en?!" I squealed, louder than was necessary, considering there were less than ten people on the train, about half of whom looked up at me after my outburst. I guess I had had a little too much to drink by this point. He suddenly looked up, startled by someone loudly calling his name at such a short range. I plopped down in the seat across the aisle from him.

"Hi Suzanne," he replied with a warm smile. Well this was promising! Usually he looked like I had caught him off guard, or like he was uncomfortable running into me.

"Why do I always run into you on the train? Are you 'observing' me or something?" I asked with a playful and happy tone in my voice. I also realized that the alcohol, sleepiness, and the quick rush brought on by the cold were making me lean in and casually touch his arm more so than I would have dared if I was sober. Generally speaking, I was a chicken when it came to men I was interested in. I'm not quite sure why that was. I didn't have a bad track record with the men I had asked out, and I generally didn't feel self-conscious or feel like I wasn't good enough to ask them out. I guess I was just a little more old fashioned. Like it was something the guy was *supposed* to do.

"Always? This is actually only the second time we've run into each other on the train," he smiled back at me with a familiarity that made my heart sing. As fun as it was to occasionally watch a man fidget nervously, I was glad to see that he seemed to be warming up to me a little bit. He took my hand that was lightly flittering around his arm, and continued, "And why are you on a train so late all by yourself?"

"Oh, I was just out with my friends and you can never catch a cab on Lincoln this time of night!"

"Still, you shouldn't be riding around alone," he responded with a truly concerned look in his eyes.

"You're right," I leaned in closer, with a breathy tone to my voice, "I could run into someone like you." I smiled a mischievous little smile and then leaned back in my seat. I glanced out the window and saw that my stop would be coming up next. As I looked back over towards Ben he was already standing up, holding his hand out to me.

"Come on, I'll walk you home." My heart raced, excited that he was here with me and that he was going to walk me home. I could finally talk to him and ask him more of my questions. Another small part of me was screaming *No! You have no clue who this person is! Why would you ever let him take you home?!* For now, I ignored that other little voice. As I had covered before in my thoughts, I figured that if he had ill intentions, he had plenty of opportunity to act already.

Without taking his hand, I cautiously stood up. "Wait, how do you know where I live?" I guess that other little voice had crept up.

"Since this is the stop you 'always' get off at, I'm assuming you live here," he responded in a lightly mocking tone. He once again offered his hand, and this time I took it. The train stopped, and we were instantly hit with an icy gush of air. Instinctively, I put my arm through his and pulled him close as we stepped out onto the platform. Noticing the loud footfalls on the wooden platform, he looked down at my shoes and chuckled.

"What?" I asked, a bit defensively.

"You women and your shoes," he laughed with a wide smile.

"Surprisingly, these really are very comfortable, and not too bad in the snow."

"I'm sure they are," he said, still smiling as we walked down the stairs. He took extra care on the steps, tightening his arm around mine in case I needed extra support. Luckily I didn't, but I smiled at the thought that he was looking out for me.

At the bottom of the stairs, he stopped and turned towards me. I took a deep breath and looked into his eyes, wondering what he was going to do next. I subtly leaned in a little bit closer, hoping he was going to lean in too. My mind had already started running away with itself, thinking about what his full, warm lips would feel like on mine.

"Which way?" he asked politely, snapping me out of my quick day dream.

"Right. Oh, um, left. Sorry, I forgot that you probably don't actually know where I live." I turned on my heel, pulling Ben towards me as we walked down the snowy street back to my house.

"So what were you and your friends doing out tonight? Any special occasion?" he asked as we started to make our way down the softly lit street. I welcomed the talking right now. It was keeping my teeth from chattering too loudly.

"Well, one of my friends was out to watch a buddy of his playing at the bar. And I met up with a friend of mine from med school who just moved back to the city."

"Did you have fun?"

"Yeah, it was good to catch up with Mandy. It's been a while since I've seen her. And I'm happy to have another girlfriend in the city. My sister is my best friend and I don't get to see her much since she moved away." I paused and looked down at the snow covering the sidewalk. "We used to get together all the time when we lived closer, but now she's in Nebraska with her family, so we don't see each other very often. You know, just around the holidays and special occasions, but we're still close. We share everything. I talk to her a couple times a week," I rambled as I looked over at him. I wasn't afraid to walk down my street at night, I did it all the time with Roxie, but I was really happy to have him here with me now.

"And have you told her about the crazy man who has been stalking you?"

"So you admit you've been stalking me?" I asked coyly, with a little extra bounce in my step.

"I'm guessing that by now *you think* I'm stalking you." He still didn't fully answer my question, but I didn't feel like pressing the issue right now. We were coming up on my house and I was hoping that he may come in and talk for a little while.

"Well, this is me," I said as we slowed down and he turned towards me.

"I should be going," he said with a very proper tone in his voice as he started to pull away from me. I held his arm tightly in mine, and he paused, looking deep into my eyes. He seemed confused, but intrigued, by my tightened hold on him.

"It's freezing out here. The least I can do is make you a cup of cocoa for your trouble. That really was nice of you to walk me home." He hesitated, trying to decide whether or not he was going to accept my invitation. I figured that maybe keeping things on a lighter note would help my case, so I added "I promise I won't bite," to which he chuckled and caved in.

As soon as we walked in the door, Roxie was yipping at our feet. I quickly grabbed her leash. She'd just get a quick little circle around our yard for now.

"Just one second. Let me get her out real quick. Make yourself at home!" Luckily Roxie didn't want to be outside any more than I did, so within one minute we were back inside. Ben was still standing in the foyer when I came back through the door. I slid my shoes off at the front door, and he quickly bent down to take his off too. I took my coat off and hung it on the hall tree, then turned to him with an outstretched arm.

"Oh thanks," he said, handing me his coat. I headed to the kitchen to get the kettle started for cocoa, then joined Ben again in the foyer. This time he was crouched down petting Roxie.

"I think you've got a new best friend now. Come on, we can sit in the living room til the water's ready." I led the way over to the soft brown leather couch. The one bad thing about leather was that it was always cold in the winter. Especially since my house was a little on the chilly side. "Sorry it's so cold in here. These old houses are awful to keep heated in the winter." I flopped down on the couch and pulled my favorite green and brown blanket over me. "There's another blanket if you need it," I said as I gestured to the one over the other arm of the couch.

"No, I'm fine," he replied, looking around the living room. "This really is a beautiful house."

"Thanks, my grandmother gave it to me, but I think I already told you that in the park," to which he nodded. I fidgeted nervously, not knowing whether I should push for answers. Luckily, amidst my thinking, I heard the kettle sound. I jumped up and headed to the kitchen. As I prepared our mugs, I thought about how to bring up some of the touchier subjects that I had been thinking about. I guess it was better to be direct than to continue to wonder about it.

I returned a few minutes later with our drinks and set his down on the edge of the coffee table next to him. "Here you go," I said with a smile.

"Thank you," he replied, picking up the cup and warming his hands on its sides.

"Can I ask you something?" The hesitancy in my voice was apparent, and I hoped he wouldn't balk at it.

"Sure. What's on your mind?" It struck me how different his tone was now than during some of our other encounters. It was much softer and warmer than it had been during most of our conversations. I wasn't sure why he had changed, but I liked it. Just then my phone rang. I couldn't think who could be calling me this late unless it was an emergency. I furrowed my eyebrows as I wondered who it could be.

"One second," I said, jumping up off the couch and heading back over to my purse. It was Colin. Crap! I had forgotten to text him when I got home. I answered the call, looking back over to Ben and holding up my finger to let him know it would just be a minute.

"Hey, sorry about that. I totally forgot to text you."

"Are you alright?" he asked with a concerned voice.

"Yeah, I'm fine, I'm just tired. I'm not used to being out late anymore."

"You made it back okay with Charlie?"

"Safe inside," I responded, intentionally keeping my answers short so that we didn't get into a drawn out conversation. I just hoped it came across as tired and not irritated.

"You're sure?"

"Yeah, everything's fine. Oh, and I expect a full report later on the Mandy situation."

"Of course you do," he said with a chuckle. His tone surprised me, and I wondered why he would be so chipper to tell me about his evening. I guess he must have really hit it off with Mandy.

"Alright, I'll catch you later Colin."

"Goodnight Suz." And I clicked the phone off, turning back to Ben.

"Sorry about that," I apologized as I turned my phone off and put it back in my purse.

"Is everything okay?"

"Yeah, I just told my friend I'd text him when I got home so he'd know I made it back alright."

"Well, that's nice of him to check up on you," Ben responded. I was glad that his tone was lighthearted. At first I was afraid that he would think the wrong thing or get jealous. Instead he continued on. "So you were going to ask me something?"

"Oh right." He could probably tell by my voice that I was starting to lose my conviction. But oh well, I may as well take full advantage of this opportunity. "It's about that boy," I said slowly, giving him the chance to interrupt and request a change of topic if he wanted to. Instead he just drank his cocoa and nodded. His eyes looked up and locked onto mine. Whether he meant to be or not, he looked so seductive right now that all I could think about was pouncing on him right here. It took me a second to regain my composure and remember what I was going to say.

"Well, you said he wasn't necessarily good, just because he was a kid," he didn't reply, but instead gave me an 'uh-huh' and another seductive glance, and waited for my question. "Oh my god, this is going to sound so stupid, I don't even think I should say anything."

"Why?" he laughed, and I didn't respond. Instead I looked down at my cup and traced the edge of the handle lightly with my thumb. He could tell I had lost my nerve, so he tried to coax me along. He leaned in and asked in a lower voice, "No really, what is it that you want to ask me."

"Well, one of my friends seems to think you're the angel of death, or something like that." I paused and looked up at him, and he just smiled a small, closed mouth smile at me, waiting for me to continue. When I didn't, he finally spoke.

"And ..." he turned his head, lowering his chin and raising his eyebrows. He was still smiling at me. I took a deep breath, but didn't answer him. Now I had to decide what to say. "What do you think?"

His lack of denial sent a shiver down my spine and I stared blankly at him. He looked down at his mug and took another drink as I raised my hand to my face, rubbing my eyebrow and then resting my chin in my hand.

"I really don't know. There's a part of me that says that's just crazy. That grim reapers don't exist, otherwise they would be documented somewhere and we would know about them."

"But that's just a part of you. What about the other part?"

"Well, that's the thing. There's no way an unscrubbed, grown man would walk into an OR and no one would see him. So, either I'm crazy and you don't even exist at all, in which case I'm talking to myself, or ..." I trailed off, not quite sure how to finish this sentence.

"Or what?" Great. He was going to make me say it, and probably then burst out laughing at me.

"Or, maybe there is something different about you."

"So, you're telling me you think I'm the grim reaper?"

"No, I don't think you're the grim reaper," I said, with true sincerity. "Because there's still Thomas." He looked at me with a puzzled look. "I'm assuming you're the one he saw too. He came in about a week before the boy. He had been in a car accident. Someone slid into him on the ice." He smiled slightly and nodded in recognition.

"Well, I'm glad to hear you don't think I'm the angel of death, considering you invited me into your house and all," he said with a smile as he continued to sit across from me and drink his cocoa.

"So, I'm guessing you're not the angel of death, because not everyone around you dies, like Thomas. But then what exactly is it that you do?"

"I observe."

"Great, the same cryptic answer as before." By this point I was a little frustrated. Now I did feel pretty foolish for having brought up the subject at all. Not that I was drunk by any means, but I had had enough to drink that my thoughts were already a little fuzzy. Trying to make sense of this difficult situation in my current state was not very easy. I took one more sip of my drink and then put it down on the table. I sighed and looked back over at Ben. I folded my arms across my chest over the top of the blanket.

"I'm sorry Suzanne. It's the rules. I can't volunteer any information." I looked over at him and I could tell there was honesty in what he said. I was facing him on the couch with my legs curled up in front of me, leaning in to our conversation. In defeat, I leaned back. So I guess this meant this was a dead subject? I couldn't imagine why he would tell me to ask away, only to tell me he couldn't talk about it … Then I perked up and smiled.

"So, you can't volunteer anything, but I can guess!" I exclaimed, not so much in a question form, but as a statement of fact. I looked over to him and saw a smile creeping across his face.

"You brat!" I said as I extended my leg and playfully kicked at him. He reached out and grabbed my foot. I felt a wave of heat rush over me. I had to remind myself to smile and to breathe. My eyes met his and his sweet, seductive smile crept across his face, then gently started to massage my foot.

"So this is your attempt to be un-bratty?" I asked with raised eyebrows.

"Maybe. Is it working?" he said with a deep kneading motion on the arch of my foot. I closed my eyes and sighed deeply. The strength of his hands made my head swim as I my mind raced off in thought.

"Oh yeah, I'd say so …" I said, pausing as I took in all of my emotions right now. "Oh, you're good." I gave him a genuine smile, feeling very relaxed and peaceful with him here right now. He reached his hand over for my other foot.

"Here, give me the other one too." I willing passed over my other foot too. We sat there for a moment in silence, before he began again. "So, no guesses for me?"

Since he had touched me I honestly hadn't even thought about the rest of my questions. I was so absorbed in the moment right now.

"Well, it changes things a little bit now that I have to play twenty questions with you. My whole lead was 'so what exactly do you do' and that seems to be shot now." He smiled at me, knowing that I was frustrated right now, but not angry with him by any means. I decided to go a different direction to keep him talking while I was thinking.

"And now for something completely different … So what were you doing on the train tonight?"

"I couldn't sleep."

"So you do sleep?"

"Yes."

"Every night?"

"Nope," he said quickly with a quick shake of the head.

"How often then?"

"Maybe once every three or four days," he answered, rather matter of factly.

"I see. Makes observing a little easier I take it?"

"Absolutely. It's kind of tough to observe if you're asleep thirty percent of the time."

"So, back to my initial question though. Why were you on the train tonight? You could have chosen a thousand other things to do if you couldn't sleep. Did you know I would be on that train?"

"Maybe," he said with a boyish smirk. He had stopped massaging my feet and now they were just resting in his lap as has hands lightly traced up and down my foot.

"And did you know I'd be on the train the last time we ran into each other? And that I'd be at The Bean?"

"Yes," as he answered his fingers stopped tracing patterns momentarily on my foot. His eyes were fixed on mine, waiting to see whether I would be flattered, mad, or scared. I definitely wasn't mad, but somewhere between flattered and scared at the moment.

"So you're following me?" I said quickly, with more of an accusatory tone than I had hoped for.

"Yes, sometimes."

"Why? As part of your job?"

"No, it's …" He opened his mouth to continue, but he didn't. Instead he closed his mouth and looked shyly down towards my feet again, squeezing them in his hands. He looked very pensive, and a little sad. I scooted towards him on the couch and put a hand on his wrist.

"Please?" I said softly, in an almost pleading tone. He let out a deep sigh.

"It's just- I like you," he said, looking directly into my eyes on 'you.' He flushed and gently removed my feet and stood up from the couch. He looked down as he ran one hand through his dark brown hair.

"I'm sorry, I should be going. It's getting really late," he said without making eye contact.

"But I thought you don't sleep?" Either I was confused, or he was trying to be polite.

"Tonight's my night to sleep." His tone was very polite, but still casual. I stood up too and followed him as he started to walk towards the foyer.

"Ben, wait," he paused as I reached my hand out and touched his forearm. He turned to look me squarely in the face. "I'm sorry I put you on the spot like that," I said in a low voice, reaching up and putting my right hand on his chest. I could feel the warmth radiate from his chest as he blushed and looked away.

"Don't worry about it. It's just," he looked away, pausing for a moment, "it's just that you're the first person in a long time that I've been interested in, so I'm a little rusty on some of this." He paused and took a step towards me, leaning in and giving me a slow and powerful kiss on the cheek. As he stepped back, he reached up and took my hand that was on his chest in his, giving it a long squeeze. He started to back away, but I squeezed his hand back, not wanting him to go just yet.

"Don't forget your coat. It's freezing out there." I realized as I spoke how sleepy I was. I imagined that my heavy eyelids probably looked like I was giving him a sensual, pleading look. Or a tipsy look. Either one was probably not the right look to get him to stay at this point. He reached past me to retrieve his coat and slowly swung it around his broad shoulders. As he buttoned it up, he gave me a small but very heartfelt smile before bending over to put his shoes back on. I watched his every movement as he got ready to leave. Even the most simple of things made me grin. He stood up steadily, with a very powerful stance. He didn't seem intimidating to me, but I could tell how strong he was.

"Good night Suzanne," he said quietly. He pulled my hand up to his mouth and kissed it, then turned quickly and walked out the front door. I stepped over to the front door and watched him through the glass inlays on the door. He walked briskly but with a certain bounce in his step, his hands stuffed deep into his pockets.

He disappeared around the edge of the stone wall and a fire welled up in my stomach and flowed upwards over my body, making me smiled. Roxie had made her way into the foyer at the sound of the door opening and now stood there looking up at me, cocking her head from side to side in an attempt to understand me. I sighed again and smiled, leaning over to pick her up and cuddle her close to my face.

"He *is* amazing, isn't he?" I cooed in her ear as I ruffled her fur and we both made our way back to the bedroom.

Chapter 10

I woke up with a warm, fuzzy feeling all over. It was nice to be able to sleep in today since I didn't have to work again until Sunday evening. Light flooded into the room from the tall windows that faced east. I opened my eyes and saw my covers and pillows tangled together all around the bed. I couldn't remember any of my dreams from the night before, but I figured they must have been pretty good. I had a huge smile that hadn't yet faded from my face and an overall sense of peace and happiness right now. I remembered back to the night before with Ben and immediately the fire glowed again in my stomach.

I rolled over and saw Roxie standing next to the bed, looking up at me silently. I knew that look of hers. She needed to go out, but didn't want to wake me just yet. I motioned for her to come up on the bed and she willingly obliged. I swept her up in my arms and laid in bed cuddling with her for a few more minutes before getting moving for the rest of the day.

In the early afternoon I decided to call Cassie. It had been far too long, relatively speaking, since I had last talked to her and she had left me three messages over the last two weeks, and I had just sent quick texts back to her. I hadn't filled her in on all of the Ben details yet, and I was dying to get her opinion on the situation. I made myself a snack and walked into the living room, grabbing the crochet blanket to curl up on the couch for what I was sure would be a pretty long conversation. It was a picture perfect moment with the room lit up from the sunlight. I could see fragments of rainbows from the stained glass window panes all over my living room and I smiled at the simple but beautiful patterns on my walls and floor. Even though it was freezing cold outside today, the sunlight made it bearable. I dialed her number and looked over to smile at Roxie, who was curled up on her bed, basking in the sunlight.

"Hi Suzy!" she exclaimed as she answered.

"Wow, you're in a perky mood today!" I said, somewhat surprised at how excited she seemed right now.

"So, do you have any big news to tell me?" I think she actually giggled like a school girl when she asked me this.

"Huh?" was all I could muster. I had no idea what she was talking about.

"About Steven! The last time we talked it sounded like things might be moving down a white dress type of a path." *Well crap.* I guess it really had been a long time since we chatted, given that I hadn't told her about the breakup. That was very odd for me to not call her for two weeks, but now that I look back on it, the times I had thought about calling her it was way too late to do that, so I had just sent her quick texts about how busy I had been but that I promised I would call soon.

She was positively beaming. I could tell from the pitch in her voice that she was probably about to pee her pants with excitement at this point. Wow, she certainly was going to be shocked when I broke the news to her. She would probably be more upset than I was right now about it.

"Well, actually Steven and I aren't together anymore," I said in a solemn tone, but not particularly sad.

"Oh my gosh, I'm so sorry! Are you okay? What happened?" Her glee had now turned to concern for me and I could genuinely hear the sadness in her voice. She knew how much my job meant to me, but she also knew what an amazing change marriage and parenthood had been for her and she legitimately wanted me to be able to find all of that happiness as well. She was never obnoxious with her questions and her prodding about relationships and plans, but I could tell she was very excited about the idea of me getting married. She probably thought this is why I was calling.

"Actually, I'm okay. It happened right after we last talked to each other. Apparently all of his 'business trips' were actually hook ups with some other girl."

"You're kidding! And right after we spoke? Why didn't you call earlier?"

"Well, I found out at three a.m. when Howard called me into the ER because Steven had gotten into a fight with this woman and she threw something at him and knocked him out."

"Serves his sorry ass right!" she barked, and we both laughed.

"Yeah, well and then I kept meaning to call you, but every time I'd think about calling it was past midnight. I didn't want to wake you guys up over some stupid asshole cheating on me."

"You know you can call whenever Suzy, but I understand. So really, how are you doing?"

"Well, funny you should ask. Of course I was upset about it when it first happened, but surprisingly I was pretty much okay after a few days. And I think part of it is this new guy that I've met."

"A new one? How'd you meet him?" I paused, thinking about how I was going to answer this. Based on my conversation with Ben last night, I don't think who or what he is was supposed to be public knowledge. I had already told Colin about it, but I didn't think he would tell anyone. Cassie would certainly tell her husband, and maybe another close friend or two. For now I'd skip the weird, mysterious types of details and go for the normal side of it.

"At the hospital. He was observing one of my cases. And I've run into him about three or four times in other random places."

"Like in a good way, or that he's creepy and stalking you?"

"No, no. Definitely in a good way. Cassie, he's got those smoldering brown eyes, and such a soft, gentle touch. I don't know, there's just something about him. Ugh! He's amazing ..." My head swam with thoughts of Ben as I tried to explain him in more generic terms for my sister.

"Are you sure this isn't too soon? I mean, you just broke up with Steven after years of being together and thinking about next steps. I wouldn't want you to get into some rebound relationship right away ..." Huh, well that wasn't exactly the response I was expecting from her on this one.

"No, it's not a rebound. Actually I met him before I found out about Steven, so I wasn't out looking for a replacement." Without realizing, I had let a somewhat bitter tone come across, which Cassie immediately picked up on.

"I didn't mean it that way. I'm sorry. I just want you to find someone who will love you and make you happy and treat you the way you deserve to be treated. Apparently Steven wasn't that guy! Who knows, maybe this new guy is him or maybe not, but you won't know if you don't give him a shot, right?" I think she was smiling, at least a little bit. She didn't sound as excited for me as I had hoped, but I guess that was to be expected. She was truly looking out for me, so I wasn't upset with her, just a little deflated by her lack of enthusiasm.

"Yeah, and I'm not trying to rush into things with Ben, but I just can't seem to shake him from my mind. When I look at him, I feel like I've known him for years. And I get that slow, smoldering fire feeling from the pit of my stomach. I'm surprisingly really happy right now, and I'm just gonna take things easy and see where they go."

"Well good, then I'm happy for you. Really, I am. If he makes you happy and he's good to you, then I'm totally cool with him. Of course, I do want to meet him the next time I'm in Chicago!" Now she sounded more like my sister!

"Absolutely! Speaking of, when are you going to be here next?"

"I'm not sure yet. Maybe some time in the next couple of months, but I'll keep you posted." From there our conversation turned to other general catch up of what had been happening over the past couple of weeks in both of our lives. After about an hour on the phone with her, we wrapped up our conversation and said our goodbyes.

I stayed there on the couch for a while, just daydreaming and thinking over everything Cassie had said. Despite her concern over this being a rebound, my feelings about Ben hadn't really changed since before our conversation. The thought of his name sent a shiver down my body and brought a smile to my face.

I shook my head. *Enough of this!* I got off the couch and decided to start getting the rest of my weekend underway. I had other things to besides just daydream.

* * *

When I got into the hospital on Sunday evening, everything seemed to be pretty low key. I did rounds, checking in on all of the post-op surgical patients before settling back in at the lounge to go over my cases for the following week. As I sat at the table by the window, the bright orange gala flyer caught my eye. My eyes fell back to the table and my mouth turned downwards. I had forgotten, at least temporarily, about the fundraiser coming up. For the first time since we had split, I was actually a little sad to have

Steven out of my life. He always went with me to events like that and he actually did make the evening more enjoyable. He was able to mingle very well at important functions like this. I mentally scolded myself for thinking these thoughts. I was so much better off without him and I couldn't let myself think otherwise.

I really did want to attend the event though, even without him. For a moment I wondered if Ben would go with me to something like this. Given that I usually only had his attention for about half an hour or less, I was guessing this could be a challenge. I contemplated going to the gala on my own. I would know plenty of other people from the hospital there, including Colin, but most of these events that I had gone to on my own had seemed awkward. Colin might be a possibility, but I wouldn't want him to pass on having a real date just so that I wouldn't feel awkward. It was still a couple of months away, so I put my thoughts on hold. There was no immediate need to get my date situation squared away right now.

I leaned back in my chair and refocused my attention on my upcoming cases. I had a couple later on in the week that would be more challenging, so I spent time reviewing them in extreme detail. With my tougher cases I would play them out in my mind several times, trying to predict what some of the twists or problems might be and how I would handle them.

I was part way through the second one when I heard my name being paged. I walked over to the phone on the coffee table and called in. I listened attentively as the operator told me that a young male in his mid-twenties had presented to the ER with a gunshot wound to the abdomen. I was to report up to OR suite two and expect him shortly.

I hurried over to my locker to return my tablet and take off my jewelry, then reported to the scrub room to start getting ready for surgery. When I arrived, there was only one other nurse there. As I scrubbed in at the sink, the other members of the surgical team trickled in and prepared for surgery. Within a few minutes, the patient was wheeled into the OR. He had been restrained and it was clear he had been given something for the pain. The anesthesiologist grabbed the chart on the side of the table to see what he had received, then made some quick adjustments before putting the mask over his face.

Most of his clothes had already been cut away by the ER team, so the nurses did a final sterilizing of his torso before giving me the nod to go ahead and begin. The major point of entry was to the left of his navel, about three inches over and three inches up. The hole itself was not particularly large, but oftentimes we would find that the damage after penetration was much worse than the visible wound would lead you to believe.

"Scalpel," I said, holding my hand out to the nurse. I cut downwards from the penetration hole. I was assuming that the person who had shot him had been standing, so the gun would be pointing downwards to penetrate waist level. If this was the case, then the damage should be below the penetration point. I was right. And the damage was more severe than I had thought it would be. Inside, there was a mess of tissue and pooled blood. I wasn't able to clearly see the bullet.

"Suction." As I suctioned away the pooling blood, the shimmering base of the bullet could be seen in the bright overhead lights. The cleared blood also revealed a tremendous amount of peripheral damage.

"Forceps and a tray please," I said, looking up at the nurse who was standing across the table from me. A dark sleeve caught my eye and I looked over to see Ben standing there, just a few feet from the table. When I made eye contact with him, he smiled patiently at me. Less than a second after I had asked for the forceps, I felt them tap against my palm and my attention snapped back to my patient.

I leaned in closer and was able to pull the mushroomed bullet from the man's body. I stared at it under the bright light of the operating table as the nurse suctioned the area again.

"Man, those hollow points are gruesome!" I remarked as I dropped the bullet onto the tray and continued to assess the damage. From this view, it looked like the left kidney, transverse colon, and possibly the pancreas were all damaged. I wasn't sure how long ago he had been shot, but it looked like he had done a significant amount of moving. Had he tried to run away after he was shot?

I went to work, methodically repairing as much of the damage as I could. As soon as I had closed up one wound, blood would start pooling from another wound. After about fifteen minutes of this 'fix and bleed,' the anesthesiologist broke in.

"Vitals are dropping," he said in an authoritative but unemotional voice. I glanced back up at Ben. He was now leaning up against the far wall with his hands in his pants pockets. I quickly took in all of the details of his face and posture, which was now void of any expression. I stiffened and looked back at my patient.

Twenty minutes later I was back in the scrub room, tossing my mask and cap into the bio-trash container in the corner of the room. One of the ER doctors walked into the scrub room as I was stripping off the blood stained scrubs.

"Jacobsen, the police want to talk to you."

"Huh?" *Real professional,* I thought to myself at my lack of being able to think of a more complete sentence. Of course they needed a report on someone who was shot and killed.

"I'll be right out," I said pleasantly and much more alert now. As I headed out of the scrub room, I saw two policemen standing against the far wall. The woman looked to be in her late twenties and the man in his mid-thirties. As I approached them, they both stood up straight and walked towards me.

"Officers," I said politely with a nod of my head as I extended my hand to shake theirs.

"Doctor," they both replied, almost in unison. The male must be the one leading the investigation as he was the one who stepped forwards and started talking. His name badge said Darrens. His partner's shoulder was slumped down as she took notes, so I wasn't able to see her name.

"Doctor ..." he trailed off in a questioning tone.

"Jacobsen. Suzanne Jacobsen."

"Thank you. We'll need an official statement from you as to what happened during the surgery, cause of death, etc. Was the bullet extracted?" I nodded and rubbed my eyebrows. "We'll also need that for forensics."

"Of course." I turned around and motioned to one of the nurses who was walking out of the OR. "Nurse, these officers need the bullet we extracted." I turned back to Officer Darrens.

"Do you have a specific evidence bag you'd like it in?"

He handed it to the nurse and she hurried off to the OR. She quickly returned with a bloodied bullet in the bottom of the small, plastic zip-lock bag.

"Generally speaking, the cause of death was blood loss due to his injuries. It looked like he had been moving around quite a bit after he was shot. Did you pick him up at the scene or had he fled?"

"I really can't comment on an ongoing investigation. Do you have his clothing as well?"

"His shirt was already off by the time he was in the OR. You'd have to check with the ED. I'm sure they still have them. I'll do my post-op report before the end of my shift. Do you have a number I can reach you at when it's done?"

Darrens handed me his card and I escorted him down to the ED so that he could get their comments as well. As soon as he left, I found the doctor who had treated the man when he first came in.

"Do you know what the deal was with that guy?"

"I dunno. We found drugs in his coat pocket when he came in, and he was rambling on about having shot someone and where was that SOB."

"A drug deal gone bad?"

"Maybe. I guess we'll just have to watch the news and find out."

I thought about this as I walked out of the ER and headed up to do my post-op write up of my most recent patient. I hit the showers before tending to my work. I had an overall dirty feeling right now and I wasn't quite sure why. I was usually more thoughtful and sad when I had lost a patient, but this wasn't quite the same type of feeling.

In the shower I thought about Ben. I must be getting used to seeing him because today I hadn't panicked or lost my concentration on what I was doing. Surprisingly, I hadn't paid him much note at all. I thought back through it to make sure he wasn't the distraction that caused me to lose this patient. After replaying every move, I determined that he wasn't. Maybe it was silly, but I actually thought I did a really good job after I noticed him there. I guess it was probably, at least in some part, due to me trying to look good in front of him. I wonder how long he had been observing me in the OR before Thomas's case. I'd have to ask him this next time I saw him.

My thoughts turned back to seeing him today in the OR. I remembered back to those few images I had of him. I traced each line in my mind, taking in each gesture. In hindsight, I guess maybe Ben's patient looking smile was more of an advanced condolence for what was going to happen.

I stepped out of the steaming hot shower and got ready for the rest of my shift. Hopefully it would be less intense for the remainder of the evening.

Chapter 11

*I*t was Tuesday morning and I was sitting in the lounge having breakfast and a cup of coffee. I had gotten to work earlier than I had expected, so I used the time to catch up on reading the newspaper. There was a small article about a drug related shooting over the weekend that I was reading with obvious interest.

"Good morning," I heard over my shoulder. I looked up to see Colin walking across the room, although I didn't need to see his face to know it was him. I could recognize his voice anywhere.

"Hi Colin!" I smiled warmly and folded my arms on the edge of the table as he sat down across from me. "So how was the rest of your night after I left?" I leaned in and raised my shoulders. He paused for a moment at my question, then laughed and shook his head.

"Hey, you told me on the phone you'd fill me in on all of the details!" I leaned back and threw my hands dramatically in the air.

"Look at you and that shit eating grin! Man, you sure cut right to the chase. Not even so much as a 'hey, how are you.' Just straight to business" he said, leaning back in his chair with a dramatic look of disappointment.

"What, I'm just curious if you two hit it off?" He smiled back at me, his head cocked to one side. He wasn't mad that I was prying, just somewhat self-conscious.

"I took her back to her place and made sure she got in alright. That's it," he declared, raising one hand in front of him as if he was taking an oath. He seemed very proud of himself on this point.

"No juicy details?" He shook his head. "Not even one?"

"She grabbed my ass and tried to make out with me, but I turned her down. So if that's a juicy detail, then there you go." He flashed a smile and took a drink of his coffee. "So how about you? Anything with you and Charlie?"

"Nope, he just walked me to the train. He totally got stiffed too. Just a hug."

"He didn't even make sure you got to your house?" His eyebrows pulled together in disappointment at his friend for not making sure I got all the way home.

"No, but that's fine. I actually ran into Ben on the train on the way back. It was pretty random."

"Ben ... the reaper?" He was clearly shocked by this turn.

"Yes, that would be the one." I looked around, somewhat self-conscious about us talking so openly about him, but there were only a few other people in the lounge and they were absorbed in their own activities.

"And he walked you home? The grim reaper walked you home? That's a weird one."

"If he was going to kill me or whatever, don't you think he would have already done it?" I sounded quite confident as I said this, mainly because I had already had this conversation in my head a dozen times.

"Unless they scout people out in advance. Maybe he's just doing this to get close to you and you're making it easy on him." Colin seemed pretty matter-of-fact about this. He wasn't teasing but he also wasn't panicked by this thought. I had to admit, he had me at a loss. I hadn't thought of this angle before, but I was sure my mind would be processing this new idea for days now.

"Well, I'm alive right now, so I think I'll focus on that."

"Good call," he said, continuing on with his breakfast.

"So," I decided to change topics back to him for a while, "it's Valentine's Day in a couple of days. Do you and Mandy have any plans?"

"Nah. It didn't even come up. She's a nice girl and all," he said slowly, looking up at me, "but honestly, I don't really feel that way about her."

"Fair enough."

"What about you? What're you up to on Thursday?"

"Oh nothing. Probably just something exciting like the grocery store." I looked up and saw him smile at me. "Yes, I know you're jealous," I added and returned his smile.

"Well, let me take you out to dinner then." I stiffened in my seat, not really knowing what to say. Before I could say anything, he quickly jumped back in. "Just as friends. You're not even gonna get a card or anything cheesy like that." I looked back up at his face. His eyes looked genuine enough and he seemed pretty harmless.

"Okay, just as friends." He seemed relieved at my acceptance, and gave a wide smile, showing a full line of teeth.

"So where do you want to go?" I asked him. As I thought about it, I was truly happy that I wouldn't be spending Valentine's Day by myself on the couch. Even though it was a holiday typically reserved for couples, it was nice to have a friend like Colin that I could share an evening with.

"There's a nice little Italian place up in Lincoln Park that I've heard good things about. Are you in an Italian-y mood?" He looked down at his coffee cup as he asked the question. I wasn't sure if he was embarrassed or nervous to be asking me to dinner, or if he was intentionally looking down so as not to come across too intense.

"Sure, I could do that. What time?"

"I'll have to see what they have in terms of reservations. We may have to go with whatever they have available. Do you have to work the next morning?"

"Nope, I've got the day off since I worked this past weekend."

"Cool, me too. I'll let you know what time and then I'll come by in a cab and pick you up on the way there. Parking's pretty bad up in that area."

"That sounds good. I'm looking forward to it," I said, getting up from the table. "Well, back to the salt mines. Catch ya later." I put my hand on his shoulder as I walked by him.

"See ya Suz," he said with a wave of his hand as I walked out of the lounge.

* * *

I came into work on Thursday morning with a little bounce in my step. I had dreamt about Ben the night before and woke up in a very happy, upbeat mood. Even though it had been almost a week now since I had seen him, with the exception of the couple of seconds in the OR, dreaming about him left me with a sense of calm and happiness that filled the void of not actually seeing him in person.

I was also looking forward to dinner tonight. Even though I wasn't trying to make something happen with Colin, I very much enjoyed his company. And, admittedly, I did occasionally think of him in that way, although I would never dare tell him that. I happened to run into him during my first round at the nurse's station. He was standing there filling out a chart for a patient, so I slid up next to him.

"Good morning," I said, with more enthusiasm than usual for eight thirty in the morning. Most of the nurses weren't within earshot, so we could talk fairly easily.

"Someone's had their Wheatie's this morning," he smiled as he finished writing up his order. He turned to face me. "I take it we're still on?"

"Of course! I wouldn't bail on you. What time?"

"It's a little later than I'd have liked, but eight was the earliest I could get. Is that alright?" He seemed concerned this would make me want to reconsider.

"That's fine for me. Gives me a chance to get home and cleaned up. I've got a full load this afternoon. I'll plan to be ready by about twenty til?"

"Sounds good. I'll see you then," he smiled as he handed the nurse the clipboard he was using and headed off down the hall.

By the time I finished up with all of my patients and got home, it was already after six. I was glad that our reservations were later in the evening. I checked my phone as I took Roxie out, making sure there were no last minute changes. My eyebrows pulled together as I saw a notice that I had one new text message. From Steven. I opened the message, fairly annoyed that he would choose today of all days to text me. *Just wanting to let you know I'm thinking about you. Can I see you?*

What an asshole! I most definitely did not want to see him, especially today. I deleted his message and hurried Roxie along and back into the house. It was still a little chilly out to be dawdling. I ate a couple of bites of food when I got in, just to tide me over until dinner. I didn't want my stomach to be growling in the cab.

I stepped into the hot shower and immediately felt a wave of relief. I hadn't realized how tired I was from the long day's work. As was my usual routine, I got out of the shower and did my make-up first, then my hair before settling on clothes for the evening. I was surprised at how long it took to pick my outfit. I wasn't quite sure how dressy to get for dinner – on Valentine's Day – with a friend. I decided to go with one of my simple-but-elegant little black dresses and a burgundy shrug.

Since they always say that you can use accessories to dress something up or down, I opted for more casual jewelry. I had tried the pearls, but they looked too formal for a dinner that I didn't exactly know the dress code for. Instead, I opted for a simple silver necklace with a delicate pendant. I spritzed on some perfume and walked into the living room. Perfect! I was, surprisingly, ready on time. I gave Roxie some food and fresh water, and a couple of minutes later heard a cab honk outside. I kissed her on the head and grabbed my coat and purse, and headed out to the cab.

As I walked down the path to the cab, Colin came around and opened my door for me.

"Wow, look at you," he said with a smile as he leaned in and kissed me on the cheek.

"You clean up pretty well yourself," I said, looking him up and down. There was a brief moment where we both stood there just looking at each other before we got in the cab and the driver took off. We chatted in the cab about the rest of our days at work and other fairly low key topics. I felt relief at how normal and casual the conversation seemed between us. While I didn't think of tonight as a date, I was not exactly sure what Colin thought. His laid back smile and the gleam in his eye made me relax a little bit. Tonight, he was just my friend Colin.

The cab pulled up in front of a quaint little Italian restaurant and I got out while he paid the driver, then slid across the seat and joined me on the sidewalk. We walked into the restaurant and were immediately greeted by the sweet smell of freshly cooked pasta and the soothing sounds of low, classical music. I looked around and was glad he had gotten us a reservation. The small restaurant was packed.

We checked our coats and I got my first good look at him. Colin was a particularly versatile person. He looked great in jeans and a t-shirt, but he honestly did clean up very well too. And the surprising part was that he looked equally as comfortable on both ends of the spectrum. Tonight he had on dark pants, a crisp white dress shirt, and a sport coat. As I glanced over him, my eyes lingered a few extra seconds on his chest where the last of the shirt buttons was done up. Underneath his shirt I could see his well-defined chest that was accentuated by his broad shoulders. I quickly blinked and looked away before he caught me staring. I smiled to myself wondering if he was doing the same thing right now, which made me become more aware of what I was wearing. I was glad I opted against the pearls. I think I matched him much better like this. And the little black dress that hugs in all the right spots didn't hurt my cause either.

The hostess came over and escorted us through the tightly packed room full of small, cozy tables with white cloth tablecloths and dripping candles. The walls had cream colored wainscoting that accented the golden gilded picture frames that held old paintings. Our table was along the far wall, in a somewhat quieter area of the restaurant under a dimly lit candelabra. Colin reached out to hold my chair for me as I took my seat.

"Why thank you sir," I said as he pushed my chair in for me.

"Hey, just cuz we're friends doesn't mean all social graces go out the window." As he passed by the side of the table, I could see a five o'clock shadow. For the most part, I didn't care for stubble on men, but on Colin it seemed to enhance his look. He looked very sexy tonight, something I'm sure he knew by the sparkle in his eye and the air of confidence about him.

Overall the dinner was going very well. I liked that the restaurant seemed to have a very relaxed pace to it. Some restaurants barely give you enough time to eat each course before they come out with the next dish and hurry you along. I would have to remember to come back to this place.

I was also thoroughly enjoying the company tonight. One of the things I liked about our conversations was the way that we would drift in and out of work related topics. We both loved our fields of work, so it was only natural to want to talk about medicine. Steven generally got the glassy look in his eyes if our medical conversations went on for more than a few minutes, so it was a nice change to have Colin actively participating.

We were towards the end of our main course when the conversation turned to more intimate topics.

"So how're you doing with the whole Steven situation?" He looked up from his plate to read my face. I took another bite to give myself a minute to get my thoughts in order. He was a close friend, so I didn't mind telling him the truth, I just hadn't really thought much about what the truth was.

"Well, overall I think I'm doing alright. I've pretty much gotten all of his stuff out of my house, so there's not that much around to remind me of him. I mean, I think about him sometimes, but I don't get too emotional about it."

"Yeah, I haven't noticed you looking upset about it at work," he added. It was nice to know he'd been looking out for me, and I was proud of myself for not being a drama queen at work. There were a few doctors and a lot of nurses at work who seemed to always have some sort of personal saga that they were lamenting at work and for the most part, the rest of us tended to not take them very seriously. I was certainly glad I hadn't become one of them after the breakup.

"Well thanks. I really haven't had too many breakdowns, except breaking the mirror in the foyer-"

"You did what?" he interrupted. He had a shocked look on his face. He had never seen me really angry or upset before, so I'm sure he was trying to picture this in his head.

"Yeah, I broke the mirror." I laughed, in a mixture of shame and pride.

"Like you put your fist through it?"

"No, I threw something at it." Now I was really smiling, all traces of shame disappearing.

"Hopefully it was something of his," he said teasingly, leaning back in his chair and reaching out for his glass of water.

"Sort of ... I was cleaning all of his stuff out and found a diamond ring in a little lacquered box." I looked up at Colin. His face dropped with this new revelation. "So I got pissed and threw the box at the mirror. I mean, what an ass! You're actively cheating on your girlfriend, yet you buy an engagement ring." I paused for a moment, looking over Colin's shoulder at a painting on the wall behind him. I continued. "So that was my only real moment of anger. After that I figured he wasn't worth me being upset about." I took a break and reached for my wine glass, taking a long and deliberate sip.

"Suz, I'm really sorry," he said, reaching over and putting his hand over my left hand that had been stretched out in front of me. I curled my thumb around his fingers and squeezed his hand.

"Yeah, well, I think the worst part was feeling like I had been so blind to it. I thought I knew him better than that. How I didn't see it sooner is beyond me. Maybe I'm just a bad judge of character," I said with an uneasy laugh.

"I think you're being a little hard on yourself. The guy turned out to be an asshole. You can't always predict that sort of thing," he said sympathetically.

"I dunno. I guess maybe I just wanted to believe him. You sacrifice so much personal time finishing up training, you know?

You put your life on hold for so long that I guess I was just ready for Mr. Right to already be in my life and to not have to keep looking for him." I caught myself looking down and away from the table, but I quickly shook my head and looked back up at him.

"Well what about me?" he asked quietly.

"No, I know you've sacrificed a lot of yourself too for the job. I'm not trying to be a martyr." After I responded, I realized that maybe that wasn't what he was asking. His silence and his gaze confirmed this for me. I continued, but very slowly and cautiously.

"But that wasn't what you were asking me, was it?" He didn't answer me, just shook his head slightly, tracing his finger over the back of my hand. His expression had turned softer now. He had a relaxed ambiance during dinner, but now he seemed to exude a quiet patience and caring that I hadn't really seen from him before, or perhaps I just hadn't noticed it until now.

I could feel a lump forming in my throat as I tried to figure out how to respond to him. I laced my fingers in between his to buy myself some extra time. I cleared my throat and got up my nerve.

"I thought we decided a long time ago it would be a bad idea to date someone we worked with." I took a drink of water, giving him a chance to respond.

"True ... but I thought a lot of that was us being new to Belvidere and wanting to be taken seriously. You know, not wanting people to think we were too busy looking for an empty supply closet to do our jobs."

"As well a good reason," I replied, in a pseudo-serious tone, gently nodding my head. We were both silent for a moment, each sizing the other one up. I let him speak first.

"Well, now that we're both well established, I figured that probably wasn't as much of an issue. We got here on our own, now we may as well relax a little bit and enjoy it." He looked down at my hand that had stopped moving over a minute ago. He gave it one final squeeze before releasing it and pulling his hand back to his side of the table. "Sorry. I didn't mean to take your hand hostage," he apologized, with a dejected look on his face. I saw this as a good opportunity for me to lighten the mood.

"You take it hostage and you're not even going to hold it for ransom?" I inquired, raising one eyebrow. "I'm *very* disappointed."

He smiled a quick, small smile, but I could tell this was a hard conversation for him. He definitely was hoping for more from me, but I wasn't sure if this was the right move for me right now. I decided to address this head on, rather than to leave him in the dark.

"You know, Colin, I just … I think the world of you, but I, I just don't know if now's the right time …" My throat tightened as I said this, and I felt like I had just been kicked in the stomach. I looked up at him to see what his reaction to this was going to be. Surprisingly, his face was holding a steady expression of disappointment but acceptance. I suppose being a physician trains you well to hold a steady expression in tough situations.

"Because of Steven?" he quickly asked. A part of me wanted to take this opportunity for the easy way out and say that Steven was the cause, but I couldn't lie to Colin. Something just felt inherently wrong with that, given how honest he was being with me.

"No, it's not that …" I trailed off. I didn't even know what to say next. I looked up to see if his expression had changed. He no longer had the dejected look about him. Instead, his expression seemed to turn back to his casual, friendly persona.

"Okay Suzy, well answer me this. Is it that you're genuinely not interested in anything romantic with me, or are you telling me the timing just isn't right? If it's that there's no interest, then I promise we'll just be friends and I won't bring it up again. If you're telling me it's a timing thing, then I won't corner you on this right now."

"So you'll just corner me later on it?" I said, folding my arms across my chest and throwing an accusing look at him. I smiled and laughed to let him know I wasn't actually irritated with him.

"You know what I mean," he answered with a smile.

"I do. And I love the fact that we can openly have this conversation," I replied warmly with a genuine smile on my face.

"Yeah, me too," he agreed.

"And for me, it's honestly an issue of timing. You are such a smart and talented, and caring person Colin." I leaned in towards him, taking a sip of my wine and eyeing him over the top of my glass. His expression had lightened and his eyes were dancing in the dim lighting. "And not to mention, ridiculously good looking!" He laughed, blushing at my compliment.

"Aww, now you're just screwing with me," he chuckled.

"Me? Never!" By now I felt like I had actually relaxed into the conversation. The lump in my through had disappeared and the words were flowing more naturally now, so I continued. "But seriously Colin, if we were going to really give this a shot, I need to be in a place where I can pour my whole self into the relationship with a clear head. My mind is going in too many crazy directions right now and I want my whole head and heart into it. You're too important to me for me to just half-ass the relationship and risk ruining what we already have. So I just want to be in a good place before we start anything. Does that sound fair?"

"Suzanne, that's more than I could have asked for." He legitimately looked shocked by my response to his questions. I felt like I owed him at least that. And I really did have feelings for him, but I wasn't sure exactly what those feelings were and how deep they ran. I was also conflicted because of Ben and not know what I thought about him and us, if there even was an "us." And lastly there was Steven. I hadn't felt like I was still particularly affected by our breakup, but I'm sure I was and I just had not put my finger on it right now. With all of the directions my mind was being pulled in, I didn't want to hurt him by saying something foolish at this point. I looked over at his eyes dancing in the dim light of the restaurant. He had a very peaceful smile and a relaxed look about him. "Thank you for being honest with me," he said with a genuinely pleased look on his face.

"Absolutely," I said as I reached across the table for his hand. He gladly offered it up, then pulled my hand up and kissed the back of it tenderly before placing it back on the table.

"So, dessert?" he asked, thus ending the serious conversation for the evening.

The rest of the evening was much more casual, with no more discussion of relationships. I was grateful that we had an open enough relationship to be able to have those conversations, and then move past them and continue to enjoy the rest of the evening without any awkwardness.

Both of us were still chatting away when the waitress brought us our check. Colin signed for it, glancing quickly at his watch.

"It's only ten thirty. Wanna grab a night cap?" he asked, clapping the leather pad closed.

"Sure, I'm not getting up early tomorrow. I saw a nice looking lounge a few buildings over. How about that?"

"Sounds good." He seemed pleased that I was willing to continue on with our evening. It probably affirmed for him that he hadn't scared me off with our dinner conversation. "Ready?"

"Yeah," I said, getting up and placing my napkin on my chair. I turned as he gestured for me to lead the way. We continued to chat as we made our way through the sea of tightly packed tables. The restaurant was still pretty full for as late as it was, so it was surprisingly loud. In an effort to hear what I was saying, Colin walked very close behind me, his hand occasionally resting on my hip as he leaned in closer to hear me.

As we were nearing the end of the dining area, I heard a loud laugh, and my ears suddenly burned. I searched the nearby tables and my eyes locked onto a man with his back to me. He laughed again and I knew in an instant that it was Steven. I froze in my tracks, but was quickly jostled out of them as Colin ran directly into me. He obviously wasn't expecting me to stop suddenly. His hands were at my waist as he leaned in.

"Are you okay?" He asked as he took a step towards my side. I could feel him look me up and down to try to see what was wrong. My eyes were fixed on the table just a few paces in front of us. Colin saw where I was looking and he followed my gaze over to the small table just in time to see Steven lean across the table to kiss his dinner date. I snarled in disgust. My feelings for Steven aside, that was an unnecessarily long kiss for a dinner in public. Colin looked back curiously towards me, so I was pretty sure he didn't recognize the back of the head that I was staring at.

I could feel the heat welling up inside me. I stormed forwards, intentionally running into the back of his chair and shoving it.

"Oh, I'm sorry," I said in the snottiest voice I could muster. His head snapped up.

"Suzy!" He was clearly shocked and didn't quite know what to do or what to say next. Granted, neither did I. Perhaps I should have thought this through a little better. "This is a surprise!"

"Well, you said earlier today you wanted to see me, although you probably didn't mean here, did you?" I replied coldly. His pupils dilated slightly but he didn't respond. Either I had actually left him speechless, or he was trying to figure out how to salvage the situation and still get lucky tonight with blondie over there. My guess was the latter.

"Steven, you remember Dr. Forrester," I said, nodding towards Colin, who had a smug look on his face by this point. He was standing very tall now, with his hands stuffed deep into his pockets. It fit my mood quite well at the moment. Steven scrambled to stand up to shake Colin's hand, but Colin didn't move. I leaned in between them and interrupted Steven's gesture.

"You'll have to excuse us. Enjoy the rest of your night." I turned my back to Steven, facing in towards Colin, desperately trying to read his face. His stoic, smug expression didn't break for a second. Instead, he held his elbow out towards me, and my eyes darted back up to his face and he winked at me. I linked my arm through his and we walked over to the coat check. Knowing that Steven had his eyes fixed on us as we walked away from him, I may have let my butt swish back and forth a little more than usual.

I was shaking as Colin helped me with my coat. The rush of the cold air over my face as we left the restaurant only mildly helped to snap me back into the moment. Instinctively my hand came up to cover my mouth as I closed my eyes and let my mind take it all in. I could feel Colin's hands on my shoulders.

"Suz, are you okay?" I didn't respond. I stood there, with images of him and that slutty girl he was with flashing in my head. Was that the girl he was cheating on me with? Had he bought the ring for her? All I could muster was a quick shake of my head. I felt him take a step towards me as he pulled me into his chest. He had one hand on the back of my head stroking my hair, and the other around my waist, holding me firmly to him. In another setting, I know my heart would be racing feeling him this close to me and being so intimate and tender with me, but in this moment all I could do was try to forget the last five minutes.

Hot tears were welling up in my eyes and I tried to fight them spilling over. I could hear Colin talking softly in my ear as he held me. We stood there in a silent embrace for a minute, and it was all

I could do to keep myself from going weak in the knees. He broke away first, taking a small step back.

"I'd love to take you out if you think a distraction is what you need, but I would totally understand if you just want to call it a night." I looked down, embarrassed that Steven had ruined our evening.

"I think that might be best," I responded, sheepishly. He smiled and took my hand as he turned out towards the street and hailed a cab. If he was disappointed, he didn't give that impression, for which I was thankful. I would have to remember to tell him sometime what a great man he is. A cab quickly pulled up and he slid across the seat, holding out a hand for me. I numbly sat down and closed the door. As the driver took off, Colin turned back to face me.

"Are you okay?" I nodded quietly, probably as much for him as it was for me. "What an asshole! I can't believe he was there making out with another girl!"

"Well, I was there with you …" Wait, was I defending him? Ughh! I made myself mad now. At least that stopped the tears from welling up.

"Yeah, but we weren't making out in a nice restaurant."

"True. Ughh!" I scowled as I shook my head and shuddered. At least I had stamped down the sadness that had been building up inside of me.

"Oh, and – not that I mind – but Dr. Forrester?" I laughed as I looked over at Colin. He had both of his eyebrows raised and a huge, crooked grin on his face. He looked relaxed with his arm up on the back of the bench seat and his body angled towards mine.

"Yeah, well, Steven always was a little intimidated by you."

"Really?" He seemed surprised by this, and then a very content smirk came over his face. Apparently not many people must have told him this before.

"Yeah, especially when we first started dating. He would always make comments or ask if I was disappointed I wasn't dating another *doctor,*" I swayed my head for dramatic emphasis.

"Ah, I see. Well I'm glad I could help."

"Yeah, thanks for playing along! That smug look on your face is an expression I haven't seen before. It was perfect!"

"That's because I've never had a reason to be smug towards you," he said in a gentle voice. I looked over at him and saw that same caring look on his face that I had seen at dinner. I felt my stomach start to burn again and I scooted over towards him and buried my head in his shoulder. I could feel his arm tumbled down around me and pull me in close to him. We rode in silence and he ran his hand up and down my arm. When we turned onto my street, he pulled back a foot or so.

"Look, you know I'm here for you. If you want, I'd be happy to come in and talk and keep you company, but I don't want you to feel weird about anything, so I'm not going to come in unless you specifically ask me to. Deal?" I smiled and nodded my head up and down. Always the gentleman.

The cab pulled up in front of my gate and we both got out. Colin gave me a big hug and started talking right away. He was saying goodnight so that I wouldn't have to.

"I know you said you're off tomorrow, so I'll call you and maybe we can grab lunch or something."

"Okay, that sounds good," I answered, looking down to take his hand, then back up at him. "And thank you for tonight. I had a really good time." I had a wistful smile on my face, but I refused to get choked up at the end of the evening. I wanted tonight to be about enjoying an even out with one of my best friends, not about Steven being a putz.

"Yeah, well at least until fifteen minutes ago!" he laughed.

"True, but that's not your fault. I'm actually relieved you were there and it wasn't just me on my own."

"Well good, I'm glad I was there. Alright, go get some sleep. I'll talk to you tomorrow," he said with a very smoldering look on his face, which made my stomach do a quick flip. I leaned in and put my hand on his cheek, giving him a kiss on the cheek and a long hug.

"Good night Colin," I said, pulling back and squeezing his hand. I turned on my heel and headed up my walkway to the house. As I unlocked and opened the door, I turned back to him and waved. He waved back and got in the cab. As I closed the door behind me, a burning tear began to roll down my cheek. I sunk back against the door, slowly sliding to the floor as I started crying.

Chapter 12

I was still crouching on the floor when Roxie cautiously approached to see what I was doing. I picked her up and took her outside, my body stiffening at the gust of cold air. I had, momentarily, regained my composure. It was a cold night, or maybe I was still shuddering from my end of the night run in, and the thought of the hot tub seemed very appealing right now. I checked the clock. It was only eleven, so I decided to put on a suit and grab a bottle of pinot.

The hot water felt comforting against my skin as I lowered myself into the water. As much as I would have loved to just sit back and not think about anything, it wasn't long before I was replaying the night in my head. My mind couldn't help but ask whether the girl that was with Steven was the one he was cheating on me with. Part of me felt compelled to know the answer, but then another part said to let it go. It didn't matter one way or the other whether this was the same girl. If it was, then she presumably already knew about me and that's why she threw whatever it was she threw at him that night. My guess was that they would end up talking about my little interruption after Colin and I left. With some luck, I had ruined their evening as well.

Remembering Steven's insecurity about Colin made me smile. I was glad that he was with me tonight, and looking fantastic I might add. Whether he intended to look that smug or not, I'm sure it had a lasting impression on Steven and will hopefully encourage him to never call me again.

And then there was my evening with Colin …

I poured myself a second glass of wine and let the chatter in my mind grow quiet as I focused on the hum of the hot tub motors. I had to admit, his suggestion was very tempting. He was simply too great of a guy to pass up, but my heart was getting pulled in another direction. Even though Colin was the safe bet, and would in no way be settling, I was drawn to Ben in a way that I couldn't really describe. I took a long drink of my wine, savoring the sweet, full taste in my mouth before swallowing. I was glad that Colin hadn't asked if there was someone else. I don't think I could have lied to him about that, but at the same time, I didn't want to tell him that I was considering choosing the 'grim reaper' over him. I'm sure it would come across that I wasn't taking his suggestion of the two of us very seriously.

Colin had said he would be patient, and I had to trust that if that was the way things were meant to be, then the timing would be right at some point down the road. But what if the timing never ended up right? What if I was just being a naïve, stupid girl thinking that Ben would come to me and sweep me off my feet? I wasn't even totally sure what he was, yet I was willing to pass on Colin for him? Now I just felt mildly pathetic …

I took another long drink of wine and laid my head back on the cushion behind me while my mind continued to battle with itself. I felt like I was being torn between two great choices and I didn't know how to make my decision. I chastised myself for being so selfish. Most people would be lucky to have even one of these options and I had both, yet I was sitting here lamenting this decision. Of course my thoughts drifted back to my comment that maybe I'm a bad judge of character. With my luck, both would turn out to be bad options …

I groaned loudly as I sank deeper and deeper into the water. The sounds of the bubbling water grew louder in my ears as I dropped below the water line. The bubbles over my face felt rough, but relaxing. From the inside, I felt like I was crying, but given that my face was already soaked, I couldn't be sure. My hands floated up to my face and my arms drifted up to the surface of the water. Over the roar of the bubbles I thought I heard someone calling my name. I scolded myself for imagining that one of my two knights in shining armor was coming to my side to make my decision for me. I tried to force myself to the realization that I would have to make the decision for myself. There was no easy way out. No one would be making it for me.

I slowly exhaled the breath I had been holding, when I suddenly felt a hand clamp down on my wrist. My body tightened and my feet squirmed to find ground beneath me. My wrist was being pulled as my other hand pushed me up and out of the water.

"Suzanne! Can you hear me?!" The voice was frantic, and it took a second for me to process what was being asked. I wiped the water out of my face as I looked towards the voice that was talking to me.

"I'm fine!" I snapped, as I slowly focused on the figure in front of me. "Ben?! What are you doing here?" I was thrilled to see him, but a wave of fear washed over me. Why was he at my house, at almost midnight? And on my back porch? Almost as if he could hear my thoughts, he began speaking.

"All of your lights were on so I thought I'd see if you wanted some company. I rang the doorbell but you didn't answer." I started to back away from him in the water. I must have had a look of horror on my face because he continued to explain himself.

"I saw the patio light on, so I came around the side and when I called your name, you didn't answer. I saw you under the water and I thought … I thought something had happened to you. I'm sorry, I didn't mean to scare you."

"No, I'm fine. You just startled me. I really wasn't expecting anyone," I answered. It was true, and I still felt mildly uncomfortable that he was here like this.

"What were you doing? You look upset."

"I'm fine. I was just thinking about some stuff."

"Do you want me to leave you to your thinking then?" he asked. He had his hands clasped in front of him, and his hands were fidgeting. He looked hopeful that I would say no, and my discomfort began to melt away

"No, that's okay. I'm done in here for tonight. Could you hand me that towel?" I said, pointing to the small table on the other side of the hot tub. This was certainly an interesting twist on the night. At least now if my eyes were puffy I had the excuse of having been in the hot tub for too long. He held up my towel for me as I got out of the water and began to dry off.

I noticed that almost immediately my inner turmoil had quieted, at least for now. Ben had a very soothing effect on me, even though a part of me felt like I should be wary of someone who always seemed to show up at all hours of the day and night. I smiled and looked down as I continued to dry myself off. He had gone over to the far side and folded back the cover and grabbed the wine bottle and glass for me as I slipped on my flip flops.

"Come on in," I gestured and started towards the sliding glass door. "I just need to go rinse off real quick. I'll be out in a minute. Help yourself," I offered, nodding to the wine bottle as I motioned towards the kitchen. I quickly headed back to the bedroom to wash off and put on some warm clothes. I opted for my warm flannel pants with polka dots and a pink thermal top. I didn't want to look obvious by redoing all of my makeup, so I settled for wiping away all of the mascara that had run off in the hot tub and applying slightly tinted lip gloss. I towel dried my hair since blow drying would take too long. It was still damp as I left the bathroom, but I didn't mind.

When I returned to the living room, Ben had started a fire and gotten himself a wine glass. I had only drunk a couple of small glasses, so there was still plenty left in the bottle. I walked slowly into the room, somewhat surprised by the setting.

"Well, this is nice ..." I said, suspiciously. I narrowed my eyes as I watching him from across the room. I generally didn't think of myself as an untrusting person, but I had also not been pursued this strongly before. Pursued? Was he really pursuing me? If I admitted that to myself, then that might have more far reaching implications than I would like to think about at this exact moment.

"I figured you might be chilled," he answered in a sweet and soft tone. He was standing in front of the fire with the poker. As he turned around to face me, he replaced the poker on the stand and a genuine smile played across his thin lips as he folded his arms across his solid chest.

"So what brought this on? I mean, you coming to see me tonight." I was leaning up against the archway into the living room, not quite sure what to do next.

"I feel bad about the way I left last time. I kind of hurried off and left you standing here. I thought you might be upset with me," he said with a slight cock of his head. I could tell his eyes were reading me, trying to decide what I was thinking. The way he was sizing me up gave me a sudden sinking feeling. What if he could read my thoughts? If he could, that would be terribly embarrassing. I pursed my lips as I thought about that.

"Why would you think that?" I was fairly intrigued as to how he would come up with that conclusion. I wondered if maybe he had seen me out with Colin and assumed I was uninterested in him and dating someone else. Who knows what he may have heard if he was right behind us at the restaurant. It wasn't like I was ever really in control of when I would get to see him, and I'm not even sure if I was always aware when he was around. For all I knew, he was within a few feet of me twenty hours a day and I just didn't see him.

"When I saw you in the OR, you looked right at me and then looked away. Usually you'll blush, or smile or something, but you just looked back down, almost like you were pretending you hadn't seen me. I didn't know what to make of it."

"Interesting," I smiled as I nodded my head thinking about what he had said. My arms were folded across my chest and I still hadn't moved from the archway. "I actually didn't respond because I've gotten used to you a little bit more. I don't freak out when I see you anymore, and you don't scare me, so I am able to go about my work without getting completely derailed like I used to. I was taking it as progress," I finished with a smile on my face.

"I suppose that makes sense … I hadn't thought about it from that perspective."

He walked forward and took a seat on the ottoman in front of the fire. He motioned for me to join him. I paused for a minute, looking deep into his dark brown eyes, searching for something, but I wasn't sure what. Misinterpreting my hesitation, he got up and walked towards the edge of the couch.

"Hey, you can have the whole thing to yourself," he said with a smile. Bashfully, I tucked my hair behind my ear and headed over towards the fire. I sat down on the ottoman, crossing my legs under me. A moment later he was walking back towards me with a blanket in his hand. He wrapped it gently around my shoulders, and as his hands came together in front of me, I reached up and clutched his hands to my chest. I whispered a quiet thank you to him, my eyes slowly closing as I retreated back to my earlier thoughts in the hot tub. I wondered again what this unspoken attraction was that I had towards Ben. There was the obvious 'mystery man' perspective, but there was something else too. Noticing my mood tonight to be quite different than the last time he was here, he squatted down in front of me, his hands still at my chest.

"Suzanne, are you okay? Maybe I should go ..." he slowly suggested as he looked up at me.

"No," I said, squeezing his hands, "I'm sorry. Please, stay." I pulled his hands over to my side and he willingly followed, taking a seat next to me. I sighed loudly.

"What?" he asked, in a soft and interested tone.

"I just ... I don't know what to do with you!"

"Why, is there something you're supposed to be doing with me?" he asked in a cheeky but curious tone.

"Well, I ..." Normally I would be afraid of sounding crazy, but apparently with the help of the wine, I didn't seem to care right now. Hey, I'd already had one pretty honest conversation tonight, may as well make it two. All of the sudden, the words started tumbling out of my mouth. "I think about you all the time, but I have no way of contacting you. But then maybe that's a good thing because frankly, I don't even hardly know you! And it's weird that you show up in random places and sometimes other people see you and sometimes they don't, which sort of makes me wonder if you're really just a figment of my imagination since I know almost nothing about you. Well, except that you observe people and often times they die, which, you can understand from my perspective, is a little confusing and sometimes makes me wonder whether I'm next on the list."

Wow. My head was still screaming at me that I had just spewed all of that in one long rant, and not a very eloquent one either. Hmm, well I had probably blown it. Replaying it in my head, I had sounded rather hysterical. I sank back a little, embarrassed at my outburst.

"So is this your way of asking me for my number?" He shot a sideways glance at me and started laughing.

"You have a phone?" I don't know why, but this completely caught me off guard.

"Well, no, but my carrier pigeon is really good." He reached over to a crossword puzzle that was sitting on the edge of the end table and scribbled down something, presumably his phone number.

"There, is that better?" he asked with a smirk, slapping the pen down emphatically on the paper.

"Well, I guess that takes care of rant part A. That just leaves the bigger, you know, more important issues." He cleared his throat and leaned forwards, resting both of his forearms across his legs and rubbing his palms together. He looked up at me gingerly before continuing.

"No, you're not on any lists Suzanne." I searched his face for any signs of teasing or playfulness, but there were none. He seemed completely serious on this point.

"Maybe not on yours-"

"No," he interrupted, "you're not on anyone's list."

"How do you know that? Are you the only one?"

"No, but I know."

My eyebrows came together as I thought about this. I wanted to enjoy my time with him, but all of my unanswered questions were echoing loudly in my head. I didn't know how much longer I would be able to be around him like this, whatever this was, without getting at least some of my questions answered. At that moment, Ben reached his hand over and ran his finger down my cheek as he gently turned my head, moving it to face him.

"Trust me. You're fine. Nothing is going to happen to you." I stared into his eyes as he spoke. I could see a deep longing in his warm eyes, and my frustrations melted away. In their place, a warm, fluttering feeling was starting to creep over me.

I could feel his warm fingers on my cheek and before I knew what I was doing, I leaned in towards him. My hand instinctively reached up for his face as I drew closer to him. I was completely consumed by the fire sweeping over me and I slid closer towards him. My lips met his with a gentle but powerful force. He was still, not knowing how to respond to my advance. A moment later, my other hand slipped below his arm and around his back. My lips moved slowly over his, and my mouth opened, my teeth gently grazing his lip. His hand quickly moved to the back of my neck and pulled me closer in to him. He leaned in to me and his tongue found mine, caressing it gently as he held me tightly. His other arm slipped around my waist and pulled me over onto his lap.

I slid my leg over to the other side of him, straddling him as we sat in front of the warm fire. Both of his arms tightened around me as he kissed me more passionately now, and my body melted into his embrace. My hands slid from his face down to his chest, and my hands clenched, grabbing on to his shirt. I let myself go in the moment, reveling in another intoxicating kiss, then I pulled back slightly from him, my fists pushing into his chest.

My head swam as I felt his hands running down my back and then around my waist again. Instinctively, my lower back gently arched. I bit my lip and closed my eyes as I inhaled deeply, holding the air in my lungs for a long minute before quietly exhaling. I could feel my eyes screaming for him to attack me, but his eyes exuded a quiet confidence and a mischievous look.

"Are you trying to get me in trouble, Dr. Jacobsen?" he asked with a playful smirk on his face. Despite the fact that he was taller than I was, I now stood about six inches above him.

"Maybe," I whispered as I pulled his face closer to me and began to kiss him again. His arms tightened around me once again as he passionately kissed me back. Abruptly, he stopped and pulled away from me, resting his forehead against my shoulder. I heard him sigh and felt his body quiver slightly. He looked back up at me with a relaxed smile on his face.

"Is it just me, or is it getting a little warm over here?" He laughed once and started to stir, so I stood up, letting him free himself. My mind raced as I wondered what he was thinking about. He grabbed the blanket and my hand and pulled me towards the couch, pushing the ottoman out of the way with his foot.

"Come here," he beckoned as he settled onto the couch, leaning against the soft leather arm with his legs outstretched in front of him. He pulled me onto the couch in front of him and wrapped his strong arms around me. He drew me back against his firm chest, keeping his arms wrapped tightly around my shoulders. He lightly kissed along the back of my neck and I could feel the fluttering in my stomach start again. With every kiss, a shiver ran through me and as he moved on, each spot he had kissed tingled with excitement and ecstasy. His lips left my neck and his hand swept slowly down my cheek. I nuzzled my face into the pocket between his shoulder and his jaw, and sighed peacefully. The gentle rise and fall of his chest was almost hypnotic.

"I'm really glad you came over tonight," I spoke softly, almost in a whisper.

"I am too," he answered, squeezing me tightly. I let my mind empty, soaking in every detail of this moment. For as much time as I had spent thinking about him over the last few weeks, my heart now skipped at the idea that he was actually here with me tonight. The fire I felt under his touch was nothing I could have imagined in my head. Being here with his arms snuggly wrapped around me, I was overcome with a feeling of being protected and an overall feeling of peace and happiness.

The wine and my sleepiness began to overtake me and I could feel myself relaxing and drifting off.

"Will you stay with me?" I cooed as I pulled his arms more tightly towards my chest.

"I'll be right here when you wake up. I promise." I felt the soft stroking of his fingers on my cheek as my mind slowly began to shut off for the night and I drifted off into sleep.

Chapter 13

I awoke the next morning to the sound of a distant siren. Without opening my eyes, I let the morning slowly creep over me. I couldn't remember any of my dreams, but I had a calm sense radiating from me. I was slowly warming up to my surroundings, and a sweet smell wafted in from the kitchen. I rolled over to find myself in my bed, slightly overheated from having my flannel pants and thermal shirt on under the heavy duvet.

I sat up in bed and rubbed my eyes, running my hands back through my hair. Roxie came scampering in and barked at me, dancing around in a circle.

"Come here," I said, holding my arms out to her. She jumped up on the bed and plodded over towards me. As I pulled her on to my lap, Ben came walking through the door. His blue button down shirt was wrinkled from the night before and his dark hair was gently tousled. I couldn't help but smile at how sexy and striking he looked in this moment.

"Good morning," he said sweetly, as he bent over to give me a long, slow kiss on the lips. "Are you hungry? I made breakfast."

"It smells good. I just need to take her out first-"

"Already done," he interrupted. "She's just whining because I haven't given her any of the food I'm making. I wasn't sure if you wanted her eating scraps."

"Thanks Ben," I said, looking up at him with adoring eyes. He smiled back at me, reaching his hand up to stroke my cheek.

"I'll be back in a minute with breakfast." He backed slowly towards the door, then spun around and headed back to the kitchen. I quickly jumped up and ran to the bathroom to wash my face and brush my teeth. I also threw on pj shorts to keep myself from overheating. I made it back to bed before he came walking in with a tray of breakfast food. I looked over the selection: muffins, pancakes, fruit and juice. He put the tray down on the already cleared off night stand. I had a sudden powerful feeling of being doted on and taken care of, and I soaked it all in.

"Where'd you scrounge this up? I'm pretty sure I didn't have any fresh fruit in my kitchen when I went to bed last night," I asked with a smile as I picked up a strawberry and bit into it.

"Well, at about four, when I brought you into the bedroom, you were pretty much out, so I used the opportunity to go get a few things. I hope you don't mind."

"Not at all!" I pulled him down on the bed next to me and leaned over to gently give him a kiss on the lips. He sighed, contently.

"Mmm, yummy," he said with a wide grin sweeping across his lips and leaning back on his elbow.

"Nah, that's just the strawberries." I smiled and fed one to Ben, who was still laying across my bed. I leaned back over to the tray to get the orange juice, and he sat up.

"Have you eaten yet?" I asked as I prepared more of my breakfast.

"Nope, I was waiting for you," he replied as he crossed his legs.

I pulled the plate of pancakes over and drown them in syrup. I put the plate down between us on the bed and handed him a fork. For the next hour or so, we casually laid around in bed, nibbling on pancakes and carrying on lighthearted conversation.

It was great to hear him tell stories about his past and about Kansas City. I didn't remember anything from my time there, and he described everything in such vivid detail. He told me about some of his favorite spots to go walking in the spring, his favorite restaurants, and other things he would do when he wasn't working. I could see in his eyes that he had been happy there. His face lit up and his posture tensed in excitement, like a little kid telling his friends about the cool camping trip he went on over the summer.

After an hour or so of chatting and pancakes, he had made his way up to the head of the bed and was now sitting next to me, leaning against the headboard with his legs outstretched in front of him.

"So," I said, plating up some muffins and fruit for us both.

"So," he responded, waiting for me to have some sort of question in mind.

"Last night was interesting." I had no idea how to start a 'serious' conversation with him.

"Interesting … That's a very non-descriptive word." He smirked at me, knowing that I wasn't sure how to begin. "I take it you have something you want to ask me," he said, smiling as he took a bite of a muffin.

"Well, you said you knew I wasn't on any lists," to which he nodded. "I was just wondering how you knew that."

"Ah, the million dollar question."

"Well," I started, somewhat defensively, "I just don't know how any of it works." I paused for a moment, allowing him to jump in, which he didn't. "I mean, I don't exactly know what you do."

"I think you probably know more than you think. Take a guess." He had a very mischievous smile on his face. He was probably laughing his ass off inside, watching me squirm as I was tiptoeing around asking him certain questions. I decided to choose my words carefully here.

"To begin with, I know you observe," I said, very diplomatically.

"True. What am I observing?" he asked, in a way to fuel the conversation and to keep me talking.

"You're observing people," I answered, with a firm certainty in my voice.

"Correct. And where am I observing them?"

"Umm, in Chicago?" I didn't quite know what he was getting at.

"Yeah, but more specifically," he said in an encouraging tone. He could have told me I was being stupid, but I appreciated that he didn't.

"In the OR?" I asked. I still wasn't sure exactly what he was getting at.

"That's one place, but you also saw me by The Bean." Well crap. That didn't exactly help my train of thought. I figured the OR would be something to do with people in distress maybe. But the Bean? Most people there always look so happy!

"You referenced it last night. What often happens to the people around me?"

"They die." There was a pregnant pause as he continued to eat his muffin, still with a slight smile on his face. "So then are you the angel of death? Do you get to decide who lives and dies?"

"I'm not sure if 'angel of death' is the right thing to call me. And no, I don't decide. I'm just the one who is there to take them." My mind raced as I actually heard him say the words. I could feel my throat tighten as I started to process this very blunt revelation. He said it so casually, that he was there to take people from this world. I set the rest of my muffin down on my plate and frowned at it before reaching over to take another drink of juice. My mind was going a hundred miles an hour as I thought about this from all angles, but then I sighed a content sigh as my mind settled on one of the important details – 'no, I don't decide.' I was glad that he wasn't the one deciding. I don't know why this should matter, but for whatever reason, it seemed like it would be too much for me to handle. Knowing that he was looking at a crowd, deciding which ones would live and which ones would die seemed to change my opinion on the matter, even though perhaps it shouldn't.

"But how do you know who to take?"

"There's a certain … aura about people," he sounded almost wistful in his answer. His expression had turned very serene as he was talking about this. I had it in my mind that he would most likely have been short and defensive on this topic, but apparently I was wrong.

"I've heard people talk about "auras" before, but I guess I never really understood what they meant. What does someone's aura look like?"

"Well that depends," he answered, very matter-of-factly.

"Depends on what?"

"Whether they're on that dreaded list or not," he replied with a cheeky smile, raising his eyebrows expressively as he answered.

"So what does your aura look like if you're on the list?"

"Depends whose list you're on." Ben was definitely in a playful mood this morning, and I liked it. He smiled a wide grin at me as he ate another strawberry. This side of him seemed so far removed from the quiet, unsure person I had spoken to on the el platform that first night. I laughed at his game.

"So, if someone's on *your* list what does their aura look like," I asked as I playfully elbowed him. He used the opportunity to pull me closer in to him and wrap his arms around me.

"It's a sort of reddish glow radiating out from them. Mainly it radiates from around the chest and head, almost like a big halo or cloud."

"Hmm … Does it have a defined shape, like a bubble?"

"Not really, it's more of just a mild haze around them."

"Does everyone have their own color?" I asked with a little bit of a shudder. Instinctively, Ben rubbed his hands up and down my arms.

"No, most people just have a light type of color, like a yellowy green kind of color."

"No, I meant others like you. The others that take people. If you see people as a reddish color, what color does everyone else see?"

"Actually, each of us sees our people as reddish. If you're on someone else's list, it's more of a bluish purple color."

"So that's why you said I wasn't on anyone else's list. Because I'm not blue, right?"

"Yep," he answered, almost triumphantly. I leaned my head against his chest as we cuddled in silence for a few minutes. My mind was still processing the idea that this is what Ben did. He took people. I wasn't sure where, but he took them. I hadn't decided yet how much I was going to probe about precisely what he did and how he did it. Granted, he was being very forthcoming with the information, but I wasn't sure if I was ready to hear the answers he would likely volunteer if I kept probing.

Part of me was burning to ask him more. As a doctor, death is one area that we truly cannot understand. I know physically what happens to the human body when you die, but the soul is a much deeper area to explore. There is no conclusive evidence to describe what or where the soul is. Ben's very presence affirms that there is something after this life. Otherwise, where is he taking these people?

I decided to stay away from some of the deeper, philosophical issues about the soul and keep to more of the mechanics.

"So ... how do you know when it's their time? I mean, I know you said their aura's red, but does that mean 'right now'?" He paused for a moment, and I immediately started to backpedal.

"I'm sorry, I'm sure I sound like a little kid asking all of these questions," I admitted, probably blushing too from embarrassment.

"No, you don't sound like a child. You're being a doctor. You're problem solving and asking questions to help explain something you don't understand. It's fine, really. I wouldn't be sitting here with you this morning if I wasn't willing to talk about this with you. Um, well, as they get closer to their time, their aura darkens. The more peop- uh, the more experience you have, the better you get at reading shades of auras. Much the same as being a doctor. Over time, you're better able to predict timeframes of various ailments and how they'll affect your patient."

I thought about that as I tried to put into perspective exactly what he does. It seemed so foreign to me that someone could be so detached about the idea of knowing exactly when a person would die and being there to take them. I suppose it's like anything else though. You sort of become desensitized to it over time. I imagine a lot of people would be shocked at how easily I can use a scalpel to cut someone open without even flinching.

I think Ben must have been able to hear the wheels slowly turning in my head.

"So, do you feel better knowing that you're not on the list?" he said in a more gentle and serious tone.

"Well, would you actually tell me if I was blue or red?" I asked, but not in an accusatory tone, just a curious one.

"We're definitely not supposed to, but I would tell you."

"Really? Wouldn't you get into trouble?"

"I don't care about that. I would want to give you a chance to say goodbye to your family. Get some sense of closure and peace. That's what people seem to regret the most."

"So, how exactly does it work? I take it you're not actually killing them, you're just taking them after they die. But how?" He paused for a very long moment. I think I may have asked more than he wanted to talk about, but rather than backpedaling, I just waited to see if he would respond.

"After someone's body dies, their soul leaves the body, somewhat by accident usually. If I'm phased, then I can grab onto their soul and take them with me, like if you grab someone's arm you can pull them with you."

"What do you mean "if I'm phased""? I asked, genuinely not understanding what he was saying to me.

"Let's go the guessing game route on this one," he said with a smile, to which I lightly jabbed at him again with my elbow. "It's a great way to get insight into how your mind works! I love it!"

"Thanks, I love being a science experiment," I retorted. He leaned in and gave me a kiss on the cheek.

"So, how does a grown, unscrubbed man walk into the OR?" he asked. I had to laugh at this. I had been wondering the same thing for quite some time.

"Maybe he was never really in the OR. Maybe he was just screwing around with my mind and I only imagined he was in there," I said with a smile. This actually was a somewhat plausible idea.

"Nope," he said with a satisfied smile on his face.

"So you were really, truly in the room?"

"Yes."

"But that doesn't make sense. Other people would have been able to see you too if you were in the OR ..." I trailed off.

"But they didn't."

"They didn't, but I did ... so ... there's something special about me?"

"Yep," he answered with a gentle squeeze.

"So you can make yourself disappear to everyone else, but I can still see you?"

"You got it. When we're there to take someone, we move to another ... I guess plane or realm. Sort of like how dogs can hear sounds that humans can't. There's another plane of existence that we use when it's someone's time because we don't want to walk right up to a total stranger on their death bed and start talking to them. You can imagine how confusing that would be for everyone in the room. This way we're there, but they can't see us until they've already died."

"So then when you're at home by yourself, which plane are you in?"

"Depends. I mean, it really isn't easier or harder to be on one plane or the other." He paused for a moment, letting what he was saying soak in, and then abruptly continued. "Breathe through your mouth," he said.

"What? Why?" I asked, as I began breathing through my mouth, not that I had realized I was breathing through my nose.

"See, you can switch between the two with almost no effort. One's not right or wrong, and you don't always breathe through your nose or always breathe through your mouth. Same thing with the form I take." A good example, I had to admit.

"But then, if I can see you when you're phased, as you call it, how come I'll see you, then a split second later you're gone?"

"Because when I concentrate fully on someone I'm observing, I ... go to another place," he said in a different, more guarded tone. Given that I hadn't expected him to answer this many questions, and so honestly, that I decided to throw him a bone and not push on.

"I see," I said cautiously. He closed his mouth and looked out the window. "So, you can be fully here where everyone can see you, or you can be phased where only I can see you, and then you can be fully phased where I can't see you and it's only the person you're there for that can see you?"

"Yeah, pretty much," he replied with a small, but happy, smile.

"Okay, that's gonna take a while for my brain to fully digest that. So for now I'm done with my interrogation, but I reserve the right to call you to the stand again for questioning," I said in a playful tone as I turned in towards him and wrapped my arms around his waist.

"Fair enough my dear," he said, leaning down to kiss me lightly as I hugged him closer to me. I shimmied up closer to his level and continued to kiss him.

"So, what do you want to do today?"

Chapter 14

On Monday morning, I was up earlier than usual. Most of the weekend had been spent on cloud nine remembering my wonderful day with Ben. After our long conversation in bed on Friday morning, we went downtown to walk around the parks and up and down Michigan Avenue. It was an unseasonably nice day, so we had to take advantage of it.

Around lunch time, Colin had texted me to see how I was feeling. I had felt a little odd answering my text messages right there in front of Ben, but he told me not to worry about it and turned towards one of the store windows, pretending to examine the mannequin's new spring wardrobe. I told Colin that I was fine and that we should do lunch on Monday at work. He agreed and didn't push the issue.

Now as I stood in front of my locker, I suddenly had butterflies in my stomach. I had to be honest with Colin, but I didn't expect that he would take it very well. It wasn't fair to him to make it seem like I may be a week or two away from being available. With my luck, I'd tell him about Ben, and then Ben would disappear and I'd end up losing them both.

Lunch time came sooner than I had hoped for. As I sat there across from Colin, I tried to stay calm and focused. I surprised myself at how well I was doing with this task.

"So, are you okay from Thursday night? You seemed kind of out of it on Friday when we were texting." I studied his face as he asked the question. There were no signs of suspicion, just interest in how I was doing.

"Yeah, I'm okay. After I got home I just soaked in the hot tub and had some wine."

"You know, you should be careful doing that," he said quickly. At first, his tone annoyed me, but I guess in hindsight it probably wasn't the best choice of late night activity given I had been drinking during dinner too.

"Well, I was only in there for about twenty minutes. And then Ben stopped by," I said, with as passé of a tone as I could muster. I looked at my sandwich as I took another bite. It was an easy excuse not to look up at Colin to gauge his reaction, but I could feel his gaze boring into me. I must have caught him in mid-bite. His jaw was firm and his expression was a mix of hurt and anger.

"Why'd you say you wanted to get a nightcap with me if he was gonna be coming over later?" he asked as he resumed chewing. His question was very direct and almost completely void of any emotion. I was not sure exactly how I expected him to respond but I was starting to get a bit anxious about this conversation.

"No, I didn't invite him over, he just stopped by. He saw the lights on and wanted to say hi." I wanted to let Colin ask whatever questions he thought he needed answered. Regardless of any relationships, he was still one of my best friends and we had always been open in the past about our personal lives. I wanted to keep that channel open.

"So is he the reason you're not interested in a relationship right now? I might as well cut to the chase, right?"

"Yeah, sure. You know you can ask me anything," I replied with a smile as I swallowed hard. "Well, to answer your question, yes and no I guess. I don't even know what Ben and I are. I wasn't looking to start anything, with anyone, but it just sort of happened. I actually met him before Steven and I broke up, I just wasn't going to do anything about it at that time. If he wasn't in the picture at all, then I would be using this time to get my head back on straight."

"That's probably a good strategy. Play one at a time, that way if it doesn't work out with him, then you haven't lost both of us, right?" His eyes were fiery now as I felt my cheeks warm, almost like I had been slapped.

"You know, that's a really shitty thing to say! You've been one of my best friends for years now, and then last week you drop it on me that you want something more and when I say the timing's not right, now I'm a terrible person?!" I threw my napkin down on the table and pushed my chair back.

"Suz, wait. I'm sorry, you're right. I guess I've been thinking about this a little bit longer than I've let on."

"I'm sorry I'm not at the same place you are right now, but I can't turn on a dime like that." There wasn't anything else for me to say, so I stood up and straightened my coat. "I've gotta get back to it. I'll see you later," I said as I was already starting to walk away. I could hear him sigh loudly as I left and I could picture his expression in my mind, but I didn't look back. Instead, I held my chin up and headed back to the hospital.

I tried to shake my grumpy mood as I made my way back to the physician lounge, but the moment I opened the door I felt my shoulders slump. The lounge was filled with residents being introduced to the doctors they would be shadowing. I had completely forgotten that Howard was assigning a resident to me for this rotation. Normally I would not mind, but my mood after lunch was not setting the stage for me being very friendly and personable today. I did enjoy mentoring, so I was hopeful this would pull me out of my funk.

"Suzanne," he beckoned me over to where he was standing with a young woman. "Dr. Jacobsen, this is Dr. Jane Paulsen. She's the resident who will be on rotation with you for the next 90 days."

Jane was a tiny black haired girl who was rail thin. She looked so fragile that I was almost afraid to shake her hand for fear I'd snap it off. I had had residents under me before for short stints, so this wasn't a completely foreign experience for me, but given my preoccupation with the Ben and Colin situation, I was a bit concerned as to how focused I would be on helping Jane. I remained optimistic though that helping someone else would help get me out of my head and make me feel better.

I remembered back to when I was a resident and how much I looked up to the other doctors. It was an exciting time in my life and it confirmed for me that this was truly what I wanted to do for the rest of my life. I reminded myself of this as I stepped forward to shake Jane's hand.

The rest of the afternoon seemed to drag, but at least her incessant stream of chatter was enough to keep me distracted from Colin and Ben. I'm sure in most other settings she was probably a fun girl to hang out with, but I was not in a particularly talkative mood. Late in the day when we were finishing up with our final few patients, she had started talking about how much fun it would be for us to hang out after work some time. In an attempt to be cordial, I nodded and agreed with her.

"Really? You want to grab a drink after work?" She sounded surprised by my acceptance of her offer.

"Yeah, we could do that sometime," I responded pleasantly.

"Well how about tonight?" she asked, practically squealing with excitement. I hoped she was just acting like this because she was nervous and excited about her first day. If she was like this all the time, this was going to be a long three months.

"Oh, I'm sorry. I actually have plans with my boyfriend tonight." I felt mildly guilty about lying through my teeth, but I didn't have the energy to spend another three hours socially with her today. I could see her shoulders sag as I said this but her tone maintained its chipper pitch.

"Oh, yeah, no problem. Maybe some time later then."

"Of course! I'd like that," I said, now feeling somewhat bad about having blown her off. We finished up the charting for our last patient and went back to the locker room to change into street clothes. Jane was still chatting with me as we walked out through the main lobby. As we approached the doors, I started thinking about which direction I wanted to go. With my luck Jane would be going in that same direction and would end up finding out I really didn't have any plans tonight.

To my pleasant surprise, I heard my name being called as we walked out the sliding door.

"Suzanne!" I turned to look towards the silky voice that was calling my name. In front of me stood Ben. He was dressed casually in khakis and a green striped button down shirt and dark brown boots. His brown coat was unzipped, giving me an excuse to look him up and down. He walked over and leaned in to give me a kiss on the cheek. I wrapped my arm around his neck as I lightly kissed him back.

"Ben, I'd like you to meet Jane. She's a new resident that's shadowing me," I said as I gestured towards her. Politely, he stepped towards her and shook her hand, exchanging pleasantries. She eagerly shook his hand and then turned back to me.

"Thanks for all of your help Dr. Jacobsen. Have a good night and I'll see you tomorrow!" With that, she waved and walked off down the street. I quickly turned to Ben.

"What're you doing here?" I asked with a smile and a gentle grab of his hand. "I'm so glad you rescued me from her!"

"Aww, she didn't seem that bad. She seemed nice."

"No, she is. She's just very high energy. Which is something I don't have a lot of right now."

He leaned forwards and hugged me as he began to respond.

"Well, you did say you have plans with your boyfriend tonight. Maybe it's a little presumptuous, but I was hoping you mean me."

"You heard that?"

"Yep."

"Do you have super power hearing or something like that that I should know about?" I asked, somewhat concerned that he might have overheard my lunch with Colin too.

"No, I was just fully phased, so you didn't see me. There was a geriatric patient that died a few hours ago, so I was here to take her. We walked by you at the nurses' station." This was something I would have to keep in mind for later. I wasn't sure what I thought about the fact that he could, theoretically, be listening in on any one of my conversations and I wouldn't know it.

"So, what are these big plans of ours for the night?"

"Ah, I suppose I did say that we had plans, didn't I? Well, I'm not really hungry, so do you want to just grab a drink?"

"Sure, your call," he said with a sexy little half smile.

Chapter 15

We walked a few blocks to small lounge called The Red Head Piano Bar. It was close enough to the hospital that it had become a popular after work spot for us, as long as we were dressed appropriately. This was not the kind of place you could wear your scrubs to. The bright classic sign out front hung over a small stairwell that led to the basement of an old building. As soon as we got to the steps we could hear the pianist playing and singing along to the piano rock version of Livin' on a Prayer, and I smiled. I loved this kind of place. As we walked up to the hostess, she took our coats and showed us to a table towards the back. This used to be a great place to come for a cigar and scotch, but since the Illinois smoking ban had been passed, the cigars had to go. Even still, the ambiance was exceptional.

The dim light from our small square table danced across the old pictures of the Hollywood greats like Sophia Loren and Cary Grant. We cozied up next to each other and started to browse through the drink menu. After a day like today, I could definitely go for a stiff martini. Within a few minutes, our waitress came over to introduce herself. She was a pretty woman in her late thirties wearing heels, what looked like a leotard, and a tuxedo coat. This place definitely had the air of an old Vegas cocktail lounge.

All of the waitresses had very slim frames and great legs, but there was a sense of class to it.

We placed our orders and she smiled brightly before turning and quickly walking away, taking small steps in her tall heels.

"So," I began, in a louder than normal voice. Ben leaned in as I spoke, but more out of politeness than straining to hear. The bar was loud enough to be energizing, but not so loud that you had to scream.

"So you were at the hospital today?"

"Yes. I'm actually at the hospital quite often," he offered, rather nonchalantly.

"Really?" I was somewhat surprised by this admission. "I thought you were there to take my patients and none of my patients died today," I said in more of a statement than a question.

"Well, yes, I take your patients, but there are others too. Trust me, you should be very worried if you have your own, dedicated taker. You'd have to be a really bad surgeon to warrant that!" He laughed at his own joke and leaned back in his chair with his hands on his hips. I knew he meant this as a positive, but something about what he said was not sitting well. I looked back over at him and he flashed a large grin at me. He seemed to be in a good enough mood, so I figured it was safe to continue and that he would likely share information with me today.

"So then how often do you take people?" It seemed a simple enough question, but he shifted in his seat, like he wasn't quite sure if he should be answering honestly, or fudge the numbers just a little bit. He smiled briefly with a polite and forced smile.

"Why do you want to know?" he asked in a fairly detached voice, leaning forwards again. He didn't seem upset about me asking, just not sure how to answer the question. Maybe I misjudged his demeanor for the day.

"I don't know. I guess it's maybe another way of asking if there are a lot of you or just a few. I mean, I know normal death toll statistics ..."

"Well, it depends on the week, but usually four or five I'd say," he answered, looking straight into my eyes, searching for some sort of reaction from me. We sat there for a minute or so in silence. I didn't know how to react to that number. I really hadn't given it much thought as to what number I thought he would say. I took a forced breath, flashed a quick polite smile and then our waitress caught my eye as she started to approach. She gently set our drinks down on the table and, sensing the quiet between us, asked if there was anything else she could help with, her gaze jumping between the two of us. Ben casually looked up to meet her gaze as he answered.

"No, this is great thank you." He then turned his focus back to me. "Suzanne, talk to me. I just told you I take four or five people a week and you haven't said a word, or even flinched for that matter."

I didn't really know what to think, so I went the humor route to hopefully direct the conversation down a more lighthearted path.

"Well, I see what you mean. If I was killing a couple hundred patients every year I should be worried!" I reached for my cosmo to buy myself a few extra seconds of thinking. When I looked back up at Ben, he had not moved a muscle. He was still leaning in towards me, arms folded across the table, eyes searching my face for some type of reaction.

"But you still haven't told me what you think about the fact that I take people from this world to the next." He now reached for his gimlet too.

"Well, I guess I don't really know what to think. It's sort of difficult to get my arms around. I mean, it's a function that must be served, right?" I asked, to which he nodded. "So, then why not you? I can't fault you for doing a required duty. But ..." I trailed off, thinking about how you would get into the field of being a Taker. He must have been able to see the wheels turning in my head. He leaned in closer, his lips almost touching my face.

"But what?" he whispered softly, then kissed my cheek. I could feel my stomach ignite as his hot breath tickled across my skin. I shook my head slightly, letting my thoughts recollect in my head.

"But, how did you come to be a Taker in the first place?" I asked with a rather sheepish feeling. I slunk down a bit in my chair as I realized the magnitude of the question I had just asked in such a naïve and childish manner. His eyes seemed to turn hard. I could detect an air of bitterness about him right now and immediately regretted my question.

"I don't really know why I'm a Taker. When I died, there was a Taker there for me. Once I finally realized that I was dead, I started asking him questions about where I was going, what to expect, all of those typical questions. He didn't really say much to me, but then when we got there, he smiled at me and said "Now it's your turn" and faded into the distance as he walked away from me."

Ben leaned back in his chair, his eyes focused on some point far off in the distance. I hadn't seen this type of expression from him before, so I wasn't quite sure how to react. Should I let him reflect back on this seemingly painful memory, or try to draw him back to the present? I opted to quietly sip my drink and shift position in my chair. He noticed my shift and turned his gaze back to me, without saying a word.

"So he just sort of left you there, by yourself?" I blurted out. While I obviously didn't have much of a frame of reference for how something like this should work, I would assume they would get training of some sort. Or at least an introduction to someone who could guide them through your new role.

"Yeah," Ben responded with a sad smile. "I found my way back to Atlanta, where I had been living before I died, and then I just ... hid out for a while. I didn't know where to go, or what to do. I couldn't go back home, because of my roommates, so I just wandered around the city and the parks. Eventually, about a month or so later, someone had noticed that I had no aura and seemed lost. She introduced herself and offered to introduce me to some of the other Takers who could help me get adjusted to my new lifestyle."

"Was she a Taker too?" I asked, leaning in to catch his every word. I had never heard him talk about any of his colleagues or friends, so I was curious as to what they were like.

"No, she's a Keeper," he said with a smile as he sipped his gimlet.

"Is she your girlfriend or your wife or something?" I asked in a somewhat accusatory tone. I hadn't meant to sound so rude, but it just sort of flowed off my tongue. I looked up at Ben's face, which seemed to have a very puzzled look about it. His eyebrows were pulled together as he was noticeably trying to figure out what I was asking him. I continued.

"Well, you said 'she's a Keeper,'" I said, with a sarcastic tone on the last part. He laughed at me and leaned forwards, putting a hand up to my cheek.

"No, not as in "I want to keep her." Keepers are like guardian angels. They make sure that people don't go before their time, or they try to anyway. Keepers and Takers tend to be friendly with each other. We really are the only ones that we can openly talk to about what we do, the challenges we face, and things like that." He leaned back again with his drink in his hand, his eyes sparkling as he watched me.

"But you told me about your situation," I said, curious as to whether I was an exception to the rule or whether this was one way that Ben would draw women in.

"Well, we're really not supposed to tell anyone about us. You're the only person I've ever been this open with about everything," he answered, looking down at his hands. On his final word, without raising his head, he lifted his gaze to meet mine through his lashes. My god was he sexy! I could feel my pulse quicken and a wave a triumph flow over me.

"And how long has that been," I responded coyly. He seemed to be offering up information so I thought I would take advantage of his mood.

"Thirty two years," he answered very matter-of-factly. Without even thinking, I kept asking questions, hoping to find out more about him.

"Wow, you look so young! How old were you when you died? *How* did you die?" I blurted out. Judging by the look on his face, I must have sounded like a rambling high schooler. This whole conversation seemed to bring out the naïve, inquisitive side of me. Usually I felt so confident and well versed but this was new territory. Something completely unfamiliar and something most people never have a chance to get answers to. "I'm sorry. That's being very nosy." Although I still did hope he would answer the questions.

"Well," he began, "my appearance can change. I appear at whatever age I project myself to be." I tilted my head to the side and raised my eyebrows as I tried to process what he had said. I suddenly felt like Roxie, tipping her head from side to side trying to understand me. I didn't have a clue as to what he was talking about, but luckily he continued. "If I'm feeling really young on a particular day, I appear as a younger man, or even a boy. If I'm feeling 'more mature' then I will appear older. That's done on purpose so that we can change ourselves for the people we are taking. We try to match their stage in life or their expectations of what awaits them in the afterlife. If I'm there to take an elderly person, showing up as a ten year old probably wouldn't be very encouraging for that person. Our whole purpose in the process is to help usher the person to the next stage of existence. If we have to spend a lot of time and effort explaining the whole process to someone, it's counterproductive."

Ben paused from his explanation, waiting for me to ask questions or respond in some way. While I did have more questions, I took a long and deliberate sip of my cosmo, thinking about what to ask him.

"So how you look right now," I began, "is that the way you usually look then? That's the only way I've seen you look before."

"Well, when I met you, this was how I felt, and that hasn't changed, and so my appearance doesn't. This is pretty close to what I looked like when I died, so it's how I usually identify with myself. When you've seen me in the OR, I'm usually in this form unless I have a good reason to be older or younger."

"But what about the little kid that fell off the roof? Wouldn't you have been a lot younger to match him better?"

"Well, he was a different situation. You know how I told you that he wasn't exactly an angel?" I nodded, remembering our conversation about him. "For kids with attitude problems like that, I see my role as less of friend ushering them along as I do a father figure or a teacher, so I don't try to match them. I've tried a few times, but then they become overly domineering. They think they can take charge of the situation and if I appear to be around the same age, they naturally think they're the alpha in the situation."

I wasn't quite sure what to think about that. As my mind started to process all of this information, Ben interrupted my thoughts. "Enough about me for now, let's talk about you and how your day went. Tell me more about this new resident you're working with."

And with that we were onto lighter topics for the rest of the evening.

Looking down at my watch after finishing our next round, I started to yawn. Even though it was only 8:30pm, it seemed much later to me. After everything that had happened over the last week, I just felt worn down. "Oh, am I boring you that much?" Ben asked with a laugh.

"No, I'm sorry, I'm just exhausted. Today's been a really long day," I replied.

"I understand. I'll walk you home," he said, motioning for the waitress that we were ready for our check. After paying, he stood up and took my hand, then we headed for the door. Even though I had driven to work today, it was an unseasonably warm evening for this time of year, so walking home sounded perfect. We started walking toward my house at a leisurely pace and continued our very relaxed and free flowing conversation. "So are you okay," he asked me timidly, holding his elbow out for me. I reached up and put my hand through his arm, resting my hand comfortably in the crook of his elbow.

"Sure, why do you ask?" I knew there was a reason, so I was hoping he would come out and say what he was getting at.

"Well, you just seemed like you were upset when you got back to the hospital after lunch," he said with a concerned tone, covering my hand with his free hand. I stiffened at his question but tried to keep walking at the same pace. I had let Colin ask whatever questions he wanted, but he was one of my best friends. I wasn't quite sure whether I wanted to go down this path yet with Ben. A part of me was also slightly irritated that he could watch me whenever he liked without me even knowing it.

"Yes, I'm fine thank you. Just had a lot on my mind," I replied curtly. We walked silently for the next block or so before I continued. "So how often do you watch me at the hospital while you're phased?" I tried not to sound too upset since he probably was just trying to make sure I was okay, but it still was not sitting well.

"Judging by your tone, I take it you're not happy about it," he answered without answering my question.

"It just feels like an invasion, that's all. I don't know when you're around and phased, so for all I know you're hanging on my every word with everyone I talk to. It makes me feel self-conscious."

"Why do you feel self-conscious? Are you saying things to other people that you wouldn't say directly to me?" he asked in a very even tone.

"I don't know, sometimes people just want to talk to their friends. You know, use them as a sounding board-" I paused, starting to feel unsure of myself for a moment. "Hey wait, this was about you and why you're watching me without my knowledge or consent, Big Brother," I said elbowing him playfully.

"Well I think that's what's wrong with so many relationships these days. People feel like they have to put on a show at the beginning instead of just saying what they really think and feel. You don't really get to know each other until you've been together for a long time. And even sometimes then, people still keep up their façade. But when you can observe people when they think no one is looking, well then you can really see what they're like." A smile spread across his lips and his eyes twinkled at me rather seductively. I couldn't help but smile back at him. Even though I did not like the idea of someone watching me without me knowing it, I could see his point. So much time was wasted with Steven pretending to be someone he wasn't, and me pretending to be a different version of myself around him too.

"But don't you think it's a little unfair that you're the only one who gets to see all the cards? How do I know you're not just pretending to be something you're not so that you can turn my head? I mean, you could have been watching me for a long time with my ex to see what I was like in relationships, what I was looking for, what I don't like, you know … Whenever I'm around, you can see me, but I can't always see you. Only when you want me to see you."

"Or feel me," he said nonchalantly. I hesitated for a moment and a shiver ran through me. I was starting to get cold walking outside, but luckily we were only a few blocks from home. If I hadn't quit smoking, I would have definitely lit up right now to keep warm. Instead I buried my other hand in my pocket to keep warm.

"Or feel you?" I repeated, to which he just nodded. "What do you mean by that?" I probed.

"Well, it's probably easier to show you, so I'll just show you when we get to your house."

"Wait a second, this isn't some weird kinky thing is it?" I said with an uneasy laugh. Ben didn't respond, but instead just looked at me. I could feel my stomach tighten.

"No, it isn't," he finally said with a chuckle. "Sorry, just thought I'd see what your reaction was first. No, what it really comes down to is this. Do you remember when I told you that there were two planes of existence?"

"Yeah," I said nodding, "you used the 'breathe through your nose, then breathe through your mouth' example."

"That's right. You have a good memory," he answered with a smile. "So if there's two planes and I can go back and forth between them, then that means that I am only physically in one plane at any given time, right?" I nodded, not wanting to interrupt him. He slowed down and began to turn towards me.

"So when I'm physically in one plane, there's a corresponding energy signature that's left in the other plane in that same place." He stopped walking, and took my hand, caressing it lovingly as he continued. "If you're standing in one specific spot and I'm phased, I can physically stand in the same spot on the other plane and you can feel me."

"Okay ..." I replied cautiously, wondering what exactly was going to happen when we got back to my house. My head began to swim as I tried to comprehend the magnitude of what he was saying. Up until now, most of what he had been telling me was all talk. He could have totally been making all of this up, since nothing he said had any physical proof to back it up. Now he was actually going to show me something that would forever change me. My breath hitched as I processed this.

"It's okay Suzanne," he reassured me, eyes smoldering. He must have been able to sense my apprehension about this. He continued delicately. "It doesn't hurt, from what I've heard. If you would rather not do this that's fine too. I just thought it would be something special for us to share," he offered with a genuine smile. His eyes were twinkling as he looked at me. I found my thoughts and continued participating in the conversation.

"So you've never done this before?" I wasn't sure if that made me nervous or if I thought that it made this extra special.

"Well," he started, taking a deep breath, "not in the way you're thinking. I've bumped into people on accident, and then when I was trying to see exactly how it worked I reached out and touched people's hands or brushed against them on purpose."

"Oh," was all I could manage to say. I wasn't exactly sure what else to say. We walked the final block in silence, slowing slightly as we got closer to my front gate. As I opened it, Ben eyed me, probably wondering whether I was going to follow through with this.

"So can I come in, or have I sufficiently scared you off yet?" he asked with that sexy smile I had grown to love, and that made me melt instantly. I fished my keys out of my purse and opened the door, looking back at him with a smile.

"Nah, you haven't scared me off. Come on," I motioned for him to follow me in. As soon as we walked through the door, Roxie was at our feet jumping and circling.

"Hey girl," Ben cooed, reaching down and petting her, "come on. Let's go outside." He grabbed for her leash and smiled at me before taking her out in the yard. I used the few minutes I had to freshen up and grab a couple of glasses of water for us and head to the living room. I turned on the stereo and settled in on the brown leather couch as Ben and Roxie came back in. He unclipped her leash and laid it on the round table in the foyer. I loved the mischievous smile he gave me as he came sauntering over. As he got closer, I could feel my breath freeze and my pulse quicken. He stopped behind the couch and gazed down at me, slowly leaning over to give me a kiss on the forehead before coming around the end of the couch to join me. My excitement about this grew with each passing moment.

"So, what do I need to do?" I asked, my voice a mixture of nervousness and anticipation.

"Just stay there. You can either lay back or sit up, either will be fine," he answered. I stretched my feet out on the couch, lying back on the arm of the couch with a smile. He rose from his seat next to me and made his way over to my head. My god! The way he looked at me gave me butterflies and made me melt all at once! He slowly knelt down next to me and I drank in every moment of his intense gaze. I could feel myself squirm a bit with desire and anticipation. His tongue slowly grazed over his lip as he as he reached out and stroked my hair. I raised up to meet him, my mouth reaching out for his. The embers that had been burning inside me ignited as his tongue met mine. His strong and sure hand slid down my cheek to my shoulder and behind my back, pulling me into him. As our kiss deepened I could feel both of our hearts pounding, and he suddenly pulled away but quickly placed his forehead against mine. He was still breathing heavily when he started talking.

"Oh, what you do to me Suzanne … Okay, let's do this while I can still concentrate! Now remember, you won't be able to hear me, but I'll still be able to hear you so please talk to me as we do this. I've never really had anyone tell me what this feels like. I've just seen their reactions."

"Okay," I nodded, taking a deep breath. As I watched him, I saw that he began to lighten and fade, then in a matter of seconds he had disappeared. I could feel the shocked expression on my face and then he quickly reappeared right in front of me in the exact same spot he was in.

"What's wrong?" he asked nervously. "Did you change your mind? Is everything okay?" he asked quickly.

"Yeah, I'm fine. I knew you were going to phase. It just looks very odd to see you fade away right in front of my eyes." I smiled sheepishly. He nodded and then disappeared again. My left hand was lying on the couch next to me, and it suddenly began to feel warm. The feeling started in the palm of my hand and began radiating outward to my fingertips. As I described the feeling out loud to Ben, the sensation started to change, like a wave of tingling and electricity passing over my skin. By now the warmth had started in my other palm as well, followed by the tingling sensation I had just felt in my left hand. As I described it to Ben, the tingling flowed up my arms in waves. It was nothing like anything I had ever felt before. My skin felt alive, like every nerve was dancing to a slow rhythm. I did my best to describe each sensation but was very soon distracted by a tingling in my nose and in my lips. I wondered to myself whether that tingling was coming from his nose and lips too.

As soon as I smiled the sensation across my lips stopped. "Where did you go?" I asked with a hint of disappointment. Almost immediately I felt a warmth that started on my chest and then deepened down through my sternum. My lips parted to describe the feeling to Ben, but I could not find the words. I let my mind drift, overcome with these new sensations. Then all of the sudden the sensation in my chest disappeared completely.

"Please don't stop. That feels amazing ... Like a warmth radiating out from my heart," I explained, with a peaceful smile spreading across my face. The feeling began again, but a little quicker this time and over a larger area. Within a matter of minutes, I could feel the warmth throughout my entire body. I did my best to describe this in as much detail as I could, but my words fell short and I was distracted by the awe of this feeling. The warmth now had a new dimension to it, and I tried my best to keep talking. To explain the feeling of fullness and pressure, like the pressure you feel diving deep under the water. As I got accustomed to the pressure, I noticed a throbbing to it. "I feel like I'm at a concert, close to a huge speaker with a thumping bass," I described, knowing that it probably didn't sound very elegant. Frankly, I was just impressed with my ability to form any sort of coherent sentence at this point. My whole mind and body were so overwhelmed I felt delirious, and I loved it!

Once I began smiling and telling him how amazing this new sensation was, I noticed the waves of fluttering over my arms returning, and my nose began to tickle. Soon after, my scalp began to prickle. I was truly breathless. All of my senses had ignited and I felt so alive! The sensation was overwhelming, but at the same time it was a peaceful and loving feeling as well. As I took a deep breath in, I noticed that the sensation of my chest moving had become weaker, almost like the feeling had been muffled. It was as if I was mentally aware of the sensation but my brain didn't feel it entirely. Soon the fluttering began to slow down and I felt a pull at my chest, then the sensation disappeared. A few moments later, Ben appeared crouched next to me by the couch. He was beaming, and caressed my hair as I blinked and pulled myself out of my dreamlike state.

"So, how was that?" he asked with curiosity, but also a sense of serenity.

"I can definitively say, that was the most exhilarating experience I've had in my entire life," I said as I sat up slowly. I could feel my cheeks flush, so I reached for my water and tried to compose myself. I placed the heavy glass back on the sandstone coaster as I looked back at him. His eyes were dancing as he looked up at me and a content smile passed over his lips. He rested his left hand on my thigh and slowly caressed it. "So what does that feel like for you?" I asked, hoping it was an equally amazing feeling for him too.

"Well," he started, but took a long pause, searching for his thoughts. "Well, it felt kind of like you were describing it from your side. The warmth and the fullness type of feeling. For me it also makes me feel sort of sluggish. Usually on the other side, you feel very light and airy, sort of carefree. This was a more grounded feeling. I can't control your body or your movements, but it's almost like I can absorb some of what you feel. So at one point I could physically feel your chest moving up and down as you were breathing," he answered with a smile.

"So what exactly were you doing? How were you sitting or lying or positioned?" I asked hurriedly. "Sorry, the detective in me is taking over now!" I laughed, and he smiled, giving me a quick kiss then joining me on the couch.

"When I very first touched you, it was my palm on your hand, then on the other hand. When your lips and nose were tingling, that's because I was kissing you." I blushed as he said that, although I'm not exactly sure why. He continued. "The fluttering on your arms? That was me running my hands up and down your arms, and then I laid down on the couch where you were," he said somewhat sheepishly. He almost looked like he was blushing. "That's why I told you to sit or lay down. I thought it would be overwhelming and I didn't want you to get disoriented or overwhelmed and fall over."

"That was probably a good idea!" I answered with a smile. I took a moment to regain myself before I continued. "That was just ... Wow, my goodness ... I can't even describe it. Thank you Ben," I said sincerely as I leaned in towards him, kissing him gently on the lips. "That was truly the most amazing experience I've ever had."

"I agree," he said with a very content smile. He rose from the couch and turned back to face me and lean down slightly to kiss my hand.

"You're not leaving are you?" I asked with perhaps a bit too much eagerness in my voice.

"No, but you seem tired. Let's go get you into bed so you can get some rest. You have to go to work tomorrow." And with that, he took my hand and led me back to the bedroom.

Chapter 16

Even though I woke up the next morning to the soothing and mellow sound of "Here's Lookin' at You," I still didn't want to have to start my day already. Since I had started hearing this song on the radio a few weeks ago, I had changed it to my alarm song. It was a calm way to wake up, and I would usually lie in bed until the song was over before getting up and moving for the morning. This morning I rolled over onto Ben's chest and enjoyed the warmth of his skin and the hypnotic rhythm of his heart beat. I could feel his fingers kneading through my hair and his hand delicately tracing up and down my back. I felt like I was in heaven here with him this morning, even if it was only for a few minutes.

As I was getting ready for the day, Ben told me that he was going to the hospital too so he would ride with me on the el. "How does that work?" I asked as I was brushing my teeth. "I mean, you can't just be walking down the street and disappear, can you? People would obviously see you." He smiled as I finished up and then answered me.

"Well, I just have to look for opportunities to phase when no one is watching. Like going into stairwells, or even just quiet hallways or rooms. It's actually not as challenging as you would think. People are so engrossed in technology these days that they are pretty oblivious to what is going on around them. I can usually find those moments within a few minutes without drawing attention to myself. Unless I'm not yet phased and the person I'm there for dies. Then I have to make a really quick exit so that I can meet them, even if it means drawing a little bit of attention."

"So how much attention are we talking about?" I asked as I starting working on my makeup.

"Well, this one time a few years ago," began with a smile, "I was following this middle aged man on a Saturday afternoon. His aura had been getting darker and darker all day and I had heard him talking to his wife about their plans to go to dinner that night. They were talking about needing to catch the 5:10 Metra into the city for their reservations, so based on the rate his aura was changing, I figured I had a few hours. So I decided to meet them at the station, and I wasn't phased. I was just sitting on a bench at the station like any passenger would. Well the station starts to fill up and he and his wife show up and are standing at the edge of the platform. Well apparently he must have done something to piss her off because they were arguing pretty vehemently and he looked like he was trying to backpedal." I looked up to see Ben's face as he was telling the story. It really was pretty fascinating to listen to him talking about his work. I smiled at him as he continued.

"So his wife is standing there with her arms tightly folded across her chest and he's hanging his head in shame, or he's trying to figure out what to do. He starts goofing around trying to cheer her up and the train whistle blows for the oncoming train. So he's still messing around and she is trying to get him to step away from the edge. Well, at the last second it looks like he's going to finally step away from the edge but then someone else stumbles on the platform and bumps into him, and he loses his balance and falls right in front of the train and gets nailed. Well pandemonium breaks out and people are looking all around screaming for help and for a doctor. So there's tons of eyes all over the place, looking for the guy who knocked into him. I couldn't very well phase because if someone had seen me and an image of my likeness made it out onto the news that would be awful," he said, making me wonder whether there was any sort of punishment or ramifications if something like that did happen.

"So what did you do?" I asked as I walked out of my bathroom to put my jewelry on.

"Well, I felt like a jerk but I pointed at someone else further down the track and said "hey, I think that's the guy" and so everyone turned and people started going after him, and I was able to sneak off and phase behind the building," he said this with almost a chuckle. I'm sure in his line of work this would be one of those stories to tell your other friends about and you would all laugh, but somehow it felt a bit unsettling to me for reasons I couldn't quite pinpoint.

"Yeah, I think I remember hearing about that a while back," I said trailing off, with a slight and polite smile. I guess this did give me some insight into how his job went, but it was not exactly what I was expecting. I suppose I was expecting it to be something more profound or revered. To think that something this monumental would be somewhat of a laughing matter for people, or more specifically for Takers, made me sad.

"What?" he asked as he looked over and noticed my demeanor. "What's bothering you?"

"No, I just thought it would be a more grandiose moment, passing from this life to the next," I answered looking down as I finished gathering my things.

"Wait Suzanne," he said, reaching out for my hand. "It is a very significant event, just like childbirth. And just like childbirth, there are stories from the delivery room that people laugh about years later. It's the same thing with the other end of the spectrum," he said with a smile. This actually did make me feel better. And it also made sense that someone would remember the more humorous ones or the ones that were out of the ordinary. How many by-the-book procedures had I done that I totally forgot about?

"Thanks Ben, that really does help," I said with a warm smile, taking his hand. He pulled me in for a hug and smoothed my hair as he did. "It's just something different for me and it sometimes catches me off-guard." I stood on my tiptoes and gave him a quick kiss before we headed out to walk towards the el station.

As we sat on the el, I started to go over my day in my mind. I knew I had a tough surgery later this morning, a bunch of post-op checks of patients, and a few pre-surgical consults. As I began preparing myself for the surgery, I couldn't help but wonder if Ben was there for my patient. Is that why he was coming to work with me this morning? I shifted uncomfortably in my seat. My mind felt so heavy today.

"Is everything alright sweetie? You seem a bit preoccupied," he asked in a sincere tone and reached for my hand. It had been a cold morning so I still had on my thin gloves. Despite the layer between us, I could feel the heat radiating off of his hand as I looked out the window. My eyes suddenly snapped down and I saw that his arm had disappeared. I nearly jumped out of my seat and pulled my hand back.

"What the hell are you doing?" I snapped, and he burst out laughing. The sound of his laugh caught me off guard, but seeing his smile made me relax back into my chair.

"Well, you didn't respond when I asked you if everything was okay, so I thought I'd see if the rest of your body was tuning me out, or just your ears," he replied with a boyish, cocky charm as he leaned back in his chair and put his arm around my shoulders, pulling me closer into him.

"I didn't know that you could partially do that," I answered truthfully. As I thought about the answer to the question he had asked me, I realized that I had also been thinking about Colin. He was working today too and I had not seen him since I walked out on him yesterday at the cafe. I honestly had no idea what to expect today. Do I ignore him? Do I try to talk to him about what happened and explain myself? Do I pretend it didn't happen? I looked back over at Ben, realizing that he was still patiently waiting for some sort of response to his question. I could tell him the truth, at least part of what I was thinking about. I didn't think I was ready to talk to him about Colin yet, especially without knowing exactly where Colin and I stood.

"I was just wondering if you were going to the hospital to take my patient today. I have surgery later this morning ..." I trailed off as I looked out the window on the other side of the el. I sat frozen, not wanting to look over at him to gauge whether I was right or not about this.

"Well, Suzanne, I really don't know. I'm not sure what her name is or even when she may be dying. Last time I was at the hospital, her aura was darkening, but she still had time. I can usually tell by how deep the hue is and how quickly it is darkening as to when to be there to take the person."

"Is it always a clear timeline, or do you have people who seem just fine and then all of a sudden they change and it's time to take them?" I asked, in full fact finding mode.

"No, it's not always that clear of a timeline. We have people who go from yellow to red at the drop of a hat, literally." He smiled a small smile. I realized that this probably was not a very easy thing to talk about. For doctors, over time we learn to talk about death in a very matter-of-fact method. That really is the only way that we are able to tell families that their loved ones did not make it. We were the ones who had to tell people the news that would shatter their world and leave them feeling empty and broken for what would seem like an eternity. To them, the doctor who bears that news must seem heartless. A stoic robot who doesn't understand and who just didn't try hard enough to save their loved one. I replayed in my head one particular conversation I had last fall with a family after I was not able to save their father, their son, her husband.

As my heart broke again reliving that moment, I decided to cut Ben some slack. I was sure this was a difficult role for him to fill too, and sometimes humor was the best way to emotionally disengage. I reached over and squeezed his hand reassuringly.

"So what happens if you're not there then? I take it they still die, right?" I whispered to him. There weren't many other people on the train right now, but I didn't want to be loud about this.

"Yeah, but if I'm not there, then they just wander around until either I get there or another Taker sees them and takes them. It's pretty rough on the person. I've seen it a few times where the Taker isn't there and the poor people just look so lost. And sometimes they don't even realize that they're dead. Whether it's denial or just the magnitude of the moment is too much to comprehend and process, they just don't understand." Ben was looking out the window as he pulled me closer to him. He appeared to be off in thought, probably remembering the times he had seen this happen. Luckily he came back to the conversation in just a couple of minutes, but this time with a light hearted tone and no more heavy discussions for the rest of the ride in to Belvidere.

We walked into the hospital, still in a light hearted mood, and walked hand in hand to the elevator to head up to begin my day. A few other people were walking by but no one else joined us in the elevator. As the doors closed, he turned towards me and leaned in, pulling me closer to him.

"I hope you have a wonderful day and I can't wait to see later," he whispered, his lips almost brushing against mine before slowly kissing me. I closed my eyes as I kissed him back. My tongue and lips began to feel warm and I could feel my heart begin to race. I smiled at the amazing sensation, but the sensation suddenly stopped. I opened my eyes to find that Ben was gone, but then felt a tingling sensation traveling up my arm. I smiled knowing that he was still here with me, even though I could not see him right now. The thought made my heart flutter and brought a smile to my face as the elevator doors opened and I stepped out into the hallway.

I took a deep breath as I approached the lounge to get settled in for the day. I knew Colin was working today but I still hadn't figured out what I was going to say to him. I didn't even know if he was going to be mad, or apologetic, or just ignore the whole thing. I could feel myself getting agitated as I started playing out the different scenarios in my head. I was brought out of my stewing by my phone buzzing in my pocket. Checking the screen, I saw Colin's name pop up and I took a breath and opened the message.

I'm sorry I was such an ass yesterday. Can I buy you lunch today?

Well, at least he realized he was the one who screwed up. I smiled and texted him back that lunch worked for me. I took a deep breath and started doing my rounds, looking forward to having lunch with Colin and getting back on the same page.

We opted for Bronze Lizard Bar & Grill a block or two away from the hospital. It was a nice, casual atmosphere with great bar food and fast service. Both of us had a full afternoon ahead, but wanted something a bit more substantial than the café we usually went to across from the hospital. After the waitress came by to take our order, Colin leaned forward, his fingers fidgeting on the table in front of him. Given that he was the one who wanted to apologize, I figured I would let him take the lead on this conversation.

"Look, Suzy," he began, still looking down at his fingers, "I don't know what got into me yesterday. That was totally uncalled for and I'm sorry. You had every right to be mad at me." He finally looked up from his hands and his eyes met mine. There was a mix of anticipation and fear in his eyes as he held his breath waiting for my response. Even though I knew I couldn't stay mad at him, I kept my face neutral and waited to respond for a few seconds. I took a drink of my water and looked back at him, still speechless.

"So ..." he pried, but still I sat silently in front of him, slowly sipping my water. He sat back in his chair with a totally dejected look. At that I just burst out laughing. "Great, so now you're laughing at me too ..." he said shaking his head.

"Sorry, sorry. I was just messing with you. You deserve it! That was really mean, what you said to me yesterday."

"I know, I know. You were totally honest with me at dinner and then yesterday too, and I just ruined that trust by behaving poorly and I'm sorry. I guess it's my fragile male ego," he said with a chuckle. "Like I said, I think I just had this on my mind longer than I let on. It wasn't fair of me to expect that, out of the blue, you happened to feel the same."

"And really Colin, I meant what I said. You *are* an amazing man and you mean the world to me. I would never want to do anything to jeopardize what we have, so starting something when I'm not in a place to put my whole heart in it just doesn't feel right."

"Yeah, I know and I would never want to push too hard on this and scare you away," he answered candidly, reaching across the table and covering my hand with his. My heart skipped a beat as he did that and I could feel a warm smile spreading across my lips. "And hey, you never know," he began again, leaning back and putting on his cocky tone, "you just may find me totally irresistible and fall head over heels in love with me one of these days." He took a drink and was smiling like a Cheshire cat as I nodded my head in an overly dramatic fashion. His tone did turn a bit more serious as he continued.

"But I suppose I do have some competition," he began. "I overheard Paulsen telling one of the other residents that she got to meet 'Dr. Jacobsen's super-hot boyfriend' last night." I looked over and he had a relaxed and joking tone about him. This was the lighthearted Colin that I had grown to know over the years. Genuine, but laid back and always ready to laugh and joke about things.

"So what part bothers you," I began as the waitress brought us our lunches, "the boyfriend part or the super-hot part?"

"Hmm, I dunno … I love the idea of you already calling some guy – correction, the grim reaper – your boyfriend after such a short period of time. But I also am totally thrilled that everyone thinks he's "super-hot" too." I could tell that this was his way of asking me how serious things were with Ben. In the past, he had never been one to flat out interrogate me about relationships, or anything really unless it had to do with one of his patients. This was more of his style to throw a comment like that out there and if I felt like answering it I would. If not, he wouldn't bring it up again.

"Okay, so the whole boyfriend thing," I began as I took a bite of my salad. "Paulsen was jabbering away about how we should go get drinks sometime after work and I was a little distracted and just being nice so I said sure, we should do that sometime. Well she got really excited and asked about that night. I was totally caught off guard so I said I had plans with my boyfriend. Ben just happened to be right outside the hospital when we walked out so I introduced them."

"He just happened to be there?" Colin asked, clearly suspicious, as he took a bite out of his burger.

"Apparently he was at the hospital yesterday and happened to overhear me say that to her, so he thought he would chance it that I meant him."

"And you didn't see him standing right behind you when you said that?"

"No, he was phased," I answered off-handedly as I took another bite.

"What?"

"Oh, right," I said as I realized I hadn't talked to him yet about this relatively new discovery. "Well, he was telling me how this stuff works the other day. There are two planes of existence, like the one we're in now, and then another one I guess after you die. He goes back and forth between them."

"So that's why you'll see him for a split second in the OR and then he's gone?"

"Yeah, and apparently I'm overly sensitive to seeing him. So even if he's on the other plane, I can usually see him unless he's really concentrating on the person he's taking." I looked up at Colin who was staring at me wide-eyed. "What?"

"You just seem so calm as you're explaining this. Like you're telling me this guy is a Hawks fan and goes fishing on the weekends ..." He looked totally shocked by this newest revelation. I hadn't realized how crazy this must sound to other people as I tried to describe Ben. I hadn't filled Cassie in on all of the details yet so I made a mental note to think it through a bit better before telling her.

"That's just a part of who he is, and I guess the way he explained it to me just made sense. I probably did a pretty crappy job of explaining it," I said sheepishly.

"No, I think I get it. But honestly, Suzy, doesn't this whole thing creep you out? I mean bouncing back and forth like that between this realm and another one? Having someone who's here but not here. That wouldn't sit well with me … I don't think I could deal with that," he said earnestly as he continued to eat his lunch.

"Well, it has taken a little bit to get used to. Probably the hardest thing is that he could literally be sitting right here and I wouldn't know it," I said as I kept eating. Colin paused from his fries as he looked at me, trying to decide how to respond.

"So he just shows up and watches you and you don't even know it?" He took a quick look around the restaurant.

"Well, if he touches me I can feel it. Yesterday, Colin, I could actually feel him inside of me," I began rambling excitedly as he pushed back in his chair, and cut me off.

"Jesus Suzy, I don't wanna hear about that shit," he said as his face scrunched up. My cheeks instantly flushed as I began backpedaling.

"No no no! I totally didn't mean it like that," I said as I blushed and kicked him under the table. I could see a wave of relief pass over his face. "We haven't, in case you're wondering. No, what I meant was that when he phases, the two of us can literally occupy the same space, so if I was sitting here and he was phased and sat in this chair too, I would be able to literally feel him inside of me. You know, taking up the same space that I am." I could feel a huge smile pass over my face as I described this recent experience in more detail to him. It still seemed to be almost dreamlike that something like that could happen to me. He did seem to listen with interest, even though I'm sure it was tough for him to hear this. I would imagine it was the curious scientist in him that was interested in hearing more about this.

By the end of our lunch, we were talking like we used to. I was relieved that we were back on the same page and that we would still be friends despite some of these hiccups. With past friends and boyfriends, it usually felt like I was walking on egg shells, so I was always on edge that any disagreement may send the relationship down an unsalvageable path. That fear of my relationships not being able to weather storms had made me feel like I had to be overly apologetic or accommodating in many of my relationships. Something I had really come to value with Colin was how we could both be ourselves and not have to put on a front for each other. We had made it through other problems before, although admittedly this was probably one of the more emotionally charged issues that had come up with us. I smiled genuinely throughout the rest of our lunch as I appreciated what an amazing friend Colin was.

After we finished our lunch and got ready to leave, he suddenly wrapped his arms around me in a big hug and leaned in close. "Suzy, just promise you'll be careful, okay?" he whispered in my ear. His sudden display of emotion was very endearing, and I told him I would. "I'll always be here for you if you need me," he said as he slowly released me and helped me with my coat.

The rest of my day went fairly smoothly and uneventfully. My patients all seemed to be doing well, and I was even having pleasant interactions with Paulsen. For whatever reason, she didn't seem to be getting on my nerves like she had the day before. The wonders of a good night of sleep I suppose.

After my day had finished, I got my things rounded up and started making my way out of the hospital to grab a smoothie from the café across the street before heading home. As soon as I stepped out, I could see the amazing site of the snow falling delicately through the crisp air. As crazy as Chicago could get, the snow falling like this always made me glad that I lived here. I stuffed my hands deep in my pockets and thought about Cassie. It had been a few weeks since I had talked to her and so much had happened. I never kept any secrets from her, so I was excited to share my experiences with Ben with her and see what her take was on it.

My conversation with her pretty much went as I expected it would. She was concerned about Ben and whether he was actually a long term potential for me, or whether he would just be gone without any word one day. I hated to admit it, but she actually had a point with that. What if he didn't have an opportunity to come back to tell me that he was going to the other side? Or worse yet, he just changed his mind and never came back?

I also filled her in on my lovely Valentine's Day encounter with Steven.

"What a pig! I can't believe he texts you earlier in the day and then is out with someone else. You definitely did the right thing ditching him," she said in a gesture of solidarity. "So who were you out at dinner with on Valentine's Day?" she asked and I could tell she had a huge smile on her face. She loved gossip and relationship stuff.

"I was actually out with Colin," I said non-challantly.

"Really? That super cute doctor you work with? I always liked him," she said, trying to see whether I had any feelings for him. "And he seemed really nice too the few times I've met him." Cassie had met him a couple of times when she was in town and she always thought highly of him. Then again, he was so easy to get along with I can't imagine anyone not thinking highly of him.

"Yeah, he's a really great guy," I began, "I just don't know if that spark is there. I mean, he's handsome, and smart, and successful and very considerate-"

"Damn, I hate those qualities in a man ..." Cassie cut me off.

"I know, right?" I joked. "But really, he's always been such a great friend, I just don't want to ruin that by jumping into a relationship so soon after Steven."

"Honey, you're talking about Ben like that's a relationship. So what's the difference there?" I thought about it for a moment before answering.

"Well, if things don't work out with Ben, I haven't exactly lost anything. I haven't known him for that long so there's not much of a loss there. With Colin, I would hate to screw things up and lose one of my best friends," I said honestly, with the harsh reality of what could happen if I screwed things up with Colin really sinking in.

"So you're penalizing Colin because he's been there by your side for years, versus someone who just came on the scene a month or so ago. Someone that you really know nothing about might I add."

"So by default Ben should lose because he's newer? I really like him Cassie and there is literally no one else like him. He is truly a unique being in this world," I said rather proud of myself on this argument that this was a once-in-a-lifetime opportunity here.

"Yeah," she began hesitantly, "but different isn't always better. If you want some 'normal' things in your life, having a ghost, for lack of a better word, may not be the right fit." She paused and waited for me to answer. I didn't really know what to say, so I just sighed.

"Ah, just my luck with men," I said sounding totally defeated. "Well, I guess we'll see what happens. Thanks for listening Cassie."

"Anytime sis," she responded and we said our goodbyes. I pressed the button on the steering wheel to end our call and a few moments later the radio came back on. I sat there listening for a few minutes, going back over my conversation with Cassie. She did have some valid points and I was grateful to have her as a sounding board. I glanced out the window as I drove through the city, taking in the wonderful ambiance that I had grown to love over the years. I tried to force myself to think about something else, but I kept coming back to my dilemma. I felt really conflicted about what I should do. Both had some wonderful qualities but I was also worried about different things with each of them.

Even as I pulled into my drive, I felt like I hadn't made any progress in my decision making. As I stepped out of the car and headed to the mailbox, I smiled to myself wondering when I may see Ben next. I seemed to run into him on the el, so maybe I needed to take that to work more often!

* * *

The next week at work drug on and on, as was usually the case in late February. Despite it being the shortest month of the year, it always seemed like the last week or so of the month took forever to pass. By that point, the bitter cold and the snow had worn out its welcome and people were just itching to get to spring time and be able to spend more time outside.

This had definitely been a long winter for me, but all of the changes in the last two months had also brought exciting new things to my life. I still hadn't made much real progress on my guy situation, despite my efforts to force things to come into focus with Ben. I knew with Colin what the hesitation was, but I had been struggling with getting my arms around the situation with Ben. It was the deeper questions of whether a future was possible, and if so what that would look like. After reaching an almost breaking point, I decided to give myself at least a few days off from the incessant thinking. I decided to just enjoy the time I spent with him and see where that took us.

On Friday evening, I came back inside from taking Roxie out and put the kettle on for cocoa as I thought about how I wanted to spend my evening. I figured I would squeeze my last few indulgences of hot chocolate before March came. After that it just seemed a little out of season. As I stood in the kitchen waiting for the water to boil, the orange flyer on my fridge caught my eye. I walked over to it and took it off the fridge, twirling the paper in my fingers. I hadn't even realized that we were coming up on the gala next weekend. I had been so preoccupied with everything with Ben and Colin that is had completely slipped my mind. I started to zone out when I began to feel my hips tingle and then a warm tingle spread across my cheek. I smiled and began to blush as Ben appeared in front of me. His hands were on my hips and he was leaning in close and kissing me on the cheek. My skin warmed in excitement as I felt his lips caressing my cheek.

"Hi there sweetheart," he said softly as he leaned back against the counter and reached out for my hands. "What do you have there?" he asked, looking down at the flyer in my hand.

"Oh this?" I said as I put it back on the fridge. "That's for the hospital fundraiser next weekend at the Planetarium. Do you want to go with me?" I smiled and felt giddy asking him out on a date. This would be the first real date for us and I was also looking forward to not going by myself. Ever since Steven had been in the ER, I felt like there were whispers and that everyone knew we had broken up. I didn't want people thinking that I was moping or traumatized by the breakup. Showing up with a gorgeous date would definitely make the evening more fun. I looked back at him as he straightened up and took a deep breath before speaking.

"Well," he sighed, "I'm not sure if that's a good idea," he said hesitantly, looking to gauge my reaction. I felt my face sink a little bit as he started to explain. "There will be a lot of hospital staff there, and if someone were to recognize me, that'd cause a big problem." He pulled my hand up and kissed my knuckles. "Sorry sweetheart," he said with a genuine tone and sympathetic look on his face.

"I thought you said people can't see you when you're phased, so how would anyone recognize you?" I asked, trying to keep my tone even. I guess this was the type of thing Cassie was talking about. The normal things I wanted in life that seemed like they may be harder to get than I thought with Ben. Just then, the kettle sounded giving me a good excuse to turn away and not have him see my disappointment.

"Well, typically they can't, but you saw me in the OR a few times. I wasn't completely phased, otherwise everyone would have seen me. You saw me even though I was just barely in your plane. There's a chance that other people over the years may have also seen me in my partial phases like that too. Usually whenever someone would get a funny look on their face, then I would be extra careful to make sure I was completely phased so that they thought they were just seeing things."

"Why did I keep seeing you then?" I asked as I stirred the cocoa powder into my cup. He laughed nervously and I could have sworn I saw him blush slightly.

"I guess I just wanted you to see me," he said with a boyish smile as I he turned to me.

"Did you want a cup?" I asked him, trying to figure out where to take this conversation. I was really disappointed and conflicted about him not coming to gala with me, but my heart sped up at thinking about him wanting me to see him. I looked over at him and he nodded, so I started busying myself making him a cup of hot chocolate as well. We gathered our cups and settled in on the sofa in the living room. Even though it was slowly beginning to warm up outside during the days, the nights were still chilly, so I pulled my brown and green chunky crochet blanket over us as we snuggled up on the couch.

As we sat there chatting, I decided I had enough of overthinking everything with Ben and Colin. For whatever reason, over the past couple of days I had gotten it into my head that I needed to make a decision right away between the two of them and it was driving me nuts. It seemed to be occupying my every free moment and it was making me read too much into everything comment, feeling and interaction. Having just gotten out of my relationship with Steven, I didn't need to take this so seriously right now. Colin had been there for me for years, so what's another week or two? And if Ben couldn't wait for a couple of weeks, then he definitely was not the right person for me either. I decided I wasn't making any decisions until after the gala. Until then, I would just enjoy myself with either one of them and see how I felt in a couple of weeks.

I moved closer to Ben and he raised up his arm so I could cuddle up next to him as we turned on a movie. He leaned over and kissed me on the top of the head as he ran his hand up and down my arm. I smiled as I felt his actual touch, enjoying the normalcy of the moment.

Chapter 17

*E*ven though Ben had told me last night that he couldn't go with me, I decided that I was going to the gala anyway. I really loved these types of things and if I didn't go, people would think I was feeling sorry for myself because of the break up. I knew a bunch of people who were going and it was good to get face time with the highers up at the hospital. I stood there looking in my closet to see what I should wear. It was Saturday morning and the gala was in a week, so if I needed to go shopping, today was the day to do it. I had a handful of dresses that I could choose from, but none of them really jumped out at me. I tried a couple of them on, but I didn't really like the way they looked. I must have been stress eating or putting on a bit of winter weight because it seemed like none of them fit me the way they used to. I definitely needed to go shopping so that I would have a great dress to wear.

I picked up my phone and looked at the time. It was 10:30am, so I texted Mandy. I always liked company for this type of shopping.

Going dress shopping today. Wanna join me? She didn't respond back right away, but she was a morning jogger, so I figured she was probably out right now. I decided to jump in the shower and start getting ready. By the time I got out, I had a reply.

Sure thing. Where do you want to meet?

Nordstrom's in an hour?
See you there!

As soon as I walked into the dress section at Nordstrom's I could hear quiet singing and I knew that Mandy was there browsing through the dresses already. As soon as she saw me she practically squealed and came bounding over to give me a hug. Her enthusiasm was contagious and that's why I loved having her come along on girly shopping trips.

"So," she said as she grabbed my hand and dragged me over to one of the racks, "are you thinking elegant?" as she ran her hand down one of the conservative dresses. "Or are you thinking sexy!?" as she reached for a slinky dress with beading down the back.

"I'm not really sure yet," I answered honestly. I hadn't thought that much about it yet.

"My vote is sexy! You want to turn heads, right?" she asked with a sparkle in her eye. That was definitely her style, and sometimes mine too. I started grabbing a variety of dresses and we headed back to the dressing room. Mandy joined me in one of the large dressing rooms as I was trying them on so we could keep talking.

"So do you have a date to the gala?" After she asked I realized I hadn't really told her anything about Ben. I wasn't sure that I wanted to tell her either. She was a pretty close friend, but she also didn't really believe in things that were outside the norm, and she was a social butterfly. If I did tell her about Ben, she would probably tell ten other people. Given his feelings about even going to the gala, I decided it was best to not say anything to Mandy.

"Nah, I'm just going to go by myself. It'll give me a chance to schmooze without having to babysit a date."

"Sounds like a good plan," she said, but I could tell there was something else she wanted to ask.

"And?" I prodded with a laugh. She blushed before she answered.

"Do you know if Colin is bringing a date?" she asked. She usually had guys falling all over her, so her asking about a guy was a bit different

"I'm not really sure. He hadn't mentioned it." After saying that, I realized that I hadn't really talked to Colin much about other things these days. I would have to remember to change that the next time we spoke. "So apparently you like him?" I asked as I slipped on another dress.

"Well, he was pretty hot, and very charming. I thought maybe there was a connection there, but I haven't heard from him since Irish Eyes and that was a month ago," she said as she held up another dress for me to try on. "Oh well, I'm guessing he's not interested for whatever reason. Here, try this one," she said with a big smile. That was one thing I had to give her. Even if she was disappointed about something like that, she was the eternal optimist. There was always someone better out there, so why dwell if one doesn't work out.

I slid on the beautiful plum, fitted chiffon dress. It was a mermaid cut with a plunging neckline, and backless with a string of silver beads at shoulder blade level that went straight across the back. Three more strings of beads draped below the cross string, making the back of the gown sparkle as I moved. The edge of the back was lined with the same silver beads with additional detail at the very base of the scoop.

"Oh my god!" she stood up and clapped her hands together. "That's perfect Suzy!"

"Are you sure?" I asked, fidgeting in place a bit. It was a gorgeous dress but I wasn't sure how much I wanted to stand out. The cut of the dress alone would make me stand out, not to mention the beads that would catch the light and sparkle. "You don't think it's too much?"

"Nah, you look great and you can totally pull it off," she reassured me with a huge smile. "Now to go look at shoes!"

After getting my dress and shoes, I was set. I already had the perfect earrings to match the beading on the dress. I had bought the earrings and a silver clutch last summer for a wedding, so I was done with my shopping for the day. I remembered how I had done my hair for that wedding too, so I planned the same style for Saturday night. I was really glad that I had gotten an afternoon out with Mandy, and that I didn't have to think about guys at all. Sometimes just a break in routine was refreshing! We said our goodbyes and I got into a cab with my dress and shoes. Now all I had to do was paint my nails on Friday night and I would be set.

* * *

Fortunately, the week went by quickly. I had a heavy patient load and managed to keep myself engrossed in my work, instead of thinking about men. I woke up with a smile on Saturday morning listening to my ringtone. I had gone to bed early the night before and gotten a good night's sleep. I rolled over and wrapped my arms around a pillow and listened to the rest of the song in a dreamy state. I heard Roxie stir, followed by a short growl and a few short barks and I sat up in bed and looked around. She scampered out of the room and I heard footsteps in the kitchen. My heart stopped and my mouth instantly felt dry.

"Hello? Who's there?" I managed to squeak out.

"Hey, it's me," Ben replied and I relaxed. I could hear his footsteps get closer as he walked down the hallway towards my bedroom. "Sorry, I let myself in. I didn't want to wake you up if you were still asleep," he said warmly. "And I brought breakfast," he said with a boyish smile as he brought a bag out from behind his back. I actually was really hungry, so that turned out to be a nice surprise.

"So what'd ya bring us?" I asked as I settled back against the headboard. It was a cream color padded leather headboard with brown buttons on it. I always loved being able to lean back against it to watch TV in bed or in cases like this, have breakfast in bed. He took long, slow strides over to the bed and set the bag down on the nightstand before leaning towards me, placing his hands on either side of me on the bed.

"Chocolate croissants," he said seductively as he leaned in and kissed me, gently at first but with a growing intensity. I reached one hand up around his back and the other in his hair, pulling him towards me. I could feel the fire starting to build inside me when he suddenly took a quick step back leaving me confused and staring at him with a puzzled look. He shot me a devilish crooked smile and spun around.

"Be right back!" he called over his shoulder.

"What? Where are you going?" I asked as I leaned forward onto my hands.

"Plates and drinks," he shouted back with a laugh. When he came back he joined me on the bed for breakfast and we spent the next several hours in bed chatting. I heard my phone chime that I had a new text message so I reached over for it. It was from Mandy. *Send me a pic when you're ready!* I looked down at the time.

"I gotta get up and moving," I said with a smile as I climbed out of bed. Ben grabbed my hand and pulled me back towards him.

"Why? Can't you stay in bed for a little while longer?" he asked as he kissed my cheek.

"Today's the gala, so I should get up-"

"It's only a little after noon," he protested before I continued.

"Well it's almost lunch time and then I need to start getting ready for tonight," I said with a smile. He let go of my hand and the corners of his lips curled down in a pout.

"I know, I just wish I could go with you," he said sadly as I started to walk towards the closet to throw on some clothes for lunch before getting in the shower. His chocolate brown eyes watched me as I walked away from him.

"If you really wanted to," I said as I turned towards him and leaned against the doorway to the closet, "then why don't you come with me?" I asked sincerely, but I'm sure there was a snotty tone to it.

"Suzanne, you know I can't go ..."

"Yeah, yeah, it's lunch time then," and I threw a sweatshirt at him as I grabbed one for myself and headed to the kitchen to make us something for lunch.

After a long hot shower, I was finally able to clear my head and get in a happy frame of mind for the gala. I had been really disappointed earlier in the day that Ben had showed up and then reminded me that he wasn't going to go with me. It did make sense but it still was disappointing. And it was exactly what Cassie was talking about. If anything ever happened to me and I had to be in the hospital, would he even come to see me or would he have to stay away because people may recognize him? After having thought about it over and over in the shower, I was finally done thinking about it and was happy to be looking forward to the party.

Once I was finished getting ready, I texted a picture to Mandy like she asked for and caught a cab to the Planetarium. I vowed to myself that I would not let myself get caught up thinking about Ben. I deserved a break and an enjoyable evening. With that determination building in me, I looked out the window for the rest of the cab ride and watched the city lights pass me by on the way to the Planetarium.

I climbed up the stone steps to the entrance and showed the doorman my ticket before heading inside. I smiled as I took in the grandiose entry hall and the buzz of the atmosphere made me smile. After checking my coat, I headed to the bar to get a glass of chardonnay and start making my rounds.

"Hey Suzanne," I heard a familiar voice call my name and I turned to see Howard and his wife walking up to join me in line. He leaned in and gave me a kiss on the cheek. "You remember my wife Maddie," he put his arm around his wife as she stepped forwards to shake my hand.

"Of course, it's good to see you again." I remember having met her a few other times and she was always a very sweet woman and quite the social butterfly at events. She was a petite woman with a slender frame, and her very toned arms showed from under her wrap. During one of our conversations at a prior event, she had told me she played tennis and played in a ladies golf league. Her hobbies definitely served her well. She had her usual winter tan which was complimented by her long, soft blond waves, and she looked stunning in her red satin gown. We made our way over to the bar, which was just inside the first hall. The room was fairly dark with soft blue lights around the ceiling that gave the whole room a relaxing hue. Normally it would have been the waiting hall for one of the domed auditoriums they use for the star shows, but today they had covered pub tables scattered throughout and benches along the walls so people could enjoy the ambiance. Along one of the walls, they also had a table with a description of the live auction items, as well as maps of the layout of the Planetarium, where to find the silent auction items and our table numbers for dinner.

We chatted as we waited in line at the bar and then I excused myself to check out the auction table and my table assignment. I loved the Planetarium so it was nice to get to come and see it in a different setting. Despite my excitement about the evening, I did have a twinge of disappointment at not having a date to sit with and to dance with later on. I groaned as I looked down at the place cards. Apparently I had forgotten to let them know Steven was not going to be joining me tonight. When I first RSVP'd to the event, we were still together. I had thought about dropping my "plus one" but had decided to see if Ben was going to come with me. After that, I must have just forgotten. That also meant that we would be one person short at our table for dinner, and I was hoping that no one would ask me about it or comment on it.

As I was tucking his place card into my purse, Jane came practically scampering over to join me at the table. I couldn't help but smile at her and her energy. Even though it could sometimes be overwhelming, in general it was a pretty contagious energy. She made small talk for a bit with me before asking me if Ben was here with me.

"No, he wasn't able to make it tonight. He had a work thing," I answered, with a sad reminder of why he actually wasn't here. Although technically I guess it was a work related reason for not being here.

"Oh, sorry to hear that. Well there's plenty of fun to be had on our own, right?" she said with a sincere smile. She lifted her glass of wine and clinked glasses with me. She was here on her own too, so we walked into the main pavilion together and continued to chat. After about ten or fifteen minutes more with Jane, I excused myself and headed over to the hors d'oeuvres table in the main hall. I talked to a few other people I recognized from work before I got another glass of wine. I meandered through the planetary exhibit that was centered around an enormous sphere through the center of the building that was painted to look like the sun. All of the other planets were constructed to scale and had their own stations with various facts and statistics, as well as some of them having interactive activities to accompany them. After about fifteen or twenty minutes of wandering around the planets, I headed off towards the moon exhibit. Space always fascinated me so I was thoroughly enjoying the educational part of the evening, as well as the party portion. But being here on my own was a bit tougher than I thought it would be. It would be nice to take a break from the pleasantries and actually have some company.

The thought pulled my mood down a level and I couldn't help but think about my predicament again. I mentally scolded myself for breaking my vow and I decided to go out onto the terrace to clear my head. It was a surprisingly beautiful Chicago night. Even though it wasn't particularly warm out, the night air was crisp and clear. As I made my way over to the railing, I saw Nurse Chapel standing by herself at one of the pub tables. Her hair was pulled back tightly, like usual, but with a bit more flare than normal, with some rhinestone pins. Her conservative navy blue dress fit her uptight personality quite well, but it was classy and timeless.

"Good evening, Nurse Chapel," I said politely as I walked towards her table on the way to the edge of the patio.

"Good evening, Doctor," she said warmly but in a tone that did not seem particularly conversational, so I kept slowly walking past her. I leaned forwards on the railing, staring out over Lake Michigan with my wine glass in my hands. I closed my eyes and took a deep breath as I focused my attention on how lucky I was to have my dream job in such an amazing city. I tried to also remind myself that I had a long life ahead of me so there was no need to rush into anything or dwell on any one detail or situation for too long. I took another deep breath in, focusing on the stillness of the moment and the sound of my breath.

I heard the patio door open and what sounded like a man's footsteps, followed by Nurse Chapel's footfalls as she walked back inside. There was a low murmur of pleasantries as the two passed each other. Just as I started to shiver, I felt the man walk up behind me.

"Cold Suzanne?" the man asked and I smiled as I heard the rich, smooth voice coming from behind me. I instantly smiled as I felt a tuxedo coat being placed over my shoulders.

"Thanks Colin," I responded without even turning to confirm that it was him. My heart fluttered as I turned to face him and my breath hitched as I took in the sight of him. He was cleanly shaven and his blue eyes danced in the moonlight. His lopsided grin and wavy blond hair made him absolutely striking, or I suppose it could have been the couple of glasses of wine weighing in as well. His broad shoulders looked divine in his dress shirt.

"You look absolutely stunning Suzy," he murmured with a smoldering gaze. I shifted my weight and blushed as he said that. "Oh sorry," he continued, "I'm not supposed to pressure you." He smiled as leaned back. "You look okay I guess," he laughed as he looked out over the black water.

"Thanks!" I said as I playfully hit him with my purse. "You pretty much look like a bum too," I chided back. We both stood there in silence for a few minutes, looking out into the inky black water and up at the stars. I finally broke the silence.

"So ... no date for tonight?" I asked, and not just to make small talk.

"Nah," he sighed, "I didn't really have anyone to ask." He looked at me with a look that cut straight through me. "Wouldn't really be appropriate to ask someone who already has a boyfriend, now would it" he said very directly, but with a wry smile. "And my heart really wasn't in it to go out looking for a date." His honesty still caught me off guard. I suppose I was used to the way Steven would spin things, or as I had come to find out recently, straight up lie to me.

"Not even Mandy? She asked about you last week you know."

"Really? I hope she didn't get the wrong idea-"

"No, she's fine. She just asked if you had a date for tonight and I said I didn't think so. So she's moving on. Trust me, she doesn't dwell!"

"That's good. But what about you?" he continued. "Where's your super-hot boyfriend?" he said with a smile.

"Well," I took a deep breath and I could see him shift, "he said he can't really go to these types of things. He said someone may recognize him, so he wouldn't be able to go with me." As I spoke, I could feel the tone in my voice shift. We both stood there in silence and I slowly nodded my head. Thankfully he let that go without another comment on the subject. A few more minutes passed with us both silently staring at the inky black water that reflected the moon so beautifully. I shivered again, but only slightly.

"Come on," Colin said, turning and putting his arm around me. "Let's get you inside and warmed up," he said as he led me inside with his hand on the small of my back.

Over the next hour, we walked in and out of the exhibits, as well as checking out one of the star theaters that the Planetarium had open for people to come and go as they pleased. After heading to the bar to get another drink, we began perusing the silent auction items. It was always interesting to see what items they were able to pull together for this event. Some years seemed dominated by sporting event tickets and memorabilia, and other years it seemed dominated by artwork that I didn't quite get. This year was a nice mixture of things, a few of which actually caught my eye. With the bidding still going for another two hours though, I wasn't going to put my name down just yet.

We made our way back into the main hall where the band had just begun playing. The hospital definitely knew how to choose a band! This year, the band had both a male and female old time crooner. As the band started playing a cover of Etta James's "At Last", Colin took our drinks and placed them on an empty pub table by the edge of the dance floor. He then silently led me out to the center, spinning me around once before putting his arm around my waist and pulling me into him.

We continued to talk lightheartedly as we danced through that song and the next two as well. I had been out dancing years ago with him and his friends, but it had been quite some time since I had danced with him and I had to admit it, he really was a very good dancer. And in a tuxedo, he had a debonair air about him that made him look even more attractive, if that was even possible.

When the next song came on, we both decided to take a break from dancing.

"I'll be right back," I said as we headed off the dance floor. "I need to go freshen up." He nodded and I made my way over to the ladies restroom. As I walked towards the mirror, I saw Maddie coming out of one of the stalls.

"Hi Suzanne," she chirped as she walked over to the sink and smiled at me. I returned the pleasantry and leaned forward to apply another coat of lipstick. "You and Colin make such a great couple," she exclaimed as she fluffed her hair.

"Oh, we're just friends," I responded shyly as I could feel my cheeks flush. I quickly grabbed for my powder.

"Really? That's too bad. You two look so natural together and I could have sworn I saw both of your eyes twinkling while you were dancing," she said with a very knowing smile. She washed her hands and reached for a hand towel.

"Really ..." I said, not knowing what else to say. I was sort of in shock that she would say that. And moreover that it would be so noticeable to someone else. It made me freeze in place for a few moments before I continued powdering.

"Oh for sure! You can definitely feel the chemistry when you two are together. If I were you, I wouldn't let him get away," she said with a smile as she tossed her towel away and walked out of the bathroom. I smiled and nodded as she left and then stood there looking at myself in the mirror. As I looked at my reflection, I was trying to picture my future five years down the road. I couldn't help but think about Colin and how great of a night I was having with him, but as I thought about it, I also missed having Ben here with me. My thoughts were interrupted as another woman walked into the bathroom, so I finished up and walked out.

As I made my way back to the main hall, I saw Colin leaning up against the wall in the hallway.

"Hi there beautiful," he said as he stood up and handed me a glass of white wine. He looked at me with those adoring eyes as he leaned in and gave me a long kiss on the cheek.

"Thanks," I responded sheepishly as I felt my pulse quicken at his touch. Even after he stepped away, I could still feel the tingle where his lips had touched my skin.

"Let's get some air," he said as he led me towards the terrace with his hand on the small of my back.

"Thank you for an amazing night Colin," I began as we stepped out onto the patio. "I really have had a good time."

"I'm glad Suzy, me too."

"And apparently other people have noticed too. In the bathroom Howard's wife told me we look really great together," I said with a laugh as I took another drink of wine.

"Is that so?" he asked with a genuinely pleased look on his face. He took the last sip of his red wine and eyed me, contemplating whether to say anything or let me take the lead on this conversation.

"Apparently," I replied simply and looked out over the edge of the railing. Two could play at that game.

"You know," he began as he slid over closer to me, his arm touching mine, "we could be if that's what you wanted. I still feel the same way I did at dinner-"

"And what way would that be?" A booming and edgy voice cut him off, startling both of us.

Chapter 18

We quickly turned back around to see Ben standing there in a tuxedo, eyeing both of us. His hands were buried deep in his pockets and his stare was icy. I hadn't felt cold before he showed up, but I felt my whole body shiver and instinctively I hugged my arms across my chest.

"Hi Ben," I began slowly as I started to walk towards him. "I thought you said you wouldn't be able to make it." I'm sure the surprise in my voice registered with him as guilt, although truthfully I didn't think I should feel guilty at all. He said he wasn't going to go with me, so I was just enjoying my evening rather than sulking at home. If he would have come with me in the first place it wouldn't be an issue. And frankly, him acting like we were exclusive rubbed me the wrong way. Never once had that conversation come up, nor had any conversation about what we really were in terms of relationship.

"Let's just say I felt like I should probably be here," he answered smugly, giving Colin an evil glare.

"And just what's that supposed to mean?" Colin asked brusquely.

"I mean, I'm tired of watching you hitting on Suzanne constantly."

"Well, maybe you should stop watching then," he retorted with a sarcastic tone, but his eyes were very serious, as opposed to the way they sparkled when he was joking around.

"Good grief," I sighed. Maybe some women would like two guys fighting over her, but this was definitely not enjoyable. I was flattered, yes, but it was also not the most attractive side of males to see this posturing, particularly when I was not in an established relationship with either one.

"Yeah, and maybe you should stop fawning over my-"

"Enough!" I cut him off. This was getting uncomfortable. I looked away and when I turned back I saw the two of them slowly making their way towards each other, chests lifted and chins up.

"Seriously?" I exclaimed in exacerbation, probably louder than I should have. I walked over towards them but was distracted by the sound of the balcony door opening. All three of us turned our heads towards the sound but Ben quickly looked away. It was Nurse Chapel heading back out.

"Nurse Chapel," Colin said politely and with as sweet of a tone as he could muster.

"I'm sorry if I disturbed you, Doctor," she began but she was looking over at Ben. Before she could even say anything he turned sharply and walked back through the doors into the Planetarium. "Who was that man that was here with you? I thought he looked familiar," she said wistfully. She had a far off look in her eyes and a small smile played across her lips before she shook her head slightly and brought herself back into our conversation.

"He's just a friend of Suzanne's. Excuse me, I need to go get a refill," he said and quickly excused himself. I was hoping he wasn't planning on doing anything stupid, like going after Ben. I know Nurse Chapel was sometimes a difficult one to engage in conversation, so I was hoping that was the only reason he was leaving right now. From what I could see, it looked like they went opposite directions after they walked through the doors, so I relaxed slightly. I would have preferred to go inside as well, but I didn't want to be rude, so I stayed in my spot while I looked back over at her.

"Well, I didn't mean to drive everyone away," she said nervously as she looked past me. I had to say, this was the most emotion I had ever seen out of her, or so it seemed.

"No, they were finishing up their conversation," I said non-challantly.

"Well, it seemed to be an argument, so I suppose it was fortuitous that I came out before things escalated." While she was in fact correct, something about the way she said that made me uncomfortable. It was as if she was inserting herself into the mix like we were all close friends.

"I suppose you're right," I responded politely with a small head nod. "I really should be getting back inside. It's rather chilly and I don't want to catch cold. Excuse me," I said politely as I walked towards the door. Right as I walked past her, I could see her emotions shift but I could not read exactly what they had shifted to. She closed her eyes as she took in a long breath and held it before loudly exhaling right as I reached for the door to the balcony.

After heading back inside, I made my way straight for the bar to get something cold to drink. I didn't want to have too much to drink and say something stupid, so I was planning on just getting a Diet Coke. As I stood in line, Jane came bounding up to me and I could tell she had been having a good time.

"So that's great that your boyfriend was able to come!" she was beaming, and she was swaying a little bit. Thank goodness she wasn't on call this weekend.

"Yeah, I'm glad he was able to make it too," I said, with sarcasm dripping from my words. Luckily she was tipsy enough to not pick up on it. It was also a little off-putting that she kept drooling over Ben. I know he did have a magnetism that I couldn't explain, but it still irritated me that she seemed to be fawning all over him almost every time she was around me.

"Look, Paulsen, I know you don't mean anything by it, but let's keep the boyfriend comments to a minimum. This is still new and we're not really sure exactly where we stand." I could tell that my tone was clipped, but I didn't mind given that I was getting annoyed with her.

"Oh my gosh Dr. Jacobsen, I'm so sorry!" she gasped, turning crimson as she began fidgeting nervously. "I really didn't mean anything and I hope I didn't say anything totally stupid." She looked mortified which made the irritation ebb, so I threw her a bone.

"No, no you're fine. I'm just not sure exactly where things stand so I don't want to be making a big deal out of this. And I try to keep my personal life out of work. I don't want to be the subject of water cooler gossip if you know what I mean." I kept my tone lighthearted so as to not come across as being too pretentious, thinking that people didn't have better things to do with their time than gossip about me.

"Right, right," she answered, sounding dejected. She clasped her hands in front of her hips and didn't say anything else. Given that I was going to have to see her a lot over the next three months, I decided to try to bail her out.

"Really, no worries," I assured her and gave her a warm smile before continuing. "So how're you enjoying your first hospital gala?" I asked, trying to change topics.

"Oh, it's been great," she smiled, but the smile didn't quite reach her eyes.

"Your dress is gorgeous!" I continued, trying to bring her back to her normal state. "Have you gotten your picture taken yet?" She shook her head no. "I would definitely get one," I said and began looking around the room. Could this drink line be any slower? I didn't want to just walk away since that would be overtly rude, but I also wasn't particularly interested in carrying on a long conversation right now with her. I was going over excuses in my head when I felt a hand on my back and I turned my head to see Colin joining us in line.

"Excuse me Dr. Paulsen, but I need to borrow Dr. Jacobsen for minute," he said with a polite smile. She nodded and thought nothing of it, which made me grateful. We walked over to one of the pub tables in the blue hued room and he leaned in close before speaking. His tone was quiet, so I could tell this wasn't going to be a good conversation.

"Suzy, what the hell is going on? You tell me this guy isn't going to be here, then he shows up like a stalker, says a few heated words and leaves?"

"Apparently so ..." I began, not really knowing how to answer. I sighed but Colin said nothing in response. He just looked at me with guarded blue eyes, waiting for something more. "He told me he wasn't coming because he didn't want to risk anyone recognizing him. I'm guessing he was there listening and was just phased. Otherwise that's a hell of a coincidence on the timing of him making an appearance."

"You know," he began carefully, but then seemed off in thought. "I think you're right. I don't remember hearing the balcony door open. Granted I may have had my mind on other things ..." he said with a smile. "But really," he continued, "are you okay with this? Him just watching you while you don't know it?" He looked very serious about this question. Not like he was trying to get me to change my mind about Ben so that he could have me, but sounding like legitimate concern for me.

"It takes a little bit of getting used to," I answered, "but I do think it's sweet to know that he's looking out for me. I feel very safe when I'm out on the el or walking around at night. I feel like I can do anything or go anywhere because he'll always be there to watch out for me." I paused and looked up at Colin to see his reaction. There was a quiet acceptance of that statement so I figured I would continue. "I realize that for a man that's probably fairly nebulous, but for women I guess that's something we think about, whether we specifically say it or not."

When I looked up and caught his eye, there was a hint of sadness to him. I wasn't sure whether it was because he thought he was losing me to Ben or if he was trying to figure out if he had something comparable to that to offer.

"You know Suzy ..." he began in a sad tone, but trailed off and then decided to change direction. "Look, it's great that you feel safe around him. I mean, that is really important, but how do you know if he really is watching out for you? I wouldn't go taking lots of risks assuming he's there to watch you. You did say he has another job to do. I just don't want to see you getting hurt, actually physically hurt, because you're banking on him being your guardian angel all day long." He still had that look of sadness in his eyes, but there was also a pleading. Pleading for me to listen to what he was saying and give it some real consideration.

"Yeah, I know. I guess ... I just ..." I stammered, not really sure of where to take the conversation. I felt my chest constrict and a dull burn in the pit of my stomach. I couldn't decide though what exactly was causing the ache that was swelling up inside. Was it because Colin was right about Ben? Or that I was starting to develop real feelings?

"Suzy, wouldn't you rather have someone who was actually there with you holding your hand late at night when you're walking home from the el? Rather than the idea that someone might be watching over you to keep you safe?" His last comment cut right to the heart of my fears after my conversation with Cassie.

I needed to clear my head and figure out where this was going. I frowned as I looked down at my fingers that had been knotting together on the table in front of me.

"Well, I think I'm going to go catch a cab," I said quietly as I looked up and gave him a sad smile.

"Look, I'm sorry. I didn't mean to upset you. You don't have to leave so early," he protested.

"No, I really do think I should get going," I responded as I scooped up my clutch and straighten up, sucking in a deep breath.

"I can share one with you. Make sure you make it home alright." Always the gentleman, but also likely lobbying for his position. And Ben's words still stung. The fact that he thought I had turned my back so quickly on him had really upset me.

"I'll be okay," I insisted. "Plus, if anyone saw that little tiff outside, I don't want them to see us leaving together in a cab. I'll be fine, promise. See you on Monday?"

"Yeah, sure," he looked rather defeated. "Have a good rest of your weekend," he smiled with sad eyes as he quickly squeezed my hand that was on the table. He gave me one last smile as he walked backward a couple of steps before turning and walking away into the main hall again. I sighed and shook my head, making my way to the coat check.

On the cab ride home, my mind was going a hundred miles an hour trying to process my feelings, particularly for and about Ben. I knew that part of the appeal was the Taker aspect of him, and maybe even a hint of wanting what you can't have. Perhaps that is what this all came down to: I couldn't have him. The part that my mind kept wrestling with, though, was whether I wanted to have him, and if I did then why? Why did this have to be so damn hard? The more I was around Colin these days the more I seemed to be drawn to him. I couldn't understand it though because we had been friends for years without any of these feelings.

He had always been a solid fixture in my life, both personally and professionally. The more I thought about it, it really was fear that was holding me back. Fear of what would happen if things didn't work out. And Ben. Ben was holding me back. I was very much attracted to him, but it almost seemed like infatuation, the way fans are drawn to celebrities. It's not necessarily the person themselves but rather what that person represents.

By the time I got home, the feelings of inner turmoil had gotten worse. If anything, I had more questions and more conflicting opinions than before. After taking Roxie out, I came back in and kicked off my silver heels next to the front door, setting my clutch on the round mahogany foyer table. I made my way into the kitchen and grabbed a glass of water before settling onto the couch with my blanket and turning on the television. I was fairly awake, so I mindlessly searched through the listings for a chick flick to zone out to while I continued thinking. I had read somewhere that couples who watched chick flicks together had higher rates of staying together, even slightly higher or on par with those who went to counseling. I chuckled to myself as I picked one and snatched Roxie up onto my lap.

As I slowly sipped my water, I came to the conclusion that I had to stop thinking about "choosing" between Ben and Colin. This wasn't a one-or-the-other scenario. I needed to make a decision on each independently. Now if I affirmatively chose both of them I would have a problem, but my intuition told me that wouldn't be the case. Given that I had reservations about both of them, I needed to be honest about my feelings and be prepared that the result may be no for both. Yes, I was certain I needed to decide firmly yes or no to each one at a time. And I told myself that answering No to the first one did not mean by default that I was choosing the second. I had already talked about this with Colin at dinner and told him I wasn't in the right place at this point, so

I opted to make my decision about Ben first. In order to make a real decision, I needed to put my feelings about Colin aside for the time being and give Ben a real shot.

By the time I finished my water, I felt at peace for the first time in days with the direction things were going. Over the next few days, I was really going to dig into my feelings for Ben and what our future may hold. If we were able to have any sort of future, he would need to start answering some important questions for me and to trust me enough for this to move forward, if that is what was meant to be. With some sense of progress, I plodded back to my bedroom, put on comfy pajamas, and curled up under the covers and drifted off to sleep.

Chapter 19

I awoke with a start and shot straight up in bed gasping. Immediately I felt arms around me and panic surged through me. I instantly whipped around and looked to see Ben's chocolate brown eyes searching my face. After a few quick gasps, I began to slowly relax. He pulled me back against him and smoothed my hair as he kissed my head. My trembling hands reached up to rest on his arms.

"It's okay sweetie," he said in a smooth, silky voice. "It was just a bad dream." I wasn't sure why, but I felt safe right now in his arms. I should have felt mad or scared that I had gone to bed alone and woke up in the middle of the night with him there, but there was an instant calming effect that his voice had on me and I melted back into him. For the first time in a long time I actually was able to relax after one of my drowning dreams and fall back asleep.

I felt a mild stirring beneath me as I awoke the next morning. I slowly opened my eyes to see Ben underneath me and as I curled up on his smooth bare chest. The sky had just begun to lighten, and the beautiful orange hue out my window made me smile. I curled in closer to Ben and kissed him gently on the lips until I saw his eyes flutter. He really was gorgeous with his strong, chiseled features and his mahogany colored hair.

"Good morning beautiful," he purred with soft, dreamy eyes. He put his free hand behind his head and smiled at me.

"Hi yourself," I replied sweetly, returning his gentle smile.

"Did you sleep alright?" he asked as his eyes searched mine.

"Surprisingly I did," I began as I propped my head up on my hand. "Usually if I have a really bad dream then I can't go back to sleep. I guess I just felt better having you here," I said honestly. The realization made a warmth stir in belly and I smiled lovingly at him.

"I'm glad," he replied. "So would you like to go out for breakfast this morning? Anywhere you'd like."

"Sure, that sounds great. There's a little café a few blocks down." I was also hoping that today maybe we could talk and I could get some answers to some of these bigger questions I had about our future and whatever that might mean. I eagerly got dressed while Ben took Roxie out and then I met him at the door with my coat on.

As we began a leisurely stroll to the café, I figured now was as good a time as any to start our conversation.

"So when did you come in last night? I went to bed by myself and then when I woke up in the middle of the night you were there," I decided to start with what I thought would be a few easier questions.

"Well, I guess it was probably about two or three in the morning," he answered pretty matter of factly. When I didn't immediately respond, he continued. "Is that okay that I came over? I mean, I didn't want to wake you up by calling in the middle of the night."

"No, yeah that's fine that you came over last night," I replied. But it still didn't exactly sit well with me that he just kept coming over unannounced. "I guess … I just … It just feels awkward that I never know when you're going to be there or not. You don't call before you come over, or even knock when you're there," I answered as I kept the leisurely pace. I also reached out and took his hand as we continued down the road in order to help keep the tension down during this conversation.

"Would you rather I call first?"

"Well …" I began, suddenly losing my confidence a bit as I was caught off guard by his very innocent and direct tone. "Yeah, I think so. I mean, it's still so new in our relationship that it just feels rushed or something. Don't you think?" I glanced towards him to see how he would react.

"I suppose for me it just feels a little different," he answered with a reassuring squeeze of my hand.

"How so?" I asked.

"I just feel like I know you so well and that we have this … connection," he said with a smile. I wasn't sure what to think. His answer did not exactly give me any insight as to why he felt so much more towards me. I felt like I was starting to get to know him, but I certainly didn't feel like I knew him very well. I furrowed my eye brows as I thought about this. We ambled down the sidewalk in silence for a few minutes, hand in hand, when it suddenly occurred to me. The only real way he could feel so much closer to me.

"Do you watch me when you're phased? Where I can't see you?" I asked quickly, attempting to keep an even tone and not sound as appalled by the idea as I really was. He did not immediately respond, so I was guessing that meant he had. "The truth Ben," I added as I stopped and pulled him towards me so that he had to look at me. He blushed quickly and his eyes flicked over my shoulder before returning to meet my gaze.

"I have," he answered sheepishly.

"How many times," I asked in a soft but assertive tone. He paused again. "I take it more than once?"

"Yes," he replied.

"Ben," I pleaded. "How many times."

"Honestly, I don't remember. But it was more than just a few times," he said looking down. I decided to keep us moving forward so I started walking towards the café again.

"So where all have you watched me then?" I swallowed, wondering if I really wanted to know the answer.

"At work. At home. Sometimes when you're out walking by yourself or out and about." Based on his body language and tone, I could tell he was mildly uncomfortable with this admission, but he didn't apologize. I kept moving myself forwards as I processed this. It felt like such a violation, but then again, wasn't this exactly what I told Colin that was great about him? That he could watch out for me and keep me safe? Some of my uneasiness began to subside, but Colin's issues of feeling like Ben was stalking me were starting to echo around in my head, giving Ben's admission an almost sinister feel to it. He continued staring straight ahead until we came upon the café, and then he looked over in my direction. "You've hardly said a word. What's on your mind?"

I was trying to get my thoughts in order as we made our way into the café and found a table by the window.

"Didn't your other girlfriends think it was weird that you watched them without them knowing?" I asked, trying to get him to give me some insight on the spying as well as how a relationship might work with him. The waitress came by and quickly took or order. Even though the place was not very busy, she seemed to be in a hurry and it seemed very awkward.

"Well," he began, "this might come as a shock to you but I don't often date or have girlfriends." He smiled sheepishly at me.

"Never?" I was not sure if I believed his answer or not. He seemed to be holding something back. The way his eyes darted as I pressed him about it made me think I was right. "Come on Ben, you were the one who said we need to be honest with each other." There was a long pause before he continued.

"I know," he let out a deep sigh before continuing. "Yeah, I had a girlfriend a while back. After things ended, I swore I wasn't going to date anyone again."

"Really? You were that heartbroken that you swore off love? How long ago was this?" I tried to keep the mocking tone down, but this really did seem a bit overly dramatic for a failed relationship. The waitress had come back with our drinks and hurried off again. Perhaps she could feel the tension between us and did not want to interrupt us.

"No, not exactly. It was more about the way that it affected her." He took a deep breath and then took a long drink of his orange juice.

"Cough it up. You spy on me when I don't know it, so you can spill the beans on this," I answered with a smile and took a sip of my mimosa, leaning back in my chair and getting ready for a long discussion.

"Well," he began slowly as he tried to pull his thoughts together, "about 10 or 15 years ago I met this woman. She saw me one day when I was partially phased. That was the first time anyone had ever noticed me, so I was naturally curious. I wasn't sure whether it was something about her, or something that I was doing differently. So I decided to try different things. I would concentrate a lot on how I was phasing and what felt different to me, and then watch for her reactions. That's how I learned to control my phasing as well as I did."

"So is there something special about you, or do all Takers do that and it was just your first time learning?" I hadn't really talked to him much about how he learned how to do the things he does.

"I asked around and I only ran into one other Taker who had said that some people could see him when he was partially phased. He had worked on learning to control his phasing too. Ronnie helped me learn to control it. He said he had spent years practicing it, so I sort of took lessons from him. Eventually, I got to the point where I thought I was pretty good, so I tried in front of her to control my phasing, and I was shocked to find out I actually had learned the skill pretty well." He sighed as he looked out the window of the café. He took a long drink of his juice before leaning back in his chair and bringing his gaze to meet mine again. He didn't speak. He just looked at me, his eyes searching mine for something. I quietly returned his stare, wondering why he was being so distant about this.

"Why are you so interested in this anyway?" he asked earnestly.

"I just want to know more about you. I feel like we talk about me a lot, and you watch me a lot, so I wanted to put you in the hot seat for a while," I answered with a smirk before continuing. "So, you found out that you're pretty good at phasing ..." I said, intentionally trailing off to spur him to continue.

"Yes, I did," he said rather coolly. "And you're not a very good liar either," he added with a curt smile. "I know there's more to this conversation than you asking about an ex-girlfriend."

"So what happened with the two of you?" I asked bluntly, guessing that he was not going to offer up any additional information without me prodding him a bit more. He sighed and shook his head before continuing.

"We dated for a couple of years, and things didn't end very well. That was what made me turn my back on relationships."

"Come on Ben," I began with a soft kick under the table and another drink of my mimosa. Our food had just arrived and we both began eating. "Are you going to talk to me or do I have to guess what happened?" He shifted in his chair and eyed me suspiciously. I could see a crease start to form on his brow and the hint of a grimace crept up along the corners of his mouth. I had never seen him like this before, and I wasn't sure whether this side of him, this vulnerable and pained side, drew me closer to him or was making me think twice about what I was doing with him.

"Suzanne, you're acting rather out of character this morning. You usually are not this curt with your responses and so ... I don't know, maybe unenthusiastic is the word. Like your interaction with me today is a chore. What's really on your mind?" he asked sincerely as he too began eating. I could hear the concern in his voice, rather than the irritation that I would have expected.

"I just ..." I began, but didn't know how to finish that thought. "I guess I want to know more about you and your past. It gives me some sense of context of what I can expect the future may hold for us." I couldn't tell whether this confession had strength behind it, or whether it was a juvenile question, so I looked down at my crepes and waited for him to answer. He let out a sigh, but then continued.

"The longer we dated, it seemed like the harder it got for her. In the beginning everything was new and exciting, so she didn't mind the Taker aspect of me, or the disappearing or not being able to go out much together. We tried to work through it, but over time it really took a toll on our relationship. Towards the end, she kept pushing on wanting to be together, like a more traditional relationship. She wanted me to spend holidays with her and her family, meet her friends, and things like that. Not that what she was wanting was anything outrageous, but it just wasn't really possible."

"Why isn't it possible? Because you don't want to do those things, or that you literally cannot do them?" This was exactly what I was needing to know and what had been making me reticent about him.

"Technically, we're not supposed to be interacting with living people in our everyday lives. People aren't supposed to know about us. That's why you never knew we existed until you and I met. If I were to be interacting with a lot of people, like a family around the holidays, then that just exposes too many people to me. That's also why I couldn't go to the gala with you," he answered with a sadness to his voice and to his eyes. He seemed to genuinely wish things could be different, but there just was not a lot to be done about it.

"So would you be in trouble if other Takers knew about you and I?"

"Probably," he answered with a smile.

"So," I began hesitantly, "what ever happened with her then?" I saw his face drop almost instantly when I asked the question, and I started to regret pushing this topic. He took another bite to buy himself some more time before answering my question.

"We kept trying to make it work, but it was wearing on her. She started to get resentful, and no matter how much we tried, we just couldn't get on the same page. She didn't like me disappearing on her all time and she became really depressed. Eventually, she tried to kill herself," he said solemnly as he looked out the window. A melancholy had spread over his face and he inhaled sharply as he shook his head slightly and looked over towards me. I had no idea how to respond to this, so I just looked back at him with what I was hoping was a sincere look.

"She said she wanted to be with me forever, and that if we were both on the same side that it would make things so much easier." He leaned back in his chair and ran his hand through his short, dark hair. His eyes had found the table next to us and he kept his attention focused there for a few moments before running his hand across his face. His fingers ran thoughtfully along his jawline, teasing at the stubble that had grown in overnight.

"Ben, I'm so sorry," I said softly as I reached across the table for his hand. He flinched as my skin touched his but he didn't pull his hand back. He looked down at our hands then up to meet my eyes.

"That's why I haven't been interested in relationships. I don't want to hurt someone else like that," he said as he looked over across the street.

"So why me then? You don't care if you hurt me?" I asked with an uneasy laugh. I looked down and took another bite of crepe so as to not see his expression. Instead I felt his hand on mine.

"No Suzanne, that's definitely not the case," he answered in a soothing tone. "I just feel a much deeper connection with you than with anyone else I've ever met." I looked at him, puzzled by his response. "And yes, that includes her too," he added with a smirk. "No, it was just different with you. I don't really know how to explain it. There was just the amazing pull towards you. You saw me when I thought I was completely phased. No one's ever done that before. Occasionally if you're partially phased, people will see you, but unless I'm deliberately focusing on you not seeing me, you usually can see me. That's why you kept catching glimpses of me in the OR. You may not see me completely but you do see me when I'm there."

I nodded as he was talking, taking in everything he had just said. It seemed like my thoughts were spinning so fast that it was hard to hang onto any one thought all the way through before another one came to mind. I looked back over at him and he was looking out the window across the street again.

"So some people can see you partially phased?" I asked him trying to keep the conversation going, but not really knowing exactly what direction to go. He nodded and turned back to me. His brown eyes met mine and I could see the emotion swimming in them. "So did Thomas see you in the OR then?"

"Thomas?" he asked cautiously. I could tell he was trying to figure out whether this is someone he should know.

"He was a patient of mine who asked me about an 'observer' during the surgery. A week or so later I saw you for the first time in the OR."

"I don't really remember him, but there's a good chance he did," he answered as his eyes flitted to the other side of the street again.

"What are you looking at over there?" I asked, somewhat annoyed that he seemed so distracted while I was trying to talk to him. He gave me a somewhat apologetic look and glanced back across the street. "Let me guess, that guy over there is red?" I asked with more bite in my tone than I intended. Ben shot me an icy stare and then returned his gaze across the street. I could see him take a sharp inhale and before he looked back at me, he began to rise from his chair.

"I'm sorry, we'll have to continue this later," he said sincerely as he leaned in and kissed me on the forehead before walking towards the restrooms. At first I was confused by him walking the other direction, and then realized how awkward that would be for him to walk into the road and then fade away. I sighed as I looked down at my plate and took the final few bites of my breakfast alone. My face felt heavy and my shoulders slumped forwards, and I imagined my expression to likely be very sad and dejected right now.

After a few minutes, the short black haired waitress stopped by to check on me and I asked for the bill with a polite smile. I had no idea how long Ben would be and if he would even be joining me again. While I didn't know exactly how long it takes to do his job, from the way he talked about it on those rare occasions, it did not sound like a quick five minute encounter. After paying for breakfast, I slowly gathered my things and walked out of the café. I looked both directions, trying to decide where I wanted to go. I didn't really have any plans since I originally thought I would have more time with Ben and that we would be having some engaging conversations this morning. As I stood there trying to decide what I wanted to do, I suddenly heard a commotion from across the street. A woman in her mid-forties was calling out for someone to call an ambulance. I turned my stare to an elderly man across the street who was lying on the ground motionless. The woman crouched over him and began frantically giving him CPR. As a doctor, my initial instinct would normally be to run over and try to help, but instead I smiled a sad acknowledgment in that direction. As I watched the scene unfolding, I caught a glimpse of Ben over in the crowd of people who had gathered around the man. I could see two younger people on their phones pacing quickly back and forth, presumably on the phone with emergency responders. The thought crossed my mind to go over to the crowd, but since Ben was there, I already knew that this man would not be surviving this episode, regardless of someone giving him CPR, or when the ambulance arrived. Part of me felt sad, but part of me thought that it would also be somewhat of a relief to know in advance which patients would be saved and which ones would not. When you are trying to save someone's life, you never know when to say enough is enough. To have some insider information could definitely take the guilt and the burden away in some cases.

I shook my head and crossed my arms across my chest as I walked down the sidewalk. I decided to walk away from the house and see where my walk would take me. I wanted some time to really think about and process what Ben shared at breakfast about his ex-girlfriend, and I felt like when I was thinking while I was walking, I actually made better progress. While trying to kill yourself seemed over the top and a little too "Romeo & Juliet," I could see how after years of being together but still feeling so alone, someone could really entertain that idea. I could only imagine how lonely that would feel to have to go through everything by yourself. To have to constantly answer questions about 'why don't you find a nice young man to settle down with' and 'oh I know the perfect person to set you up with!' After hearing that for years, I would think it would drive anyone crazy, let alone a person who had a partner, just one that they could not admit to having. I could feel the pit of my stomach begin to tighten with this new revelation. Could I really handle that? Or would I snap too, like his ex did? I would like to think that I'm stronger than that, but part of me knew better. The small part of me that held onto the memory of Steven, even after I found out about him cheating on me. The part of me that cried and wished he was back, even though that side only showed it's ugly head for a few short hours. What would I do in the depths of my desperation?

I shuddered at the thought and picked up the pace. I rounded the corner of the next block and headed home. I wanted to talk to Cassie about this and see what she thought. I always trusted her opinion on things like this and I felt like I was inching towards a decision.

"Hi Cassie," I said as I walked in the house, "what's new with you?" She began filling me in on everything that was happening with her and her family. I felt like I had dominated our conversations recently, so I wanted to make sure I talked about her first.

"So, how's the guy situation going over there?" she asked about fifteen minutes into our conversation, changing the focus back to me.

"Oh, I'm still struggling with trying to decide what to do," I answered honestly. I filled her in on the strange conversation with Ben, and then how he had to walk out in the middle. "You know, if I hadn't seen the guy across the street keeled over on the sidewalk, I might have thought he just used that as a line to get out of an awkward conversation!" I said with a laugh. As I said it though, I thought about how I would never really know if he was using that as an excuse to avoid tough situations, or if he legitimately had to go.

"Well, not to defend the guy, but you sometimes get paged by the hospital in emergencies," she retorted.

"Hey, aren't you supposed to be on my side?" I asked, not entirely offended, but a little surprised since she seemed to be in Colin's corner most of the time.

"I am on your side, but being on your side means helping you see all points of view so that you can make the best decision for you. It's not just blindly agreeing with everything that comes out of your mouth you know," she said with a smile that I could see in my mind just by hearing her tone.

"Yeah, you're right. Damn, why are you always so much smarter than I am when it comes to this sort of thing?" I always loved getting her opinion on things, but I also found it very frustrating sometimes. In my day to day life, I usually didn't feel like the dumb one in conversations, but sometimes I felt like that with Cassie. She was typically gracious enough to not brag about it or throw it in my face, so that helped, but I still felt like I was a child and she was imparting this wisdom on me.

"I'm just in a different place in life and can see things differently than you can. But answer this for me. Why are you so fixated on trying to make things work with Ben?" I took a long pause before answering her. I really didn't think that I was fixated on making Ben the ultimate winner in this situation. Especially based on the way I started this conversation. "I can tell by your tone that you're very disappointed that things seem like they may not work with him, and I'm just curious why. You've only known him a few months. It's not like you've sunk years and years into the relationship and just found out something that you have to decide if you can live with. You're in a pretty unique situation right now. You can see what the toughest part of the relationship will be up front. You can make a more rational decision now instead of finding it out down the road."

"Yeah, that's true … I just … I don't know. I will honestly never again meet someone like him. It just seems like a once-in-a-lifetime chance and I don't want to turn my back on it because I'm scared or I'm getting caught up in unimportant details."

"Suz, just because he's unique, that doesn't mean by default that he's better. You of all people should know that."

"What do you mean by that?"

"Well, as a doctor, you see all types of people, right? So, if someone has a super-rare condition, that's probably not a good thing is it?"

"I suppose not …" I trail off.

"Right, because you have very little experience with that condition. And there may not be a very large body of research on it either. So at the end of the day, being "unique" could actually hurt you."

"Yeah, but think how boring it would be as a doctor to see the same old coughs and sore throats all day. That's why I wanted to be a surgeon. I wanted something more exciting than that."

"Yeah, Suzy, but don't confuse average with mediocre. Common doesn't necessarily mean dull. I mean, Bob's not an angel or a rock star and I still love him more than anything. My life may be ordinary but it's mine and I love it just the way it is," she said with a sense of pride. Pride in a life that had meaning to her, even if the rest of the world wouldn't necessarily rank it as the most exciting adventure imaginable.

"No, no. Sorry Cassie. I didn't mean to imply that your life was dull or subpar or anything like that," I said, trying to backpedal. Did she really think I was talking down about her life? The last thing I wanted to do was hurt her feelings like that.

"I know you didn't sweetie. I'm just trying to make you see that Colin, even though he's a regular guy, may give your life more meaning and happiness than you think. Exotic doesn't always work out. I mean, look at how you're feeling right now. You're hurt that he left in the middle of your serious discussion, right?" I agreed as she continued on. "It's only going to get more frustrating over time, not less frustrating. If you get into a relationship thinking that you can change someone, you just end up hurt by it."

"You're right," I conceded, letting out a long sigh. "Ben may not be the right guy for me, I just don't know … I guess I need to keep thinking about it," I said, resigning myself to that thought. More processing and thinking was not what I was hoping for. I was hoping for clarity that would make this decision easier and the answer more apparent to me.

"Just remember though, no one is perfect. Every man you meet will have a flaw, so it's just a matter of figuring out which flaws you can live with and which ones are deal breakers."

"Ah, the million dollar question … Well you always give me something to think about. Thanks for the talk Cassie. And don't forget to call mom tomorrow."

"You're welcome. Love you sis," she said, with a smile.

"Love you too."

Chapter 20

I poured myself a glass of cabernet and made my way over to the couch. I curled up with a big crocheted blanket and turned on a rom-com in the background while I thought back over the conversation earlier in the day with my sister. Even though I knew she was right, that every man I meet would have some sort of flaw, I couldn't ignore the doubts that were creeping in about Ben. And if my past had taught me anything, it was to trust my instincts more.

As I sat there watching the movie with Roxie, I felt my lips begin to get warm and then tingle. Soon the tingling spread to my shoulders and then waves of flutters swept over my arms. I couldn't help but smile and feel a warm, satisfied feeling pass over my entire body.

"Hi there handsome," I said quietly with a peaceful smile on my face. In a matter of moments, I saw Ben phase, sitting next to me on the couch. He reached over and kissed the back of my hand.

"Hi yourself," he smiled an easy going and enamored smile. "I'm sorry I had to leave earlier. Business calls," he said with an apologetic smile.

"Well, at least it was business and it wasn't that you decided you were getting tired of our conversation," I said raising my eyebrows emphatically. I took another drink of my wine to give me a few moments to see how he would react. Sometimes I enjoyed our game of cat and mouse, but now after all of my thinking today I felt different. Like I was assessing him in a different light now rather than just letting things flow smoothly.

"Of course not. I just had to go. You saw the man across the street after you left the café," he answered, sounding wounded by my statement.

"Yeah, I get it. It's just hard to adjust to it, that's all. That was the first time you've left in the middle of a conversation like that, so I wasn't quite sure how to take it.

"This is just a part of who I am," he began, but I cut him off, already starting to feel agitated.

"No, I understand. I get paged by the hospital too, but I do get days off where I know I won't get called away and I can focus on whoever or whatever I want to. Do Takers get to have days off?"

"No, we don't," he answered curtly.

"Well, would it really be the end of the world if you just didn't take someone? I'm sure the person would figure it out on their own." His expression made me feel like I had just slapped him across the face. I rushed to try to take my foot out of my mouth.

"I mean, can there really be a Taker there to get everyone? What about the people who die out at sea or on some remote island? I doubt a Taker would just happen to walk by someone right as they're dying in the middle of the desert, right?"

"That's not quite the way it works," he replied. His tone was almost condescending, which was a feeling I was not used to. And I was not particularly pleased with the way he acted as if I should know these things when he, in fact, was the one who had not shared the information with me in the first place.

"Enlighten me then," I replied brazenly. I felt a boldness come over me that I normally would not have this early on in a relationship. I suppose when you're on the fence and need to make a decision, you cannot stick to surface level questions and pleasantries.

"How much have you had to drink tonight?" He asked as he glanced at my almost empty wine glass in my hand.

"What? Are you serious?" I asked in an incredulous tone.

"You really haven't seemed like yourself today. First at breakfast and now this conversation. I just don't know what to make of it," he answered as he got up and started to pace around the room. He shook his head in frustration.

"I just want to know how it works. Why can't you just ignore the person? So their aura's red. Why do you have to go? Are you the one that literally has to kill them or something?" I put my glass down firmly on the table and stood up across from him.

"No. No Suzanne, that's not it at all," he said, running his right hand through his dark hair. His left hand squeezed his hip firmly, like he could wring an answer out of himself. His inability to directly answer my questions made my mind feel like it was slowly slipping backwards. What was he trying to cover up by not answering me? I took a deep breath and just stared back at him, waiting for his answer. "We're just … drawn to the person we're supposed to take. I don't really know how to describe it except that you physically feel pulled towards that person. That's how people out in the middle of nowhere who die have a Taker there for them. Ignoring that feeling and what you're supposed to do is literally painful to endure," he explained. He raised his eyes to meet mine, trying to evaluate what I thought of this.

"So I guess this happens pretty far in advance then? So you're saying people are fated to die at a certain place and time?" His quizzical look meant that he was having a hard time seeing how I made my way from one thought to the next in this sequence, so I went on to explain myself.

"Well, you said that you're pulled towards someone. If you were being pulled to someone in Alaska, it would take you a while to get there from Chicago. So I'm guessing that's where the fate part comes into play."

"True," he answered abruptly, "some things can't be changed." This answer seemed to have an air of sadness to it.

"Have you ever tried? I mean … to change fate?"

"Yeah, once I did. I saved the person I was supposed to take. It was a young girl, and I just didn't have the heart to do it, so I reached out and helped her instead," he said, his eyes glassy at the memory.

"What happened after that? Did you get in trouble?" If he could save people, then why wouldn't he? As a doctor, I couldn't imagine having the opportunity to save someone and rejecting that opportunity.

"Let's just say, when I said it physically *hurts*, I meant it. And then when you're not playing by the rules, somehow you end up getting the worst cases assigned to you," he answered somberly. He sat down in front of me, his elbows on his knees.

"What do you mean the worst cases? How are some better than others?"

"Taking old people who have lived a full and happy life and are surrounded by loved ones, those are the easy takes. They're usually prepared for death and they're not really as afraid. They're more excited about what comes next. In the case of children, particularly abused, starving, neglected children, it's much different. They're confused and scared and they don't want to go. Those are the cases Takers hate to get. Or people taken in their prime, or by someone else's selfishness or stupidity."

My heart hurt as I watched his face sag talking about this. I hadn't given much thought to how difficult this job must be for someone. Just like I hated having to operate on children or, worse yet, having to tell the parents that their child did not make it, he must have those same types of feelings. Even if he didn't have to tell the family about their loved one passing, he had to see them. He would have to see them fall to pieces. While families were upset when I gave them the news, they typically tried to hold themselves together somewhat, saving their total collapse for a private moment. His job definitely took a toll on him and I didn't think I gave it the respect that it deserved. At least I had people to talk to about it. Ben didn't really seem to have people to talk to. I had heard him talk about a few other Takers, but not many and it did not sound like they still saw each other regularly.

"I'm sorry," I answered weakly. I truly meant it, but the words seemed inadequate for the gravity of the situation.

"For what?" There was a smugness to his tone that I couldn't quite pin down. Was he hurt by thinking back on a painful memory, or was it because of me and my attitude this evening?

"For not realizing how hard this must be for you. I didn't really appreciate the challenges you face." I crossed the room and sat down next to him, resting my head against his shoulder. We sat there for a few more moments in silence before he began talking.

"So what's been going on with you today? You seemed like you were pushing on issues and just generally out of character." I didn't answer right away, trying to figure out what I was going to say in response to him. "Is it that other guy?" My face burned as he said that. I was not sure whether he had been listening in on private conversations I had been having recently or just a gut instinct. Either way, I could feel myself getting defensive.

"Why would you think it's about him?" I responded and straightened up next to him.

"Given what happened last night at the gala," he answered simply. I shot him a quizzical look so he continued. "You seemed to be having a good time with him until I showed up, and then you got upset that I was there. Not quite the reaction I was hoping for …" I noticed how he had not taken any responsibility for it, but merely pointed out that I may be upset.

"Yeah, and if the situations were reversed I bet you would be upset about it too," I replied, looking over at him and making strong eye contact. I did not feel a need to apologize for being upset about the situation, and I wanted to make sure my eye contact conveyed that to him.

"Why, did I interrupt something with the two of you?" with a slightly accusatory tone.

"No, you were spying on me. That's what is upsetting," I answered, trying to sound as detached as I could, despite how angry I was starting to become. He legitimately seemed to not understand why I would be upset by this. And that was a huge part of why I felt like this may not end up working out with us. He did not seem to understand things like boundaries and the pace of a relationship. "I was disappointed when you said you weren't going to go with me in the first place, but I decided to go and have a good time anyway. Then halfway through you show up out of thin air and make a scene with one of my best friends. It came across like you were setting up the whole thing to essentially spy on me."

"I wasn't spying Suzanne. I felt bad that I didn't go with you so I wanted to surprise you. Imagine my surprise when it seemed like you were happier to be there without me."

"That's not the case," I jumped in right away. And I actually meant it too. "I just wasn't going to go to the party and then pout in the corner all night that you weren't there."

"I've seen the way you two are together and it … it is very off-putting. Then you were going on and on today about my ex-girlfriend. I didn't know what to make of it or what you were getting at."

"You talk about honesty," I began cautiously, but with a growing sense of confidence, "so here goes. I'm worried about what the future would be like with you. If a future is even really possible. That's why I was asking what happened in your past relationship. I wanted to see what things would be like a few years down the road."

That was the first time in my life that I had ever really put it all out there like that in a relationship, especially so early on. I felt scared but at the same time stronger than I thought I was. After all, why beat around the bush and play those silly games when you can just be honest and see how the person reacts?

"I see," was all he answered with. I could see the conflicting emotions playing across his face. I could see the disappointment when I said I needed to see if a future was possible. But at the same time, I could see the anticipation and excitement about the idea of a future together too. I did not want to give him the impression that I was backpedaling on anything, so I opted not to break our silence.

"So you thought our future would be dictated by my past?"

"Not entirely, but yes, it seems to make sense that there would be similarities." I could feel my pulse start to quicken at this conversation. This may very well be the end of us. I had thought about it and was fairly confident in my decision, but now as Ben stood there in front of me, I doubted myself. I normally was not one to second guess myself, so I was not sure where this doubt was coming from now.

"You really think you would try to kill yourself?" he sneered at me. "You're not that weak Suzanne." The way he said it sounded like it should be a compliment, but I could also hear the disdain in his voice, although it was likely aimed towards her and not me.

"No, of course not. I guess the similarities I was talking about was about what your life was like. That you still never got to a point of being able to have a normal life with her. To do the normal things together." There was a hollowness to my words as I spoke them. This was a hollowness that mirrored how I felt right now. I almost felt like I was detached from the conversation. Normally I would be very spooled up and emotionally engaged in a conversation like this, but it felt more like I was watching myself having this conversation with Ben.

"But that *is* what's normal for Takers ... That's where things broke down with the two of us. She thought that our lives would be like her version of a normal relationship, but I'm only capable of what is considered normal by my standards." He turned to face me and took my hands in his. The warmth coming from him immediately made my heart flutter, so I closed my eyes and took a deep breath as he continued. "Look, today has been a long day. Let's just call it a night and we can talk about this again tomorrow with a clear head."

"I have to work tomorrow, so I'll be leaving to drive in fairly early in the morning."

"Okay, well I'll see you tomorrow morning then," he replied with a warm smile. I looked into his chocolate eyes and he gave me a quick, chaste kiss on the lips and then on my cheek before taking my hand. He gently kissed it, then he began to phase, sending warm tingling waves across the back of my hand. I smiled a quick, small smile thinking this could be the last time I felt that.

I awoke in the middle of the night, shaking and covered by my sweat soaked sheets. This time, my bed was empty so I decided to get up and go to the kitchen for a drink of water and to shake the images from my dream. Even after getting settled back into bed, I could still hear that silky voice shouting at me to swim. I readjusted my pillow and kept thinking about the dream, or kept thinking about trying to not think about it. I remember having had that dream periodically growing up, and even through college, but it seemed to be once every year or so. The fact that I was now having this dream much more regularly was very unnerving. I hadn't been thinking about swimming an extraordinary amount lately or anything that would make me dwell on that point in my life. The harder I tried to fall back asleep, the more futile it seemed. My head buzzed with trying to figure out why this dream kept surfacing now, and trying to think metaphorically about the dream. Was I waiting for someone to just reach out now and save me from this dilemma? If so, which one was it that I was waiting for? I had kept calling Cassie about my predicament, so maybe I was waiting for her to save me.

After dwelling on that thought for quite some time, I resolved to not just wait around for someone else to save me. If my past was going to color my future, I did not want it to be from a position of weakness. I did not want to have to wait until I was literally on death's doorstep and then count on someone else to rescue me.

Chapter 21

*M*orning had come too early for me. After mulling things over for quite some time in the middle of the night, I felt like I was ready to move past this stage of churning and analyzing, and doubting myself. I climbed into my car and let it run for a few minutes to warm up. As I sat there checking the weather and my email on my phone, my hand started to tingle and I instantly smiled. Why did that always make me smile? Part of me was irritated with myself that it would get that same reaction out of me every time. My eyes were looking down at my hands as he phased next to me.

"Good morning," he said cheerfully, but rather quietly. "How did you sleep last night?"

"Horribly," I answered abruptly. "How about you?"

"I had other things to do last night after I left," he answered in a concerned tone as he raised my hand up to kiss it.

"So is that really why you said we should talk in the morning? Because you had someone else to take last night, so you would have to leave anyway?" I asked with a tired tone. When I raised my eyes up to meet his, they had a sad expression in them. He didn't answer my question, and I took his silence for a yes, so I put my seatbelt on and put the car in gear.

"No seatbelt?" I asked him as we made our way down the quiet street.

"Would you prefer I wear one for appearance sake?" he asked, not in a condescending way, but with a smile. At least it did make me laugh, which was a nice break from the scowl I had.

"No I suppose it doesn't really matter does it?" We rode in silence for a few moments down the dark, empty street before I continued. "I'm sorry for all of the weird conversations yesterday. I'm just trying to figure out how I really feel about things before getting too far in, you know what I mean? This is a unique situation and if there's any chance of it working, I have to feel comfortable with what that relationship would look like. Truthfully, that's something I'm struggling with," I said cogently.

"I can appreciate that," he answered and gave my hand a squeeze.

We pulled up to a stoplight and I pulled up my phone, dialing my mom's cell phone number.

"Sorry, I just need to make a quick call," I said as I put the phone on hands free and heard the other end ringing. Ben had been looking out the window with his chin resting on his fist, but when the screen lit up with a picture of my mom, it caught his eye and he looked down at my phone. He stiffened in his seat and squeezed my hand as it started to go to voicemail. I shot a confused look at him and then returned my focus to the road and the purpose for my call.

"Hi mom, it's me. I just thought I would let you know that I'm thinking about you and dad today, and that I love you both very much. I have to work today but I'll be around later this evening. Love you and talk to you soon. Bye."

We drove a few more blocks in silence, before Ben started to speak again.

"What was that about?" he asked in a quiet tone. I let out a long, sad sigh.

"Today's the anniversary of my sister's death," I answered, shoulders sagging a bit. I didn't think of Lenora very often anymore. Truthfully, I hadn't really known her. She was four years older than I was and had died when I was just three. I could picture her face, but I wasn't entirely sure whether that was from a real memory I had of her, or whether it was from the pictures I had seen and a scene that my mind had created later as a way to hold onto her. What I do remember in shocking clarity was my parents reactions, mainly my mother's, over the next few years after her death. Cassie was only one when it happened, but even she remembers some of the aftermath. I remember walking by my parents room and seeing my mom sobbing quietly into her pillow. Even once I was old enough to go to school, I remember coming home around Easter time with my school art projects to show her and a few times seeing her in her pajamas with a box of tissues next to her. In my own life, I had a limited experience in dealing with real loss, and this was something even as an adult that I could not possibly fathom. The loss of a child.

"What happened to her?" Ben asked with an uneasy look on his face.

"She was killed by a drunk driver. My dad was driving her home from a friend's birthday party and this guy T'ed into the side of their car at an intersection. She was sitting in the back seat, but he slammed into the passenger side and she died in the ambulance on the way to the hospital. My dad was fine, physically anyway," I said, trailing off. Ben shifted uncomfortably in his seat. "What, you didn't take her did you?" I asked sarcastically. He gave me a dry, weary laugh as we pulled into the parking garage at the hospital. I hadn't really thought about someone taking her before, but I guess this was one of those "tough" types of cases he had mentioned.

"I'm sorry about your sister," he said very somberly. I looked over to see his chocolate brown eyes looking like they were going to melt before me. His expression did strike me as odd. He said he takes multiple people every week to the other side, but then he acted like he was legitimately moved by my sister dying when I was younger. My mind was trying to settle on whether I thought that was sweet or whether I thought it was hypocritical. Maybe it was because he could sympathize with the Taker who was there for her.

"Such is life, right?" I answered as I tuned the engine off and got out of the car.

I did my rounds that morning, checking back on all of my recent surgical cases. I had chosen a soft, blue V-neck sweater that day and dark brown dress pants. On this day, I always wore blue. I was guessing that was Lenora's favorite color because in all three of the pictures that my parents had displayed of her, she was wearing blue. While today didn't make me devastatingly sad, like it still sometimes did with my mom, it did make me reflect more on life and the choices we all make. Not just the choice of the driver to get behind the wheel after having had too much to drink, but even my family's choices. My mother chose to spend her life with a man who absolutely adored her and would do anything for her. I can't recall what their relationship was like prior to the accident, or even the few years right after. What I do recall though was how every year when they would go to the cemetery to pay their respects, my dad was always so strong for my mom. That evening, he would make dinner for Cassie and I, and do something fun and special with us. The times when my mother was almost incapacitated with sadness, he would take care of her and dote on her. I could see the love in his eyes and in the soft kisses he placed on her forehead or her cheeks. I could literally feel the love they shared and that is what I always wanted. I wanted to feel that closeness that I saw from my parents. I had never asked them whether that closeness came in the aftermath of Lenora's death, or whether it had always been there. I liked to believe that it was always there, although perhaps it was deepened by that life altering event that brought them even closer together.

I was standing at the nurses' station when Jane came cheerfully walking up.

"Good morning, Dr. Jacobsen," he said with a big smile. Even though overly cheery people first thing in the morning would sometimes grind on my nerves, particularly when I was exhausted, today her energy was a welcome presence.

"Good morning, Dr. Paulsen. So how'd you like your first Belvidere Gala?" I asked with a smile. I had seen her at the party and she looked like she had been mildly over-served, but not acting ridiculous like some of the residents end up acting. Granted, I left early, so who knows what happened after later in the evening.

"Oh it was great!" she said beaming. "I got to meet a bunch of great people that work here who I haven't met before. And Dr. Barrett's wife! She's such a nice lady!"

"She really is, isn't she?" I answered genuinely.

"So what's this about my wife?" I heard Howard's deep voice coming from behind us and turned to see him walking towards Jane and me. He had a relaxed look about him and a big smile across his boxy jawline.

"Dr. Paulsen was just telling me that she got the chance to meet Maddie at the gala. She really is a great woman."

"Why she's with me, I'll never understand!" he said with a laugh before moving onto business. "There's a case this morning that I want you and Forrester to include Paulsen on. Wasn't one of your scheduled cases but it came in through the ER last night. Patient is stable and is being prepped."

"Sounds like a plan, Chief," I said as I turned back to Jane.

"Is that going to be awkward?" she asked wide-eyed.

"Huh?" I was very much caught off guard by her question.

"Well, with you and Dr. Forrester and your boyfriend at the gala-" I held up my hand to cut her off.

"Paulsen, remember what we talked about? This isn't a sorority house. Stop gossiping," I said in an authoritative, but not mean, tone. She instantly flushed. "Your skills are good, but you need to remember to keep a certain level of professionalism on the job. Save the gossip for your friends who don't work here. Being a gossip is the fastest way to alienate people," I said as we turned back to the desk at the nurses' station.

"I … I'm sorry," she responded sheepishly. "I know you did mention that on Saturday night." I could see her cheeks flush with embarrassment.

"I know and I can tell by your expression that you didn't mean anything by it. It's just something you need to work on," I said with a quick, purse-lipped smile before grabbing by tablet and walking away from the nurse's station.

Chapter 22

I stood at the scrub sink outside the OR looking down at my hands as I kept working the brush back and forth on a spot under one of my fingernail. I chatted idly with Jane as she scrubbed in next to me. I began going over the case in more detail and what her role in the procedure would be. This was the first emergency surgery that we had together so she would mainly be assisting me and observing.

I started to head into the operating suite when Colin came in behind us and began scrubbing up too. I could hear him reviewing the case with Jane as well but from the cardiac perspective. She wouldn't have much of an opportunity to observe him during the procedure but it was important for her to be aware of what her colleagues in the suite would be doing. He would also be observing her from across the table so he wanted a chance to begin building a rapport with her. After her rotation with me, she would also be doing a rotation with Colin and the rest of the trauma team.

By the time they joined me in the OR, I was already settled in and ready to begin my pre-surgical checklist. Colin would be starting first and as I was going over the instrument count on our tray. I saw her eyes dart away and over towards the head of the table, so I turned my head to see what she was looking at. Colin was holding the saw up in the air and pumped it twice as the anesthesiologist removed the mask from the patient, allowing the lungs to deflate.

"Paulsen," I said sharply to draw her attention back to what we were doing. She quickly shook her head and when her eyes locked on mine, she flushed in embarrassment.

"Sorry," she said sheepishly as she looked back down at our tray. Colin's eyes flicked up to meet mine for a split second as he was cutting through to get access to the woman's heart.

"Watch your concentration. I know it's easy to get distracted but we've got to stay focused," I said in an authoritative tone but not overly critical. I remember my first surgery. The sights and sounds, even the smell. It's very easy to get distracted, but repetition helped to take the newness out of it and help keep you on track.

"It won't happen again," she said confidently with her chest and chin held high. I hoped that would be the case. She seemed to be a very promising doctor from what I had seen so far of her, as long as she could keep focused and stop gossing.

The surgery was going smoothly. After the initial distraction, Jane had been spot on and I had not seen her miss a beat or falter in any way. I was making a mental note of this when I began to feel a slight warmth on my shoulders and across my neck. I shifted position, thinking it was just the lights making me warm. As I shifted, though, I noticed a fluttering sensation on my arms and I knew it was not the lights making me warm. My heartbeat began to pick up as I thought about Ben being here with me now. I knew he had watched me before in surgery but for some reason, today this made me feel a little giddy that he was here. Was it because I was not only operating, but also mentoring Jane at the same time? My emotions felt out of place right now though given the way our car ride went, and I then became slightly annoyed with myself for always caving so quickly whenever I felt him touch me like that. I guess a part of me just couldn't help it. I would have to reflect back on it later because I wasn't going to let myself get side tracked in the middle of surgery.

I could feel the fluttering continue down my arms and I smiled as I looked down at my gloved hands. I heard Colin clear his throat from the other end of the table and glanced up quickly at him, but his eyes were down, looking intently at his work in front of him. As I returned my gaze to my work I called for suction, reexamining our patient. I leaned towards Jane to point something out and then shifted back to my original position. I could feel my forearms and the backs of my hands fluttering and I blushed again.

"Scalpel," I called and placed my right hand out towards Jane, and I instantly felt a playful tickle of electricity tease across my right hand and it flinched, involuntarily closing as I gasped. The scalpel fell only an inch before Paulsen grabbed it. My heart shot into my throat and my pulse soared. Luckily she caught it before it cut into anyone inadvertently.

"I'm so sorry doctor!" she exclaimed as she tapped the handle of the scalpel loudly into place in my palm, holding it for a few extra seconds to make sure I had it. "I thought you had it," she continued.

"No, that's okay," I replied. "These things happen," I said with a soft smile before continuing to work on our patient.

"What's going on down there?" I heard in a firm and agitated voice.

"Nothing, just a rough handoff," I said as non-challantly as I could. I looked up to see a look of concern and of irritation in Colin's eyes. I held his glance for only a moment before looking back down. His cold eyes seemed very distant, and I could clearly see something brewing below the surface. I snuck a quick peek back at him and saw him giving Jane a quick evaluation as well.

I mentally shook it off and continued with my work. After another ten minutes or so, I took a half step back from the table and arched my back, stretching it out from being poised over the patient. When I relaxed my shoulders, my head returned forward again, but not before seeing Ben in the corner of the suite, giving me a lopsided smile. He blew me a quick kiss before he started making his way to the door, fading away as he went. I could feel my cheeks flush and a smile play across my lips as I turned my focus back to my work and began wrapping things up.

After I finished up, I had Jane do some of the closing as I carefully watched her work. I peered through my lashes to see Colin taking a few steps closer towards us since he had finished with his portion of the surgery. He watched attentively as Jane took care to get the incision closed properly and with small and deliberate stitches. As she knotted her final stitch, he looked over at her and nodded.

"Good work Paulsen," he said as he quickly exited the OR. By the time we finished up and I made my way to the scrub room, Colin was already out the door. I quickly stripped out of my dirty scrubs and took off down the hall after him.

He ducked into the emergency stairwell up ahead and I hurried to follow him. He was already down the first part of the stairs and was approaching the landing by the time I came through the door.

"Colin," I called to him and he looked up at me, but kept moving. "Wait up," I called out, but I could see that he was seething. I started down the stairs towards him, trying not to get caught up in his emotion for the time being.

"What gives?" I asked bluntly, shrugging my shoulders as I casually continued down the stairs. I wasn't mad but I also was not exactly sure why he was so agitated right now. He stared blankly at me, not answering at first.

"What gives? Seriously? After that bullshit in the OR you're gonna ask me what gives?" He was livid at this point and overly articulating his words. His eyes had a fierceness to them that I had not seen before from Colin. He stood there with his hands on his hips, searching my face for something that I could not quite pinpoint yet. I couldn't decide whether his stare was icy or fiery. Despite how angry he was, I caught myself admiring how sexy he looked standing there like that. Given the nature of our conversation though, I quickly dismissed the thought.

"What do you mean? There was a not-so-perfect exchange with a resident. It happens all the time and we recovered quickly-" He held his hand up, cutting me off and began speaking as I slowly continued down the stairs to join him on the landing.

"No, that's what you tell Howard when he asks what went wrong when a resident screwed up but you don't want to throw them under the bus. I'm talking about your boyfriend," he said totally deadpan as his eyes met mine. I felt as if I had been slapped. How could he have known that Ben was there? And where did he get off lecturing me? I stood there silently, reminding myself to keep breathing, but I too was starting to get spooled up the longer I stood there across from him.

"You think I didn't notice you smiling and flushed behind your mask? Or the way your hands were trembling or your arms shuddering? I know you well enough to know that wasn't nerves that was making your hands shake like that." I paused at the compliment that was intertwined with his accusation.

"So what bothers you about it? That I was distracted during surgery or that it was *him* distracting me?!" I retorted, not quite shouting but much louder than I should have.

"He's a distraction Suzanne, plain and simple," he answered with a coldness to his voice that betrayed his eyes. But a coldness that made me shiver none the less. His eyes were locked on mine and unflinching. I could feel my heart beating faster with the intensity of this conversation.

"Like you've never lost focus for a second during surgery," I snapped back, folding my arms across my chest. I couldn't believe the tone of my words. Why was I being so hostile towards him? I had not meant to unleash this sort of emotion right now, especially not at him.

"I'm not talking about playing footsie under the table at dinner. This is twice now that asshole has distracted you in surgery. You've had an impeccable record of keeping focused, and this is twice in the last two months now that you've done this," he said, closing the distance between us until we were only a couple feet apart. He was starting to breathe heavily as he became increasingly angry. "Maybe he doesn't value human life but I sure as hell do and I'll be damned if someone dies on the table because he thinks it's cute to distract you and give you little love taps in the middle of the OR!" he growled at me.

"Why are you so furious about this? Nothing happened and everything was fine!"

"That's not the point and you know it. It's unprofessional, not to mention if something would have gone wrong, now I'm in the middle of this with Howard having to bail your ass out because you think it's a good idea to date the goddamn angel of death!" He had resorted to pacing back and forth in front of me now, his hands gripping his hips. I could feel my pulse quicken as he glared at me. I wasn't quite sure why I was so mad, particularly given the way I had been feeling about Ben over the last couple of days. It wasn't upset because he was judging what he perceived my relationship with Ben to be, but I was getting so angry that I couldn't even focus on figuring out why.

"Everyone's entitled to have a life Colin, as much as you may hope that I don't get to have one unless it involves you," I barked back at him. Now I was fuming, my cheeks heating up the angrier I got. I could even feel my insides shaking. I was being incredibly harsh with him and would have normally felt guilty, but right now my anger was overshadowing that. Although by the look on his face, he didn't seem particularly phased by my mood or my temper. Maybe it was giving him an excuse to vent.

"A life? You seriously you think you can have a life with this guy?" he said waving his hand in the direction of the door we had come out of. He turned around and ran his hands down his face in exasperation as he continued, slowly turning back to face me. "He's not even a guy Suzy! He's a fucking ghost! You think he's gonna want to settle down with you, buy a house in the burbs and start a family? Do you even think that's possible?" His voice had quieted slightly but he was still irate and his liquid blue eyes blazed as he looked at me. He ran his fingers through his wavy blond hair as he stood there trying to regain his composure. As much as I wanted to shout back at him, he was right. What sort of a life would I have with a man like Ben? Could I even have one with him on this side? From the way our conversations had been going over the last couple of days, I was starting to think more and more that it would not be possible.

I said nothing. I had nothing to say to that. He was right but there was entirely too much adrenaline surging through me to be able to say that calmly right now. I could feel my cheeks flush as I stood there looking at Colin. Part of me was angry at him for saying these things, but mostly I was mad at myself for believing in things with Ben and for not taking a more realistic view of the relationship. And goddammit why was Colin looking at me like that?! Both of us drew in ragged breaths as we stood watching each other for a minute, not wanting to break the silence. As the tension grew, I saw a subtle shift in his body language and then he started to move towards the stairs, shaking his head.

"Colin, wait," I said in an exasperated tone. I was still shaking with anger or whatever this feeling was, but I didn't want him to leave like that. He kept walking though. Either he had not heard me or he was ignoring me, and I was guessing it was the latter. I turned and grabbed his wrist as he walked by and his body went rigid as he turned to look at me. His eyes were burning with a mixture of anger, intensity and something else. The longer he looked at me, the more I could see the hurt and the love in his eyes. My feet were frozen to the ground as I looked deep in his eyes, searching for some clarity on this outburst. I could feel my insides ignite as he continued to hold my gaze, slowly realizing what all of this was about.

"Don't … Don't look at me like that Suzy," he said softly but with a very heated undertone. His eyes dropped to where my hand was on his wrist. "Not unless you mean it" he continued. I had no idea what to do. I stood there paralyzed, my lips sealed. I felt like my body was practically shaking after this encounter and my mind seemed detached from what was going on around me. All of this interaction had been driven by pure instinct and from the heart, without my mind having time to chime in.

I squeezed his wrist tighter and his eyes met mine. In one long stride he had closed the gap between us and was right in front of me. In one more fluid move I felt him grab my wrists as he pushed me back hard against the wall, pinning my wrists above my head. He pressed against my body as he looked down at me. I could feel him getting excited as we stood there, eyes fixed on each other and I felt myself melt beneath his touch. His chest quickly rose and fell as he tried to control his ragged breathing. I felt breathless, whether it was from being pushed against the wall, or whether it was this man here before me I couldn't tell. I no longer felt angry, instead my shaking had turned to desire. He said nothing as his fiery blue eyes searched mine for some sort of answer. At this proximity, I could feel his heart racing against me, matching my wildly pounding heart. With each passing moment the fire continued to build inside of me.

"It's your call Suzanne," he said virtually panting as he continued to press against me. I could hear his words, but it was as if my mind could not process what he was saying. What he was asking of me. I stood there searching his vivid blue eyes for the answer. His eyes widened as he stood there growing more excited, more carnal. I started to move my hands slightly and he tightened his grip and pressed himself harder against me. In a brief five minutes, he had taken me from furious to an almost frenzied state, making me weak in the knees. "It's always been up to you. You're the one pulling all the strings," he said, just as we heard the door two flights above us open and someone step into the stairwell. Both of us redirected our eyes upwards, but neither of us moved from our current position.

In a very composed voice he started talking. "Well, I guess we should debrief with the resident about that case." He gave me a devilish smile, not breaking our hold or our gaze for one moment. He definitely was enjoying this game, more than I would have expected. I was still unable to speak, overwhelmed by the past five minutes. Colin mouthed *you better answer* to me and flashed me his gorgeous smile, his eyes still devouring me. I was hypnotized by his lips but somehow managed to answer as I slowly closed my eyes.

"Yeah. Yeah let's review with her," I said as we heard the person exit the stairwell on the next floor. As soon as the door shut, I dropped my arms down, burying my face in my hands. Colin had let my wrists go and was now bracing himself against the wall behind me, one hand on either side of me at shoulder height.

"Well, I guess we don't have to worry about people finding us in the supply closet," he joked as I groaned and leaned my forehead against his sculpted chest. I could feel his heart still pounding in his chest and I immersed myself in the hypnotic rhythm. He moved his hands to my arms and started casually running his hands up and down my upper arms. My overly sensitive skin felt like it was tingling with every touch. My face was still against his chest when I could feel him softly shudder as he laughed at the situation.

"What? Thanks for laughing at me you brat," I said as we stood there so close to each other.

"Hey, I never said I fight fair," he answered. I leaned back against the wall and playfully shoved his chest.

"Yeah, no kidding! I think I need a cold shower after that," I replied with arched eyebrows as I brought one hand to my forehead and crossed the other arm over my chest. My entire body was still trembling. Colin shifted in front of me but did not back away. His whole posture had changed since just a few minutes ago. He was no longer the angry, hyper-assertive man who was about to rip my clothes off. He had turned into the tender, gentle man who would take care of me and love me. The dichotomy was breathtaking, as he fit both sides so perfectly.

"Hey, look at me Suzy," he said softly as he gently lifted my chin with one hand and ran his other hand down my shoulder. My god, my skin still felt like it was burning wherever he touched me. "Are you okay? I didn't scare you did I, or hurt you when I shoved you back against the wall?" he asked me in a serious tone, his eyes hopefully that our encounter hadn't ruined anything.

"No, no. I'm fine," I said as I tried, fairly unsuccessfully, to control my breathing. I smiled a genuine smile, letting him know everything was fine.

"Sure you are," he smirked as he took a step back, his expression turning to ornery again. "So residents?" he said raising his eyebrows.

"Tell her 15 minutes. I really do need a shower you know," I responded, slowly shaking my head as I tried to regain strength in my shaking legs. He laughed at me, making me blush.

"No problem," he said with a smile as he leaned forward and kissed my forehead before turning and walking toward the stairs heading down. He stopped and turned at the top and said "Oh, and Suzanne?" I looked up and smiled at him, "hot and bothered is a good look on you." His whole face lit up as he flashed me his gorgeous smile and winked at me, then bounded down the half flight of stairs.

Chapter 23

I pulled my hair back into a loose bun as I stepped into the shower. The cool water felt heavenly as I washed away my earlier arousal and cooled the fire that had been building up in me from my encounter in the stairwell with Colin. As I closed my eyes, all I saw was his smoldering blue eyes and I could feel my insides clench again thinking about him. A huge smile passed across my lips as I let the water cascade over me. I reveled in the memory of our encounter for a few more minutes but was brought back to the present when I remembered that we were meeting with Jane shortly to debrief on the case. *I should have told him 20 minutes,* I thought to myself with a smile. I quickly finished my shower and turned off the water.

I reached my hand out from behind the curtain and began feeling for my towel when I suddenly felt my hand begin to get warm and tingle. The suddenness of the feeling made me jump and jerk my hand back inside the shower. I carefully peered out around the edge of the shower curtain but there was no one there.

"Ben?" I whispered. "Is that you?" I didn't want anyone else to hear me. Men were not supposed to be in the ladies locker room so I didn't want to have to explain anything. In a matter of moments he materialized in front of me sitting on the bench in the changing stall outside of my shower.

"Oh my god!" I screamed, but in whisper. "What are you do-ing here?" I gasped as I grabbed for my towel that he was holding up for me. He smiled playfully at me as I tried to quickly cover myself up.

"A little shy, Dr. Jacobsen," he said as he stood up and leaned in to give me a kiss on the cheek. My mind started racing. Had he seen our encounter in the stairwell? And why was he here now?

"Ben, you can't just show up in the shower. That's not right and it's very uncomfortable." I said, for the first time wishing he would just disappear.

"It's just a body Suzanne. It's nothing new," he said so non-chal-lantly. Normally as a doctor I would agree, but there had to be some boundaries, and certainly popping into the locker room unexpectedly and uninvited was one of them.

"We need to talk about this later. We're not at this stage in our relationship and I don't like you popping in like this. I have to meet with a resident in a few minutes, so you need to phase back now," I commanded him rather matter-of-factly.

His face sagged, noticeably disappointed in my response, but he said nothing. I could see his mind racing, trying to figure out what to do or say next. He raised his eyebrows and they came together in a furrow and he pursed his lips, the corners turning down. "As you wish," and with that he disappeared.

I sat next to Colin as he did a recap with Jane about our case that we had just finished, grateful that he had much better com-posure than I did right now. I couldn't believe how seemingly oblivious he was to the last half hour. I didn't know whether to be in awe or to be disappointed that I must not have left much of an impression on him. He must have been able to tell what was on my mind because in a brief moment when Paulsen looked away while she was talking, Colin leaned forward but ran his hand along the top of my thigh subtly as he brought both of his hands to rest on the table in front of him. The small contact made my heart surge and my breath hitch as I looked over at him and saw that devilish smile pass across his lips once again. I made sure to interject here and there to make it seem like I was dynamically engaged in the conversation, but truthfully I couldn't get Colin out of my mind. There were so many things I had not noticed about him before today. Like the strength of his hands, how expressive his eyes were, and how his pants hung off his hips in the most seductive way. Had he always been this way and I was just now seeing it? Or was he working harder to get my attention these days?

After what seemed like an excruciatingly long meeting, which was only actually fifteen minutes, Jane got up to leave and go meet up with some of the other residents for lunch. Colin turned to face me, on the verge of laughing at me again. I didn't mind though, because it brought out such amazing, charming expressions on him when his face lit up.

"So, way to lead that debrief there, Doctor," he teased me.

"You seemed more focused, so I figured I would let you run with it this time," I answered as my lips began to curl up. Colin rose as he started talking again.

"It's almost lunch time. Wanna grab a bite across the street," he asked. He looked relaxed and not overly eager or awkward, to which I was pleasantly surprised. I opened my mouth getting ready to respond when I was cut off by a gruff voice I knew too well.

"She has plans today," Ben declared coldly. I looked at him, puzzled not only by him thinking we had plans but how he managed to sneak up on us at the table without either one of us noticing. I raised an eyebrow quizzically. He shot an icy glare at Colin before turning to face me. "Well, earlier in the shower you said you wanted to talk to me later, so I thought I would come by and take you out to lunch," he said as he came around the edge of the table and put his arm around my waist, like he was claiming his stake in front of Colin. I bristled at the gesture and took a deep breath, not wanting to create a scene right now.

Without missing a beat, Colin shrugged. "No biggie. See ya around," and walked off without a second glance.

The thought of going out to lunch with Ben actually made my stomach turn. I did want to talk to him, but I thought I would have more time to get my thoughts in order before having such a serious, and awkward, conversation with him. I grabbed my coat and purse and we headed over to the deli across the street for a quick lunch. I opted for soup and an apple. I figured I could make myself eat the soup, even though I wasn't really hungry, and I could always take the apple back to the hospital with me for later in the afternoon. I hadn't thought much of this conversation through yet but I wanted to be the one controlling it, not the other way around.

"So Ben, why exactly did you appear in the shower today?" I said calmly as I began eating. I surprised even myself with how blunt I was being now. I suppose I didn't have the energy at the moment to sugarcoat it.

"I just wanted to surprise you," he answered as his eyes drifted down and away from the table.

"By showing up in my shower–"

"Outside your shower," he interjected. I shot an icy look at him.

"Semantics. Fine, outside my shower at work? We're nowhere near that stage in our relationship. Why would you think that would be a good idea?" He said nothing but he kept his eyes fixed on mine.

"And then with that little show in the lounge?"

"What? You said you wanted to talk about it later, and lunchtime was later," he said with an even expression.

"It seems an awful lot like male posturing to me," I said smugly as I continued eating. We sat in silence for a few minutes, but I was not going to let myself talk to fill the emptiness. The past few days had left nothing but more questions about a future with Ben and even though some of the fluttering touches made me smile and made me feel close to him, they still weren't enough to push out the other doubts that were slowly invading my thoughts.

"I don't like the way the two of you act together," he said eventually and I could see the hurt in his eyes as he said this. My heart did feel for him as I saw him shifting in his chair. I was trying to put some context and meaning to the way I was feeling when I heard screeching tires and horns blaring. I looked out the window and saw a man on a bicycle lying on the ground. I looked over at Ben who shook his head and quickly got up and kissed me on the forehead.

"I've gotta go. Can we continue this conversation later?" he asked earnestly.

"Sure," I said despondently. I didn't even look up at him as he walked away to wherever he was going to phase. Even though he had a reason to go, I was getting tired of our discussions being interrupted. I wondered to myself why we had not experienced this until recently when our conversations started getting more serious. Did he have some control over it and was choosing to let himself be pulled away to avoid these awkward conversations? Or he also mentioned that Takers hate getting the tough cases, like they had been assigned to them. If the cases really did get 'assigned' then perhaps our relationship had drawn too much attention already. Perhaps the powers that be were trying to keep our relationship from getting as serious as his previous relationship had gotten by making it maddeningly difficult for us to communicate effectively on tough topics.

Regardless, I was getting frustrated and my patience on this was already wearing thin. After everything that Cassie had said on our last couple of phone calls, I really felt like perhaps I was trying too hard to make something work just for the novelty of it. I finished up my soup alone and in silence, not caring that the sadness was visible on my face.

After lunch my day seemed to creep by slowly. I didn't hear anything else from Ben, although after the way our lunch went I would not be overly eager to communicate either. While my encounter in the stairwell earlier had definitely pushed my mind farther along with Colin, I felt resigned to the fact that things were not going to work out with Ben. Knowing that I would have to have an uncomfortable talk with him, and that I had no idea how he would take it, had put me in a sullen mood. I tried to keep myself focused on my work and see the small things that would make me smile and help turn my mood around. The grateful wife who was so happy to see her husband doing better after his surgery. The grandmother that was smiling ear to ear at the drawing her granddaughter had made for her while she was in the hospital. The way Colin smiled at me as I walked by him while he was talking to another doctor at the nurse's station.

By the middle of the afternoon, I felt like I was back to my happy self, having pushed all of those deep, saddening thoughts from my mind. I looked down at my phone and saw a message from Colin.

I really would like to talk to you (and just you) if you're free later. RHPB @ 6:30?

I felt that delicious clinching and replied back. This definitely gave me an extra pep in my step for the rest of the afternoon and now I felt like I was the one with the contagious smile.

Chapter 24

I got to the piano bar a bit early and went to the bathroom to primp as best I could before finding a table. I quickly ordered a glass of wine to calm my rising nerves and hopefully take the edge off. I just prayed it didn't make things worse and turn me into a bumbling idiot.

Right on time, Colin showed up and came over to give me kiss on the cheek before taking a seat across from me at our table.

"So … How about that day today?" I asked nervously. "May as well talk about the elephant in the room, right?" I said as I took another long drink from my glass.

"I don't know, you tell me," he said coyly, his eyes dancing at this game. He nodded at the waitress and she came over to get his drink order as well.

"Well, that was quite a bold move today. Considering how angry I was, why did you do that? That was pretty risky," I stated, somewhat in awe of the fact that he would make that bold of a move.

"Nah, I could tell you weren't mad when you reached for my wrist."

"Oh really?" I retorted. "And how could you tell?"

"Well, there was the ragged breathing," he began hesitantly, "as well as the pounding heart."

"Which are often signs of being very angry," I contended. "I was so mad I was shaking and you couldn't tell that?" I asked in disbelief.

"You weren't shaking because you were mad," he said confidently as the waitress brought his drink over.

"I wasn't?" I said skeptically.

"Nope," he said with a victorious smile.

"You seem pretty cocky. How can you be so sure," I asked, curious as to what he would come up with. His confidence was rather charming, I had to admit.

"I've held you before when you were so mad you were shaking. On Valentine's Day" he said very directly and with an almost sad look on his face. "Earlier today it was different. It wasn't anger."

"Then what was it," I said very seductively, just to see whether I could make him squirm.

"It was arousal," he said, sizing me up. My heart skipped and I instantly felt flush. He lifted his glass up but held it shoulder high before finishing his thought. "And you weren't shaking. You were quivering," he said with a sexy half smile before he took a drink of his gin and tonic.

"And what, pray tell, would be the difference between shaking and quivering," I asked with raised eyebrows. Some of this questioning wasn't even that I didn't believe him, but rather that listening to him explain our interaction in the stairwell gave me great insight into how he thinks about things like this. As friends, we had not really talked about these subjects in much detail before tonight.

"Well, shaking is just a general twitching almost in place. Quivering has a rhythm and flow to it. Like a wave flowing down your body."

"Oh really?" I asked as I nodded along to what he was saying. I had never thought about it before, but his explanation did seem to make sense to me. "You seem pretty confident that you had me all excited. I know you were. I mean, it's not exactly subtle when you're wearing scrubs and pressed up against me, so maybe it was just wishful thinking that you had the same effect on me" I said playfully as I took another sip of my wine. I watched him through my lashes as his eyes took in every inch of me. Seeing him gaze at me like that made my pulse quicken and my insides begin to melt.

"Well, remember that when I was pressed up against you, I could feel every move of yours," he began explaining as he moved to the seat closest to me. He leaned in close and put his arm over the back of my chair and leaned in towards me, almost whispering in my ear. "And that includes when you're clenching down there as you get excited," he said before giving me a slow sensual kiss on my cheek. "With just thin scrubs on I could feel your muscles twitching." His eyes danced as he looked me in the eye to try to read my reaction.

"Okay, there is NO way you could have felt that! How did you know-" and with that he burst out laughing. "What?" I continued, "there's no way you could have felt that!"

"I didn't," he answered with a triumphant smile as he leaned back and took another drink.

"Then how did you know?"

"You just told me!" he said with a laugh, his eyes dancing and huge sexy smile filled his face.

"You jerk!" I squealed as I hit him in the arm. "I can't believe you duped me into saying that." I buried my face in my hands.

"Why are you so embarrassed anyway? Think how humiliating and demoralizing that would be if I didn't get any response from you." I started to go weak again as I listened to the smooth, melodic sound of his voice. He did have a point and I started to relax, giving him a genuine smile. He slid his chair back a few feet so that we were facing each other again, and a huge smile teased across his lips.

"And there was one other thing too. Your eyes totally gave it away. When you grabbed my wrist, I looked back at you and could see your pupils dilating. By the time I pushed you back against the wall your eyes were huge," he declared with a very satisfied smile as the tip of his tongue licked his lips.

"Ha! Yeah, I guess that was pretty obvious and hard to confuse with something else," I sighed as I relaxed a bit more. "You really do pay attention to details, don't you? Is this how you woo all of your women?" He shook his head slightly and he spoke quietly.

"Only you," he replied honestly with a tender look in his eyes. He shifted and I could tell from the rest of his body language how engaged he was in this conversation and in me as we were connecting this evening. The thought of that made my heart skip a beat and I took a deep breath. It still caught me off-guard how easily one of my best friends could get me so flustered.

"So why didn't you kiss me then?" I leaned forward across the table, only about a foot away from Colin's face.

"Well, I told you Suzy, it's all up to you. I would never do anything that you didn't want me to do. When I had you pinned up against the wall, it wasn't about overpowering you," he explained as he took another long draw of his drink. "I could have very easily done that if I wanted. What made it so hot was that you had me frozen in place with just a look."

"Or you were afraid I would get scared off or not return your sentiment."

"No, it wasn't fear that stopped me. Quite the opposite," he said quietly as his eyes drifted up to meet mine. I could hear his breath hitch. At that last confession, I immediately started to get nervous. That was a much more serious tone than I was expecting and I didn't know how to respond. I started readying myself to come up with some sort of a response but he continued before I had a chance.

"Like you said Suzy, this relationship is too important to half ass it. And I do have to beat someone who is literally an angel! I figured I needed to lay it all out there, no regrets. I didn't want you to think that I was just some nice guy who is a great friend but nothing more. A relationship needs that fire, that passion, in order to work. I just wanted you to be able to see that. I wanted you to be able to see that we have that before you make your decision."

"So, did you set up that whole thing then?" At first I started to get worried, thinking that maybe all of that was just an elaborate staging for me but he quickly squelched those fears.

"No," he shook his head, "I meant every word of what I said, but when I saw that raw emotion coursing between us, I couldn't help it. It's not like I haven't thought about those types of moments before," he said as he started to gaze off slightly past the edge of our table.

Suddenly my right hand that had been resting on the table started to get warm and tingle. I jumped slightly as I looked around in a very paranoid fashion.

"Suzy, what's wrong?" Colin asked, very concerned and now on high alert based on my change in posture. I looked back at my hand and moved it sharply to my lap.

"Nothing," I lied, "I'm fine. It's just a chill," I said as I took another drink of my wine.

"You're a horrible liar Suz. It's him, isn't it? Ben's here."

I looked over at Colin who had a mixture of disappointment and irritation on his face. I didn't know what to think about Ben showing up here right now. Who knows how long he had been here. The part of me that once thought it was sweet that he would look out for me all the time was now beginning to think it was sort of creepy how he was always there and I didn't know it, like in the shower earlier today. I knew I had to say something to Colin though.

"Yeah, he's here. I could feel him touching my hand," I said softly, not wanting to draw any attention to us.

"Oh really?" Colin asked, almost angrily. "So he spies on you without you knowing. Was that supposed to be reassuring to you that he was here or a warning? Why don't you just show yourself tough guy?" he asked looking around our table. Luckily we were in a corner and the place was pretty empty at 7:00 on a weekday. Suddenly my hand started to tingle again and as I looked over, Ben was phasing out in the open in a very public place. I was shocked to say the least. He had an icy stare that I had never seen from him before, even when he was having to take people to the other side.

"What the hell are you doing here," Colin asked in a calm but pointed tone.

"Making sure some guy doesn't try to steal my girlfriend," he said sardonically as he caressed the back of my hand with his thumb. I really didn't like the feeling of being a pawn in their little game, so I moved my hand back to my lap.

"Really, because I thought the only reason you were considered her 'boyfriend' was that she was trying to get out of-"

"Knock it off, both of you!" I interjected. "I don't want to be having this conversation right now."

"Maybe if your boyfriend wasn't being such a sick peeping tom we wouldn't have to be having this conversation," Colin replied. I hated the way Colin said the word 'boyfriend' and it made me cringe too at how often Ben would throw that word out, despite our conversation about it. I could tell Colin was getting agitated but his expression stayed cold as he stared Ben down. Ben, on the other hand, was starting to get more worked up.

"Well if you weren't hitting on my girlfriend incessantly then I wouldn't even be here!" His voice was tense and he was starting to stand as he was saying this. Out of the corner of my eye I could see the bouncer, dressed nicely in a black suit, start to make his way over to our table. The loud voices had no doubt drawn attention to us, especially on a night that wasn't very crowded.

"Excuse me gentlemen," he began, very politely, "but could you please take your conversation outside? It appears you have some things to discuss." His eyes were very friendly, but it was clear that they would not tolerate this sort of behavior in their establishment and I could respect that. As the two of them began to walk out with the bouncer, I dug through my purse and paid the waitress. I wasn't quite sure how much the bill would be so I intentionally overpaid, and because I felt bad for making a scene.

By the time I got outside of the bar, the two of them were already at it again. They were standing only a few feet away from each other, clearly having both been overrun with testosterone. Well, if Ben could even be overrun with hormones. I wasn't even focusing on what specifically they were saying. Not that they were fighting over me, rather it seemed they were having a general male pissing match. Or were they honestly arguing over me? I quickly shook that thought off. I didn't want anyone fighting over me, so I stepped in between them, holding a hand up to each.

"Both of you, knock it off! This is ridiculous! You're arguing like a couple of teenagers!" I said, exasperated by the situation. I looked over at Colin, who smirked at me.

"Well he started it," he said sarcastically, winking at me. "If he would just trust you and stop spying on you then we wouldn't have a problem," he said very assertively as he looked back over at Ben. His face suddenly fell and he took a step back.

"What the hell is going on?!" he said as he blanched, looking over at Ben.

"What?" I snapped back, tired of this little squabble. As soon as I turned to face Ben, I could see why Colin was startled. Ben's face was subtly changing right before our eyes. Ben had said that he could become older or younger, but I had never seen him look any different. Tonight, though, right in front of us he was visibly becoming younger. His cheek bones were becoming a little less sculpted and his skin started to have a more youthful glow. The small creases around his eyes and his mouth were smoothing out, and his hair seemed to be getting a little longer and wavier. While it wasn't a huge, dramatic shift, it was still rather jarring. I looked back at Colin who was taking a couple steps back, not really sure what to think since I was pretty certain that I had not shared this detail with him before. By the time I looked back at Ben, his teen-age version of himself stopped me dead in my tracks. I couldn't breathe and I could almost feel my heart stop beating.

"It was you," I whispered, clutching my chest with my right hand as I put my left hand out for balance. "It was you in the pool, wasn't it?" I gasped. I felt like I couldn't breathe. I looked up to see him nodding at me, and things suddenly started to get fuzzy. I looked around and everything looked checkered as my legs started to feel weak. There was a bench along the edge of the sidewalk and I tried making my way toward it.

"Oh shit Suzanne, you're red!" I heard Ben yell, almost in a frantic tone as he started grabbing for my free hand. I shook him away as I moved to turn around, but everything started to sound muffled around me and I was rapidly feeling queasy and unsteady. I felt my foot catch on something and then everything was dark as I felt myself falling to the ground. Off in the distance I could hear the muffled sound of a car horn, but it was getting closer. It echoed around in my head like a train whistle in a tunnel. My fingers and arms quickly began to tingle and my whole body spontaneously became warm. I felt a gentle bump on my left hip, like a wave in the ocean that pushes you back onshore, followed by a soft blow to my head. It was unlike anything else I had ever felt, but it reminded me of a pillow fight. My thoughts drifted off to Cassie and I playing on my parent's bed having pillow fights and giggling. I smiled at the memories and felt a happiness spread through me. Then stillness took over me and I could hear muffled sounds all around me and the sounds of scuffles and movement everywhere. Somewhere off to my right I could hear Colin's familiar voice, only he seemed panicked.

"Where the fuck did Ben go?!" He seemed very angry and I tried to reach over to put my hand on him to calm him down, but I couldn't feel his arm underneath my hand. He must be just out of arm's reach, but I couldn't quite will myself to move closer to him. This sluggish feeling was very disorienting and starting to take over my senses.

"Who's Ben?" I heard another man ask. He sounded jumpy but I did not recognize his voice, so maybe he was just naturally like that. "I'll call for an ambulance" the man continued and I could hear more shuffling of feet around me. As he said that, I could feel the warmth abruptly leave my body and the sounds around me became crystal clear. Some of the sensations around me began to return, though still somewhat muffled. Colin's breath was shaky and I could feel soft gentle touches along my wrists and along my neck. What was he doing? Why was he getting so upset about me tripping and falling? I know he'd seen me do this at least a half a dozen other times, albeit ice or drinking was usually involved.

"Jesus Suzy, don't do this. Stay with me," he pleaded. But why was he so far away? It seemed like he was blocks away from me at this point. The back of my head felt warm and I resisted the urge to just take a nap in the puddle I must have landed in, but it kept beckoning me. I tried to reach up as I felt my nose itch, followed by my mouth having pressure around it. I just wanted to swat away whatever hands were all around me but I could tell I was getting tired. Colin's voice became even more distant and muffled as I noticed a strange rhythmic pressure in my chest. In the far off distance, I could hear sirens getting a bit louder, but then the sounds started to fade away and the pressure in my chest dissipated. I tried to reach out for Colin, out in the darkness that had surrounded me but I couldn't will my muscles to move. I couldn't hear anything around me anymore. I let the warm blanket of sleep come over me.

"Suzanne ..." I heard a silky, smooth voice call out for me. I lay there motionless, wondering if I had imagined it. "Suzanne ..." I heard it again, but this time the voice was coming from all around me. I felt a surge of electricity through me, like a lightning bolt and I opened my eyes. For a moment, I thought that I *had* been struck by lightning. All I could see was pure white light for a split second before everything settled back to a normal hue. But as I looked around, nothing in the scene around me appeared as it should. The moisture on the hood of the parked cars seemed to gleam, and the streetlight overhead twinkled like I had never seen before. Even the sign outside of the Red Head Piano Bar had a lush, deep red glow to it that I was sure was not there when we walked in. All of the colors around me were richer and more vibrant. Every drop of water, whether pooled on the ground or droplets on the nearby benches, seemed to hold a rainbow in it. I could see the entire color spectrum in just a few tiny drops.

As I looked around me, I could see a gathering of people along the sidewalk and an ambulance with obnoxious, glaring lights. Next to the ambulance there was a small cluster of people crouched over someone and a gurney was on the ground while the techs quickly worked on their patient. Mixed in amongst them was a familiar figure that I would recognize anywhere. It was Colin. He moved swiftly but I could tell that he was completely strung out. I had seen him work enough to know his body language, and it was telling me that this person was not doing very well. He ran his hand nervously through his hair and I could hear him talking to the techs, but none of the words he was saying were making any sense to me. He grabbed one of their arms and they all stood up and raised the gurney to load it into the ambulance. Colin jumped into the back of the ambulance first and I started to walk towards them.

"I'm a doctor, I need to help them," I said aloud, although I wasn't quite sure who I was saying this to.

"Suzanne ..." I heard the melodic voice all around me again. This time I turned a complete circle, looking for where that voice had come from. As I faced the opposite direction of the commotion, my eyes came to a stop on a beautiful body before me. There in front of me was Ben. I stood there for a moment, just taking him in. I knew he was gorgeous with his tanned skin and short dark hair, but there was a different energy emanating from him now. And from those chocolate brown eyes that still made me weak every time I gazed into them, despite some of our conversations lately. As quickly as the memory of all of the hard talks we had had over the last week came to mind, they vanished and I was left with the same happy and giddy feelings I had the first time we spoke. And the first time he kissed me. He had a soft and loving smile play across his lips, and his eyes sparkled as they met mine.

"My God, you're beautiful," I said, almost breathlessly. He started to laugh and I couldn't take my eyes off of him as I watched his face light up. While he slowly started to walk toward me, I noticed every detail about him that I hadn't seen a short time ago amidst the argument that was going on. I noticed the alluring way his jeans hung off of his hips, especially as he was sauntering over towards me. The crisp, white button down shirt he was wearing was opened just far enough at the top to make me bite my lip thinking about what was underneath it. As he got closer to me, I nervously looked down at my feet. Until now, I had not yet looked at myself, but even my skin seemed to have a slight radiance to it. I turned my hands over in front of me just to be sure I was not seeing things.

Ben slowly closed the distance between us, in a very deliberate but casual way. The tender look in his eyes made me melt and blush as I returned his loving gaze.

"And you are absolutely breathtaking my darling," he replied as he leaned in and kissed my cheek very sensually. I reveled in the warm, tingling sensation of his lips on my cheek. Even the soft breath of his exhale on my skin felt exhilarating. Instinctively, I flushed and raised my shoulders in a shy gesture.

"Shall we?" he asked, looking optimistically at me. I looked around, confused by his question.

"What do you mean? Shall we what?" I asked, although as I looked around I could see that the crowd had dissipated and the ambulance was gone. It was just Ben and I along the sidewalk and a few casual pedestrians. I felt like something was pulling me backwards, away from Ben, but when I looked him in the eye all of those other feelings were overpowered. There was a calm voice inside me that was pushing me to follow Ben. I knew him well enough to trust him. He exuded a serenity that had instantly put me at ease, despite some of the inner panic that was trying to rear its head.

"It's time Suzanne," he said in a very warm tone as he held out his hand to me. I looked from his hand back up to his eyes and I instantly knew what he meant. I hesitantly lifted my hand up, admiring how silky and luminescent my skin looked. Then I turned my gaze to his eyes and smiled as I gently placed my hand in his and we began walking into the darkness together …

Stay tuned for the next
installment in Suzanne's journey!

Beyond the Light

About the Author

*K*athryn is a full time insurance professional, as well as a mother in a very full household! Creative expression is her passion and she uses it to relax at the end of her busy days. In addition to writing, Kathryn also is an avid bellydancer. Kathryn lived in Europe and in Chicago, but she now calls central Illinois home. Red Aura is her debut novel.